"Serve the light and seek the truth resting in darkness. Aid those in need, to the utmost of your power. Learn the avenues of magic and protect the secrets of the Association whenever possible. Risk your own life before putting the life of another in danger."

– The Oath of the Association of
Magical Arts and Sorcery

Also by T. Thorn Coyle

Novels

Like Water

The Panther Chronicles

To Raise a Clenched Fist to the Sky
To Wrest Our Bodies From the Fire
To Drown This Fury in the Sea
To Stand With Power on This Ground

Collections

Alighting on His Shoulders
Break Apart the Stone

TO WREST OUR BODIES FROM THE FIRE

BOOK 2 OF
THE PANTHER CHRONICLES

T. THORN COYLE

TO WREST OUR BODIES FROM THE FIRE
Panther Chronicles, Book Two

ISBN-13: 978-1-946476-02-9 (trade paperback)
ISBN-10: 1-946476-02-1 (trade paperback)

To Wrest Our bodies From the Fire

"The walls, the bars, the guns and the guards
can never encircle or hold down the idea of the people."

– *Huey P. Newton*

"The only way somebody can enslave you is that you don't fight back."

– *Roland Freeman*

CHAPTER ZERO
LIZARD

Lizard thought that he was dreaming. There was pounding…and then, with a rush of air to the lungs, he was awake and coughing.

The smell of cordite and gunpowder assaulted him as the noise established itself as not inside his head, but just above.

A strange thumping sound, like boots kicking, coming from up on the roof, and the *whump whump whump* of a helicopter rotor.

Then Cotton's voice shouted from downstairs.

"Wake up! Wake up! They're coming in!" followed quickly by the *bam, bam, bam* and the splintering crash of wood exploding inward. The downstairs door was being battered down.

Lizard shook himself upright on the raspy carpeted floor, raking a hand across his eyes to clear them. His other hand was already on the rifle he'd fallen asleep next to. The rapid fire of automatics, punctuated with the carefully placed shots from a .45, cracked through the small building from downstairs.

Light flashed through the doorway every time a gun fired. The light was jagged, smoky. Gunfire was the only light aside from the streetlights outside the chicken-wire–reinforced windows. The skylight in the center of the room was a black rectangle of night.

What time was it? The flashing gunfire shattered the room as he scanned for movement with night-adjusted eyes.

There was the table where they put together propaganda and held meetings. The ersatz kitchen on a card table in the corner. The odd assortment of chairs.

And the sandbags forming little squares just big enough to hold a man or two near the windows, stacked three feet high. Not as well fortified as the ground floor, but protected all the same.

Was anyone else in the room? PeeWee nodded at him from his place against the far wall. Lizard could just make out his bulky shape, his ragged natural, and the handgun, point up, ready to level at the first person who dared come up.

"Go," PeeWee breathed out. Lizard crawled toward the door at the top of the stairs, crouching just beside it, ready for whatever came through. The scent of discharged guns wafted up the stairs. What the hell was going on down there?

A shot ricocheted off the outside of the doorframe. Bracing his shoulder against the wood, rifle reaching around the corner, Lizard fired down the stairs. No clue if he hit anyone.

More shots came toward him; bullets lodged in the ceiling and a shard from the doorframe nicked his ear.

Lizard hissed out and shot another round at the boots coming up the stairs. There was a grunt, and a body slammed against the wall. Got something that time.

"They're shooting back!" he heard. Then more boots on the floor. The stairs? Coming up? No. No. Going out. The pigs were leaving.

PeeWee's eyes got wide at that. Lizard bet his were, too.

He exhaled. A moment of relative quiet. The house settled. Some rustling. Breathing. The ringing in his ears. The right one stung. He chanced a hand up. Blood.

Then Geronimo Pratt's voice came from downstairs. "Okay! We got a few minutes. Get what you need!"

PeeWee told Lizard to hold on and ran, combat boots thumping down the wooden steps.

He came back shortly. "More ammo is coming. Stay put."

Lizard itched to open the gun slats in the walls, but the light would only draw fire. It was so fucking dark still. The glowing tips of the hands on his watch face pointed to 5:20. Damn.

Peaches and Tommye thundered up the stairs, heading to the far corner where desks were set up with phones. The women dragged heavy rotary phones off the desks and crouched in the spaces underneath, shoving the chairs aside.

Immediately, they began making calls, the phone dials rasping and clicking in cycles of short, long, long, long, short, short, long.

Peaches must have been calling for backup; her low voice was urgent, words cutting in and out of Lizard's awareness, warring with Tommye's softer voice, somehow calm in the middle of all the mess. Tommye must've been talking to the news. Reporters down with the cause. Or at least holding out some sympathy for a group of Panthers getting shot out by the pigs.

The panting of his own breath sounded loud in the relative quiet, and he fought to slow his breath down. That Chinese shit Geronimo Pratt was always on about in training. "Quiet the body, you quiet the mind."

That cat had given him the gun he held now at 2:30 that morning, around the time Lizard bunked down on the floor.

Just a few hours ago.

Roland Freeman ran up the stairs with fresh bullets, carrying his own rifle. The comrades downstairs would also have Molotovs and pipe bombs. Lizard knew that, because he'd made up a bunch just days before. They'd be useful if the pigs made it back into the house. Keep them out of the room. No use upstairs though, with the chicken wire in the way.

Noise started up again. Not deafening, but confusing to the mind. Helicopters whumping. Shouting men. More gunfire. The women's voices raising as much as they dared, trying to cut through the clamor to the people on the other end of the line, without giving exact physical positions away to the pigs just outside the building.

Shifting onto his knees, Lizard got the balls of his feet under him and crouched in a run across the room toward the windows.

Once there, he struggled to reload, sweat running down his body. There was still barely any light.

Must be 5:30 in the morning and he was crouched next to a door in a room fortified with sand in the walls and sandbags around every window, a rifle slick in his hands. He didn't want to pause to wipe them, but his grip kept slipping. Should've wiped the whole gun down, but there wasn't any time.

His hands rasped down the chinos he'd slept in, one at a time, then back to the wooden stock, leaning against those bags packed tight against the walls, three feet high.

The bags that were keeping him alive.

An incendiary burst against the window, punching the glass. Lizard ducked his head on impact, to save himself a face full of glass knives. The chicken wire held. The incendiary didn't make it through.

Someone shouted "Fuck!" and an explosion happened down below, in the street.

More shouting. More gunfire. Walkie-talkies crackling through the open window.

"*Ssshhhhhupp!*" and the clink of a projectile against chicken wire. Tear gas seeping through. Damn. One hand on his rifle, the other patted pockets. No smokes. His eyes started to sting.

"Any smokes in the room?" Lizard called out. PeeWee tossed a packet over. He slid out two, then tossed the packet toward the women under the desks.

Quickly breaking the cigarettes off near the base, he shoved the filters up his nose. The scent of tobacco and mint warred with the scents of gunpowder and gas.

CHAPTER ONE
JASMINE

The magic pricked at my fingertips, ready to burst out and drown someone's ass. Any minute now.

My bare feet were practically wearing a hole into the flowered rug on the floor of my small white bedroom off Aunt Doreen's kitchen. I paced, black rotary phone dangling from my right hand, receiver held up to my ear with my left.

There wasn't much room for the pacing. From my door, to the single bed with its white chenille spread and pile of paisley and denim pillows, past the student desk under the window reflecting morning dark beneath its sheer white curtains.

Che Guevara looked down at me from the wall, alongside an op art poster of a gorgeous woman, whose perfectly round natural was framed by flower mandalas. *Black is Beautiful,* the poster read. She gazed at me from beneath the orange and yellow flowers framing her head.

I sighed. May all the Powers damn Terrance Sterling, head of the Association of Magical Arts and Sorcery, whose clipped voice was now lecturing in my ear.

Heat rose off my skin like boiling water, despite the chill of an Oakland, California, December morning. That was the sorcery, rising on my anger, wanting out. I was figuring out one of the perils of being a

Water Sorcerer was that the more my powers increased, the more they played with my emotions.

I needed air.

I set the heavy black phone down on the desk, Terrance's voice still squawking in my ear. At 6:30 on a rainy Monday morning, the little desk lamp cast a pool of light over the books and desk, forming a golden puddle that spilled over on the roses hooked into the rug.

Leaning across the narrow, white-painted wood desk, I cracked the window open, letting in the fresh scent of rain tinged with the brackish water of the bay. Rain pattered onto the glass. There was the added note of biscuits baking coming in from under the door.

That would be Aunt Doreen, baking away her fury. My stomach growled at the warm, yeasty smell of the biscuits, and the percolating coffee. I hadn't really eaten for a couple of days. Too tense to keep much down.

"You have to…"

Damn. Terrance never did like to let anyone talk. Especially a member of "the younger generation" as he called it. Younger generation my ass. He was going to listen.

"Terrance…" The man was still going.

"No. *You* have to listen!" I yelled. "I don't care how much more magical experience you have! *You* and the rest of your cronies up on your fine hill in that fine mansion don't know *anything* about what is going on *in your own backyard!*"

The streets of Los Angeles felt like they had been on fire for three years. But the white folks with money seemed to neither know, nor care.

"No. It can't 'wait until later in the day.' You think I'm happy to be up this early, hearing that folks are getting shot to hell down there?"

A particularly large crash sounded from the kitchen. Aunt Doreen must be picking up on my frustration through the door. Either that, or I said that last bit much louder than I thought.

Really, listening to Terrance go on and on about our responsibility to one another, and to the magic, and for the good of the Association itself, and how we couldn't get involved in politics because we remembered what happened last time....

I was pretty much ready to send a strong magical zap down the phone wires and into his ear. This cat was so full of crap. My middle class upbringing be damned.

Bourgeois folks never noticed much until something exploded across the newspaper headlines as they sipped fresh squeezed orange juice from tiny curved glasses. They would tsk and turn the page as they dipped their toast into the runny yolk of a perfectly cooked egg.

I wasn't far from that, growing up. My parents tried to shelter me from the realities of the world outside our white-picket–fenced neighborhood. Yes, I got the talk about avoiding being alone with white men, and always walking home from school with a friend.

And I knew my father sometimes had trouble getting jobs, and my mother had things she just never told me about.

But it still wasn't the reality I saw people living with every day since the Panthers had woken me up. It was all around me here in Oakland, and now that I could see it, it was down in Watts and the parts of South Central my family just never much made it into.

The sorcery was still rising on my skin, and the scent of ocean grew stronger. So was the taste of cinnamon...Aunt Doreen again. That was the scent of her Fire. She was all up in here with me, inside my energy field, closer than usual. We only got that intertwined when something had us both upset at the same time. Usually we kept better walls around our magic. Took care to not spill over. Control the bleed.

But this was big. The cops were in the middle of raiding the LA Panther's HQ as we spoke. I'd woken instantly, on the first ring of the phone in the kitchen, knowing it meant trouble because I'd smelled the gunpowder in my dreams.

Aunt Doreen had met me in the kitchen when I was still on the phone with my boyfriend, Jimmy, who was calling from Oakland HQ with the news from Los Angeles.

We had argued about who should call Terrance Sterling and alert the Association that there was a magical need.

"He'll listen to you, Doreen. You're in his age group while I'm still considered wet behind the ears."

"But I'm more likely to *kill* that man," she said, full lips pressing almost straight into a line. "You better make the call. If you can't convince him, I'll get on the phone and wup his behind."

So here I was, with the long phone cord snaking under my bedroom door, shut to try to muffle the increased banging from the kitchen. I was trying to convince a wealthy white man whose life had been too comfortable for too many years that people were in immediate danger a forty-minute drive from his fancy home.

Trying to convince a man who had spent too many years exercising the arts of magical diplomacy. Keeping the peace among once-hating factions who had finally agreed to work together.

"We can't be sure who is right in this situation, Jasmine. And you know the Association doesn't involve itself in these sorts of disputes." His voice grated my spine like tin on a chalkboard.

Yeah. That was Terrance all right. Mister "I once was a powerful sorcerer, but now I find it best to not get involved." A honky with too much money and power who never did a damn thing with either.

I was sick of that. It was time to force his hand.

We didn't need diplomacy; we needed folks angry enough to throw some magic up between the tear gas and the bullets in order to save some people's lives.

It was time to bring the Association into this thing my friends in the Party were calling a war.

And it wasn't going to happen through Terrance Sterling.

"Goodbye, Terrance." I cut the call short.

I looked at the pile of books and my notes from last night. Damn. I should have been working on a paper this morning instead of dealing with crisis. I also had a statistics test to study for.

It was the last week of classes and I couldn't care less.

"Welcome to the real world, Jasmine Jones," I said. The real world where cops shot at my friends, my boyfriend was an actual shape-shifting panther, and there was out–and-out war in the streets.

I needed my sorcery. Listening to the rain, and smelling the distant bay, I began to breathe water into my pores and exhale it out again. The power of it built inside my belly and rose until it cascaded down my arms and toward my hands.

To become a badass sorcerer, I needed to be free.

To be free, I needed this connection to the Element that had marked me at my birth.

To be a badass sorcerer, I couldn't let Terrance and his hang-ups hang *me* up. That cat was too beholden to the Man. For every little thing.

The whole Association of Magical Arts and Sorcery were hip deep in the muck of the oppressors. Even though the Association always insisted we didn't work in politics, no one in America got that much money from keeping their hands clean.

Well, the Association was just going to have to deal with Jasmine Jones.

CHAPTER TWO
DOREEN

Up to her elbows in soapy hot water, Doreen scrubbed at the mixing bowls and spoons. The water scalded her hands but that felt good in a perverse way. It stoked her irritation.

That damn Terrance Sterling. She slammed the spoons into the rinse water and leaned on the sink, staring out the window into the dark and rain. The sky was barely growing lighter, the black night turned dark gray. It would likely stay that way all day because she had to go out in the weather to work at the florist shop.

The red-and-white–striped kitchen curtains framed the darkness with too much cheer. That was irritating, too. Her face looked back at her, slightly wavery. A forty-three-year-old woman with a pale blue satin wrap protecting her hair, the lines deeper around her mouth than they used to be.

She supposed she was still a good looking woman overall, and her lover, Patrice, certainly told her she was, but at the moment Doreen didn't much look like it, or care.

The fury wasn't leaving. It only increased. It shook inside the slender layer of fat hard-packed around her middle-aged waistline, and stomped itself out through her feet in their crocheted slippers on the linoleum floor.

Fire was Doreen's Element, unlike her niece, who was Water, deep and strong.

She could smell salt water still rolling out under Jasmine's door, although she must have hung up by now because Doreen no longer heard the occasional sharp cracking of the girl's voice, like a mighty wave smacking the side of a rock.

The immovable rock that was Terrance Sterling's perfectly groomed silver-gray head. Doreen couldn't recall the last time she'd been so pissed off.

She wanted to blast Terrance's head clean off his neck. But he'd probably like that. It would be proof that Doreen was using magic again.

Terrance was conveniently ignoring the major piece of magic she and Jasmine had just orchestrated days ago.

There had been a standoff with the police at DeFremary Park, where they and the community had worked together to build a dome of light, water, and fire as the Black Panthers—both shifter and human—roared and the cops' bullets bounced off the shield.

The people were victorious that day. The police had rolled out, leaving a celebration behind in the city park.

They had proved that sorcery and politics not only mixed, but were effective.

After years away, Doreen was smack dab in the middle of magic again, training people for battle who shouldn't have to ever fight. People like Patrice, a woman who had been a close, beloved friend for years, until the power of magic and danger had unlocked some lust beneath the love.

And Drake, a thirteen-year-old boy who should have nothing more on his mind than school and playing baseball or reading comic books.

But if they didn't fight, what else were they going to do? Jasmine had convinced Doreen of that, at least.

"Black people have to fight back, Aunt Doreen. Otherwise, they'll make us slaves again."

She had the truth of it, there. Smart girl. And brave. Kind of like Doreen used to be before they shot her Hector in the dry, gold hills of Southern California, then chopped his gorgeous, mountain lion head off, leaving his carcass to rot.

She bowed her head. By all the magic in her soul, she couldn't let that happen again.

"Okay, Aunt Doreen. Finish your dishes and get the biscuits out the oven before they burn," Jasmine's voice said from behind her.

Doreen pulled the plugs on the big double sink and wiped her hands on a clean terry towel while the water sucked itself down the drain.

Grabbing two red quilted hot pads, she pulled the trays out of the oven.

Jasmine was dressed already, in purple cords and an orange turtleneck that brought out the warm highlights in that beautiful face of hers. She'd thrown a black-and-purple V-neck poncho over the whole ensemble, warding off the morning chill.

Doreen was all too conscious of the fact that she was still in her blue chenille robe.

"Coffee's done," Doreen said. "Pour me one, too, please."

Jasmine strode across the kitchen floor in her stocking feet—never could get the girl to wear her slippers—and took two coffee cups from the cupboard.

"I need some of this in me before I start to talk, okay?" Jasmine said.

"Fine with me, girl. Sit yourself down. But get the jam and butter out first. And some cream."

They were both buying time so they wouldn't start shouting, but their Elements crashed up against each other all the same. Doreen sighed and reined her Fire in a bit. When two sorcerers were upset, it was easy for things to escalate.

No need for extra drama until she knew what was what.

As she pulled out a chair at the red-topped Formica table, Doreen could tell Jasmine struggled to tamp down the blue, watery energy that favored her.

Stirring some cream into the coffee, Doreen finally spoke. "What did he say?"

Jasmine smeared butter onto a biscuit she'd pulled apart. "Bunch of bullshit."

"Oh girl, that mouth of yours."

Jasmine eyed the strawberry jam. "I'm just not sure what else to call it, Doreen. That man is so full of it. It makes me angry and then makes me tired. Him and that whole damn Association can kiss my ass. Their bourgeois bullshit is gonna get more folks killed. Folks who don't have to die. If only they'd get off their magical asses and actually help someone other than themselves for a minute."

Her hooded eyes met Doreen's. So young. So angry. Doreen knew that feeling.

"Am I going to need to talk to him, then?"

"You're gonna need to kick his ass, is what you're gonna need to do. But I'm not even sure if that'll help."

Doreen bit into a biscuit. Oh yes. Perfect. A little flaky around the edges from the lard. Soft and warm in the center. Needed some jam.

Her body had distracted her mind, and in that moment, her consciousness shifted, allowing the magic in the room to form itself around her. Doreen paused a moment, knife poised over the jam jar.

She could almost see all the threads spreading out, from Los Angeles to Oakland. From Oakland to Chicago. From Chicago to Philly. Philly to New Orleans. Back to Memphis. To Atlanta. To Los Angeles.

Something big was trying to form itself into a pattern.

Doreen could also feel and almost *taste* something else. Something… like a brown stain on a pale yellow sundress, or a cloud passing over the sun. There was interference forming, too, running alongside the spreading threads, riding on their fibers, like hatchling white spiders parachuting through the air.

Doreen was going to have to look into that. She was getting the feeling there was a big, fat momma spider in the center of it all. Somewhere.

"What are you seeing?" Jasmine asked.

Doreen put the knife down. "The pattern. Didn't Carol say Terrance had been practically foaming at the mouth down there, and Ernesto was killing spiders at the Association Mansion?"

Jasmine set her half eaten biscuit back on her plate.

"Yeah. You seeing something about that?"

Doreen nodded thoughtfully.

"There's some bad magic happening, Jasmine. Well, we knew that already. But these spiders, that snake that's been attacking you…there's some connection between them all. And it makes me wonder if these attacks on the Panthers aren't connected with it too."

Jasmine picked up her coffee, taking a long sip before speaking again.

"What are we gonna do about all this, Aunt Doreen?"

"First thing is, I'm calling Los Angeles and talking with your mother, Cecelia, today, before I head to work. She'll help us if it's the last thing she does."

CHAPTER THREE
LIZARD

Lizard could barely believe this was happening. Only his second night staying at HQ and they weren't just being raided, they were in a prolonged skirmish.

The stink of tear gas and gunpowder was all over him; he could even smell it through the mint that lingered on the filter he'd broken off the Kools and shoved up his nose…how long ago? He spared a glance at his watch, visible now in the morning light finally coming through the skylight. 9 a.m. Four hours they'd been at this now.

The pounding hadn't let up. He kept hearing booms from downstairs, and assumed they were throwing pipe bombs out the door. Someone said a car outside was on fire. Everything was moving so fast. Tommye and Peaches weren't calling anymore. They were crouched against the wall opposite him, trying to stay out of the way. Roland was writhing on the floor. He'd been hit during the last round, after he'd come upstairs to bring them more ammo.

Snipers were shooting through the skylight. Lizard felt the bullet and rolled away before it embedded itself into the wall where his shoulder had been seconds ago.

Something felt wrong.

Then things grew still above Lizard's head. For around sixty seconds, all Lizard could hear was Tommye and Peaches whispering in the corner, trying to plan something. Shots still rang downstairs, but the pigs on the roof were silent.

"Roland, how you doin', man?" Lizard called, softly.

A grunt sounded, and Lizard swiveled his head away from the sky-light to look at his fallen comrade. Shorter and stockier than his brother, Ronald, Roland Freeman was still a presence to be reckoned with, when he wasn't lying shot on the floor.

He was an integral part of LA leadership. Lizard hoped he was gonna make it through.

"They got me, but I think I'm gonna be okay."

That didn't seem quite right, either. Lizard could see the shredded cloth of Roland's camo pants and his T-shirt. Looked like he'd taken multiple shots in his legs and crotch. How the hell was the man not passed out, screaming, or dead?

Then the world ended.

Shrieking wood and metal. A flash and explosion left Lizard's eyes strob-ing and eardrums booming as he dove deeper behind the sandbags. Whole pieces of roof crashed to the floor. Tar paper. Chunks of plaster. A splinter as big as an arm embedded itself in the sandbag near Lizard's head, sending a jet of dirt into his face. The women were screaming; Roland, too. A mighty yell.

Lizard could hear panicked voices down below. Tommye and Peaches ran for the door. PeeWee raised his automatic and shouted, "Grab Roland!" as he pointed the gun toward the gaping hole where the roof had been. Lizard saw the salmon and purple of the morning sky through the ragged opening.

Slinging his rifle across his shoulder, Lizard grabbed Roland under his armpits, dragging him toward the door. Roland was in bad shape now. A big piece of plaster had bashed his right temple and it looked like a piece of roofing had crushed his chest. He screamed as Lizard dragged him over the debris on the floor.

"Sorry, man. Gotta get you downstairs."

Roland was dead weight, but Lizard didn't dare get him into a fire-man's carry. They needed to stay as low to the ground as possible.

As they hit the door, bullets started puncturing the room again, bouncing off the floors and shattering the walls.

At least the huge hole had let out the tear gas and cordite. Lizard could breathe a little easier.

His shoulders pulling, his hands slipped with his own sweat and the sweat, blood, and debris on Roland's shirt. He kept trying to get a grip under muscles around the other man's shoulder blades, but couldn't keep purchase there for long.

Every time Lizard grabbed him, Roland keened a little. A high-pitched little whine of breath, like a man trying to hold in a scream so powerful it would break his throat. His pants were in shreds from the bullets. Damn.

"Okay. This is gonna hurt like a bitch, man. But I gotta drag you down the stairs."

"Do. It," Roland got out through gritted teeth.

"I got his feet, man." Wayne ran up the stairs and grabbed Roland around the knees, which caused an actual scream.

"Careful, man. He's hit bad."

The two men got him down the stairs and up against some sandbags. There was no space in one of the little bunkers for him, but it was better than leaving him completely exposed.

Lizard got back into position, trying to cover Roland and the rammed-in front door. He was crouched near Tommye, who had wedged herself into a corner, legs out across the floor.

The light coming through the windows lay in a stripe across Tommye's legs. She needed to move.

Lizard was about to yell at her to shift her legs when a line of bullets rained across the floor, hitting her in the thighs. Tommye cried out and Peaches struggled to get her closer to the wall.

The Panthers sent a barrage of bullets back out the windows and the door.

"We almost out, man!"

Yeah. Lizard was out, for sure, after that last round. PeeWee and the others had abandoned the upstairs by this time. It was too hard to keep it covered with the hole punched in the roof.

"What we gonna do?"

"I'm not surrendering after close to five hours of battle, man," Geronimo said. Lizard was with him on that. His ears rang and his eyes ached from the cordite and tear gas. He wasn't sure how the hell they could continue to defend the building, but something inside his heart and belly wouldn't let him give himself up. Not like this. Not to those pigs out there.

"Tommye and Roland are hit, man, they're gonna need a doctor."

"Yeah, man, I feel that. But we can't just give them over to the pigs!"

The discussion was hurried. Emphatic. No one was sure what to do. All Lizard knew was these were his comrades. He would die for them if necessary. His mom would miss him, but she knew as soon as he took up with the Panthers that someday he just might not come home. She said she was proud of him anyway.

His eighteen years had been good. Strong. Full of love from his mom. Full of bullshit and harassment from the fucking pigs. Full of dismissal from the fucking schools.

Full of hope, this last six months since he found the Party. There was nothin' else he'd rather be doing than this.

This revolution. Slowly he raised his right fist.

"All power to the people," Lizard said.

"All power to the people." Every other voice in the room answered, except for Tommye and Roland, who were conserving what breath they had.

They were all quiet for a moment after that. Walkie-talkies crackled outside. Tinny voices saying there was enough back-up and they were going in again.

They needed to make a decision soon.

Then Peaches cleared her throat. "I'll go."

CHAPTER FOUR
SNAKES AND SPIDERS

*S*amuels felt the syphoning of life force as it spiraled out from the edges of his skin, joining the skein of power, sixteen strands, one from each dark-suited man, as it formed a rope that wrapped around The Master's solar plexus.

The Master drew on the energy of his men, and slammed his fist into the face of the closest operative.

A string of spittle arced through the air from the man's mouth as his head snapped to the side. The crack of fist on jaw was audible in the secluded park area behind FBI headquarters.

There was no way a man of his age should have been able to pack a punch like that. When you leeched magic off enough people, Samuels thought, anything became possible.

A squirrel barked and chittered from the massive elm overhead. The branches shook as it ran, bending near the tips as it sprung to next tree over, complaining all the while.

"What do you mean he's not dead?" the Master roared into the otherwise still air of the park where he insisted on having some of his most delicate conversations.

Even the lead-lined walls of the Master's office suite weren't completely soundproof around the doors. He trusted no place outside his own mind, of course, but he had to talk to the humans somewhere.

Humans. Samuels supposed the Master had been one once upon a time. Underneath the magic that coursed in the blood beneath Hoover's pasty skin, Samuel supposed he still was. Maybe.

The operative sunk to his knees on the manicured grass with an "oof." The man panted, head bowed under the gathering storm clouds that painted the Capitol gray.

The other three men in black blanched paler than they already were beneath their shades, the one black operative going mildly gray. They stood as still as possible, wrist held in hand, spines straighter than the trees. A mild breeze set up, barely ruffling their perfectly cut hair.

Samuels swallowed the bile rising from his gullet and stepped forward.

Forty years old, and trim and muscular as a man who exercised every day of his life, Samuels was always the one deputized to speak, being the highest ranking magician in their squad. Exercise every morning, and magic every night, without fail, no matter how brutal his day had been.

And they often were.

None of the others trusted that they'd remain alive long if they were to speak with the Master about anything other than the most basic assignment report backs. Samuels sneered at them sometimes, but he also understood. Twenty years ago, he'd been the same.

The Master really was a creep. All the spooks said so. But he was also the most powerful spook in the nation, maybe even in the world. As a magician, Samuels had to respect that. As distasteful as he found the Master, the man had power. Samuels wouldn't mind being that feared himself one day.

"Mr. Hoover, sir, I saw the rooms myself. They were riddled with bullets, all from the direction of police guns. There was no way anyone could survive that onslaught."

"And yet someone did. More than one! That fucking Panther coon and his bitch survived. I want them both. And I want the whelp inside her belly."

The Master ground up the turf beneath his shiny black shoes, his face quivering with malice and hatred.

And anger. So much anger that the Master's skin was red with it, and practically steaming. Magic roiled around his body, puce, and muddy red, and black. The colors of rending and decay. His fists were still clenched, and everyone but Samuels stayed well outside of punching range. Though if the Master decided to use magic, no one there was safe.

Not that they ever were.

"Yes sir," Samuels replied.

"How did you allow this to happen? Who the hell was there? Neophytes? Was anyone there carrying salt and rowan?"

Silence met the Master.

"Nothing?" The Master turned his eyes on Samuels, who trembled on the green turf, and raised one of his fingers. The turf started smoking under Samuels's feet. Sweat popped out on his pale face, mouth turning to a rictus as he tried to control the urge to flee. Or to combat the Master's magic with his own.

"Only. Bullets. Sir."

The Master dropped his finger and Samuels sagged from the relief, catching himself right before he collapsed to the grass like his colleague. Samuels bolstered his bones with his magic. The magic of serpents. The magic to shed and renew.

Samuels had developed a taste for power at age thirteen, when he first saw that he could control his friends by just giving his suggestions a little nudge.

Samuels would be the Master someday if it killed him.

If he didn't kill the Master first.

Chapter Five
Jasmine

En route to my first class, I paused for a moment to enjoy the copse of redwoods, needles soft beneath my boots, leather coat protecting me from the chill. My black beret was perched on my head, even though it made my professors nervous.

It *should* make them a little nervous. I was a member of the Black Panther party, and a little nervous was okay. Fear and power walked hand in hand. If they couldn't be bothered to find out that black beret signified that I was feeding children breakfast several times a week, that just wasn't my problem.

Crenshaw Jasmine spent a lot of time coddling white folks' feelings. Oakland Jasmine was starting to not care.

Sneezing hard into my leather sleeve, I fumbled for a handkerchief, crouching to dig through that voluminous fringed bag of mine. Damn. Hopefully I wasn't getting sick. Did I have time to stop by the People's Clinic? Doreen had badgered me about getting a routine checkup from "those Panther doctors" as she called them, but I hadn't bothered.

Nineteen and healthy, I thought those were just middle-aged–woman worries. My fingers found the soft white cloth and grabbed it and I blew my nose.

I flipped my coat collar up to protect myself from the rising wind that sent needles and leaves tapping against the leather and winging past my head.

Something wasn't right. I shouldered my bag again and sent my senses outward.

That.

That strange tingling sensation that started at the base of my skull. They were following me again.

I say "they" because I couldn't tell if it was one person, or two people. Or if they were even people at all.

But I had a stinking suspicion…that behind the papery snake smell I was catching even under the giant redwoods I was walking under, and the cat piss smell of the stand of eucalyptus across the way, there was a human being.

Every single time, it smelled the same. Human and snake skin. Snake and human.

They had sent that astral serpent to attack me at Panther headquarters the week before. They'd been following me for more than a month now. I was thinking they were behind other recent attacks, too.

Carol had spiders in Los Angeles, and up here we had snakes. All creatures that lived under rocks, hid in shadows, and struck when a person least expected.

But I was ready for them this time.

A slow hissing sound came through the trees. I turned, carefully, wrapping my fingers around the quartz crystal in my right coat pocket. If I needed it, I could channel the bay through it, giving the water-fed blue flame of energy more focus and reach.

And there he was. A man in sharp black suit and white shirt, some subtle patterned tie knotted close around his neck. Dark glasses covered up his eyes despite the gloom under the redwood canopy.

I throttled back the urge to sneeze again. No way was I closing my eyes around this man.

He stood between two redwoods, just past the stream. Hands loose at his sides. Feet parted. To most people, he would just look like a man standing there. But I knew a fighting stance when I saw one.

I'd seen it on Leroy and the other Panther security forces. My boyfriend, Jimmy, too. And I was starting to feel it in my own body, from the little bits of training I'd had so far.

But mostly? I knew the fighting stance of a sorcerer or magician. We stayed strong, loose, and wary, too.

He was as Aunt Doreen had described him from her encounter. Average height. Average white skin. Slight build. Black hair slicked back with too much pomade. Nose thin and long, a little large. About the only thing about him that stood out.

If it weren't for the weird dark glasses, he might even pass for normal.

I turned to my second sight, looking around his head. There was strange patterning. Some Solomonic shit, looked like. High church magic, we sometimes called it, all geometry and chanting. This was stuff I'd read about, and sat through interminable lectures about when I was fifteen and just wanted to go outside, or blow shit up in the lab.

But I'd never actually seen it before.

The man was moving toward me. I brought the crystal out of my pocket, keeping that hand close to my side. If he came any closer, I'd drop my leather bag.

Part of me was saying I should run, but I was too curious and too pissed off to listen. Doreen and my mother, Cecelia, always told me I was stubborn. Well. That ran in the family, didn't it?

The trees moved slightly, bowing out away from the man as he walked between them. He wasn't on any path, but made a path with such ease. Like he was gliding. Just like a snake.

The hissing sound grew louder, coming from inside my ears.

My heart pounded in my chest and I swallowed hard, planting my boots more firmly in the needles, leaves, and soil. Slowly, steadily, I drew on the water in the soil, connecting it drop by drop to the waters in the air and in the bay.

Water filled my body. Water cascaded out into my energy fields in a stream. I pulled on it like taffy, drew it deeper, let it spread.

The man kept moving toward me.

I dropped the heavy fringed leather bag off of my shoulder, never taking my eyes off his pale, pale face. It fell with a thump by my feet.

I wished I could see his eyes.

Focusing on the feeling of liquid moving through me, I concentrated the energy into the tip of the crystal, where it would form into an extension of my own power, shifting Elemental Water into a blue fire that could burst forth like salt from a rifle, or focus as fine as a scalpel cutting through.

I didn't need any chanting or geometry. I *was* chanting and geometry. I was all the water in the universe. All I had to do was ask.

"I'm asking now," I whispered softly to the trees. They sent a rain of moisture onto my head, soaking into the felt of the black beret and running down my skin.

This was power.

He stopped two yards from me. Was he sweating? Or was that just the moisture I had called, condensing on his skin? Strange that such a dry, papery-feeling man could sweat. And in this cold.

He wasn't scared. Which meant he must be expending some effort. Effort on what?

Shit.

Something started squeezing at me, gripping my calves and rising toward my knees. I tried to step out of it. Tried to stomp it down. Never taking my eyes from his face.

I slashed down with the crystal, sending streams of blue fire to whatever the hell was gripping at my legs.

The squeezing let up a little. I pushed more of the water in me outward, making the energy around me larger.

It was such a strange feeling. I could sense something squeezing the very edges of my aura, seeking purchase, seeking *me*. It wanted closer in. It wanted to climb up my body and squeeze until my lungs burst in my ribs and my heart stopped beating in my chest.

Well, I wasn't going to let it, was I? Time to shift tactics.

On a mighty yell, I flung a blue burst of Water-powered fire out from the crystal, heading straight for those dark glasses.

The man moved his head, but not fast enough. One of the lenses cracked diagonally, then shattered, the pieces falling onto the needle-carpeted ground.

The man blinked rapidly, like his eye hurt. Like the gloomy gray day was desert bright.

Like he was used to living in some cave.

I caught a movement at his breastbone and braced myself for attack. He threw his arms up and started pushing his hands toward one another, as though he was pressing on a giant invisible ball that resisted his hands.

The pressure around me increased.

I shot another bolt of blue, this time aiming for the space between his hands.

A giant cracking sound pierced my ears and a burst of light shot upward toward the trees. The man fell to his knees.

The squeezing stopped.

I grabbed my fringed bag and ran.

Chapter Six
Doreen

Doreen and Patrice were up the attic. It was far less dusty than only a few weeks before, and there was finally a shade over the central bulb. Doreen had found a glass globe tinted a pale umber that reduced the glare, washing the broad fir planks and the wood beams of the rafters in a golden glow.

Jasmine and Drake had dragged some low bookcases up, lining one of the knee walls, making a place for the unpacked books and magical objects.

The ancestors were knocking around the house, and Doreen had started making offerings every morning, at a small altar she set up in the sitting room.

But the ancestors wanted a bigger altar, a magic altar. One that would draw on the Powers from Angola, and bring the spirits home.

Jasmine should have been here, helping, but she was always so busy. She would be here for the dedication, but for now, Patrice said she would help unpack and clean.

Patrice looked good. She was wearing slacks tonight, which she rarely did. Doreen admired her friend's lush backside under the burgundy gabardine. The slacks and the thick, cable-knit cardigan in prosaic navy were both concessions to the fact that they were in an attic and likely to get dirty.

It felt good, what was growing between them. After years of Patrice being there for Doreen when she was recovering, so slowly, from Hector's death, Doreen was finally ready to see Patrice for what she was. Not only a friend, but a companion who could love her through the coming years.

"This mask is gorgeous!" Patrice said, breaking into Doreen's thoughts. "Where did it come from?"

Patrice held up a black mask, cylindrical, with a large oval framing the face like a halo. Red eyes like big cowrie shells, surrounded by white. The red stripe of a nose between them. The mouth was also large and red, with sharp white teeth. The halo was decorated with blue, red, and white, patterns that Doreen couldn't read, but knew were significant.

"Hector found that for me in a hole-in-the-wall-shop in LA, he said."

Doreen remembered the day he brought it home. When he took the piece of sackcloth off the thing, her knees almost buckled. It took her breath away.

She *recognized* it. Even though she'd never seen anything like it before.

Doreen cleared her throat. "It's Chokwe. From Angola. That's where my people come from."

Patrice shook her head in wonder, and placed the mask on the table they were using to stage the altar.

"I wish I knew where my people were from," she said.

Doreen polished Momma's crystal ball. The cloudy sphere was heavy in her hands. Everyone in the community used to come see Momma when they needed visioning. She was the most powerful sorcerer and seer Doreen had ever met.

"We could do some divination about it someday. Ask the cards. Or I've been meaning to get back to practicing with the bones."

"Huh. You could do that?" Patrice asked. "Figure out where my ancestors are from, just by asking a pack of cards?"

Doreen laughed at that.

"After what you saw in the park, girl, and the things I've been teaching you? You still think things need to make sense?"

Patrice humphed a bit at that, but she smiled. Then walked over to Doreen, sensible heels—for once—pocking softly on the Douglas fir planks. Raising both her hands to Doreen's cheeks, she leaned in and kissed her.

Oh my. My my my. Doreen did like that. So different than Hector. And that was good. She didn't need another Hector. Doreen just needed…whatever the thing percolating with this woman was.

Patrice's lips were sticky with mauve lipstick. She smelled of talcum, Queen Helene's cocoa butter, and Aqua Net. And the other, lower note that was just Patrice's skin.

Doreen fumbled to set the crystal ball on the table, but then thought the better of it. She didn't want Momma's sphere to roll away.

Right then, Patrice started to laugh, breath buzzing against Doreen's lips.

"Am I distracting you?" She turned her head and murmured in Doreen's ear.

"You know you are," Doreen replied. "But that's all right. It's been a lot of years with no distractions at all."

They stood like that for a moment, holding one another, belly to belly, breast to breast, before Patrice stepped away.

"Do you have altar cloths?" she asked.

Doreen took a breath, willing the tingling in her body to join the rest of the flow of her magic. They still had so much work to do.

"In that box over there." She pointed to a lidded cardboard carton covered in old silver-and-red wrapping paper.

Patrice snapped out a large, plain black cloth and spread it on the card table they were going to use as an altar. She rummaged in the box a bit, finally coming out with a woven cloth, black with a pale diamond pattern. She held it up.

"This?"

Doreen nodded. "Yes. Here." She handed Patrice a large, sturdy cigar box. The flat, rectangular kind.

"Use this as a riser. You can drape that cloth over it."

That done, Doreen set the stand for Beatrice's crystal on the cloth, and placed the sphere reverently in the center.

Then she gestured for the mask. Patrice set it in her hands. Doreen looked into the red, cowrie-shaped eyes and took a breath. Finding center. Connecting to her people.

Then she set the mask on the altar.

Jar candles came next. Red. Black. White. Patrice placed them on the table just in front of the covered cigar box and the mask.

Doreen started to feel dizzy, gray spots swimming at the edges of her eyes.

"Patrice…"

She felt the other woman's hand grab her wrist, right before Doreen fell to her knees.

And she was staring at a thick trunked tree with branches reaching out from the top like tiny arms and hands. There were mountains in the distance, and red, rocky earth, dotted with green.

She could smell water, but couldn't see it. Mostly, she smelled earth and whatever the strange tree was.

A flock of small, black, finch-like birds with red-painted wings darted among the upper branches, making a cheerful racket.

There was motion from the direction of the distant mountains. A woman walked toward her, a blue-, yellow-, and red-patterned cloth wrapped around her hips and swaying gracefully down to her feet. Her hair was in elaborate coils, colored by the red mud, and row upon row of tiny colored beads, reflecting the colors of her hip wrap, wound themselves around her neck.

She looked like Momma around the eyes and nose, but her mouth was her own, lips carved in two sharp peaks on her dark face.

When the woman reached Doreen, she held out her hands, fists closed around small objects.

Doreen held out her own hands, palms up, open. Ready to receive.

The woman's fingers were surprisingly cool and smooth, despite the hot air that pressed at Doreen's skin.

In Doreen's left hand, she deposited a small, brown, curling mollusk shell. In her right, some sort of rough brown seedpod.

"Life and life," the woman said. Those weren't the sounds that came out of her mouth, but they were the words Doreen felt echo in her head. She supposed the woman spoke some Bantu dialect, but didn't really know.

"Life and life," Doreen said back. The woman smiled at that, showing a row of white teeth, with a dark gap where her left incisor was missing.

And then the woman was gone. So was the scene. Doreen was aware she was on her knees on hard wood. And Patrice's hands were on her shoulders.

"Doreen! Are you with me?"

Doreen coughed. "Water?"

Patrice's hands were gone. Doreen couldn't seem to open her eyes. Or she didn't want to.

"All I have is some tea in the thermos." Patrice's voice came from behind her. "Can you wait for me to get downstairs for water?"

"Tea."

Doreen heard Patrice pouring liquid into a cup. Then felt her hands under her armpits.

"Let's get you in a chair," she said. "But you need to open your eyes."

Doreen struggled. Fluttering her eyelids. When she finally opened her eyes, the mask was staring down at her. She felt something in her hands. Her fingers were wrapped so tightly around whatever it was, it was starting to hurt.

Opening up her aching hands, she saw the tiny shell. And a seedpod. "How?"

"Come on, baby. Let's get you up."

"Patrice." Doreen stopped her. "Look."

She held out her hands.

Patrice got down on her knees beside Doreen, and held her hands in her own.

She looked into Doreen's eyes.

"How is that even possible? You didn't have those before, right? What happened?"

Doreen set the shell and the pod up on the altar, underneath the stand for Momma's crystal ball.

"I'm not sure," she said. "I actually have no idea. But I think I just met an ancestor from Angola."

CHAPTER SEVEN
CAROL

Carol was back, having run down the hallway to catch the phone before it stopped ringing, or before one of the ten students currently in residence at the large, Spanish-style Mansion picked it up.

They were all supposed to be in class, but you never knew.

Carol paused in the doorway of the big workroom, trying to slow the pounding of her heart.

Ernesto was still at one of the long wooden tables in the middle of the goldenrod-painted room, light from the tall, arched Spanish-style windows glinting off his dark black hair and light brown skin.

Her binders and yellow legal pads were where she'd left them, next to a partially eaten triangle of toast smeared with liverwurst.

The box of old books and papers Ernesto had been working through still sat waiting. It looked like he hadn't done much while she was out of the room.

Ernesto was pouring coffee from his blue plaid thermos into two white, blue-patterned Pyrex coffee cups he'd brought in from the kitchen.

Ernesto looked up, beautiful dark brown eyes staring at her behind his tortoiseshell glasses, brow furrowed slightly with concern. He wore a red shirt today, tucked neatly into black trousers.

He looked good in that shade of red.

She held up a hand to forestall the questions she could see forming on his face. Then Carol tucked her stick-straight blond hair behind her ears and shut the door.

"It was Jasmine. Things are bad. Like Chicago bad…"

"What's happening?"

She stood by the long work table, taking one of the cups of coffee, welcoming the warmth in her hands. Welcoming the slightly bitter taste, cut through with sugar and heavy cream.

"It's…" She exhaled a heavy breath, trying to release some of the tension and fear thrumming through her body. "It's happening practically down the street, Ernesto."

"Carol…" He rounded the table and reached out, circling his fingers around her arm and guiding her to sit.

"What is happening?" he repeated.

"The Panthers. Police surrounded headquarters down here. At South Central, Jasmine said. At 41st, I think? There's been a shootout."

"Mierda."

"Should we go down there?"

Ernesto shook his head. "Running in at this point? We're not prepared for that."

"She also said some man just attacked her on campus. Looked like he was from the FBI."

Ernesto shoved aside the box of papers and sat down.

"I feel like this has something to do with whatever's going on with you," Ernesto said. "The sigils coming through… The visions? Right?"

A shaft of late morning sunlight reflected off his glasses, making patterns over his eyes. Carol could feel the Elements shifting around him, dominated by Air, but feathering out toward Fire, Water, and her own Element, Earth.

She reached for the power of growth and soil encoded in the wooden floor boards beneath her feet. Carol needed some comfort. Strength.

The power of the trees answered her energy, rising to meet her.

"I…don't know," she replied. "I'm honestly not clear about what's going on with me. But a firefight between the police and the Panthers doesn't seem good. Jasmine sounded freaked out. The man who just attacked her was the one who's been sending those astral snakes."

The coffee was a little sweeter than she usually drank it, but it tasted good. And the warm, solid cup helped ground her.

"So we figure out how to help. Starting with what you were telling me before the phone rang," Ernesto said.

Carol started to protest. This time he held up a hand.

"It's a good a place to start as any. The thing about sorcery is, we can't go haring off after everything that arises. We need to maintain our focus, or they win. Claro?"

Carol's hair had fallen in her face again. She swiped it behind her ears.

"What if that's what they want, though? For us to be like Terrance and Helen? Doing nothing? What if we end up being too careful?"

"We'll keep asking ourselves those questions," he replied.

Carol guessed that would have to be good enough for now. Frankly, she was relieved he didn't want to head to South Central. Stepping into a firefight? Carol wasn't ready for that. No matter *what* Jasmine Jones said.

"Okay." She let out a breath. "Jasmine and I have been talking."

Carol gestured at the binders and the legal pad. "I've been trying to research what I think might help her. Her and Doreen."

Ernesto's bushy eyebrows raised a bit at that, causing tiny lines around his eyes to fan out.

"But the more I think about it, the more slippery it all becomes."

Carol took a bite of liverwurst toast and chewed. Stalling for time again because she wasn't exactly sure how to talk about this.

Ernesto didn't say a word, just sipped at his coffee.

He gestured for her to continue.

She sighed.

"No matter how clear I am, by the time I sit down to work on a problem, it's like I only half remember it. Or am remembering it wrong."

Carol gestured at the yellow pad again. "I've been taking notes, but it's like I've written them in Theban or something. Even though the English words are clear to see."

"And the sigils are coming to you again?"

"It's not that, no, but it feels similar to that. The way the sigils took me over, and I didn't even know I was writing them? This…this is like that. But almost the opposite. Instead of the information taking me over, it's hiding from my mind."

Carol rotated her head, stretching the tendons in her neck. Everything felt so tight.

"Jasmine and Doreen are working out more ways to protect people. That battle in the park in Oakland wasn't the end of things. I guess this morning's attacks made that more clear, right?"

Ernesto's brow furrowed a bit at that. "It *is* part of the Association's job to protect people."

"So, Jasmine and Doreen have been fighting with Terrance about that, but he's been digging in his heels, insisting it isn't about magic. We're starting to suspect it's *all* about magic. The snakes, and the spiders, yeah, but the cops, too."

She threw the triangle of liverwurst toast down on the plate, not hungry anymore.

"Do you have to eat that thing?" Ernesto said.

"Sorry!" Carol shoved the plate further down the table.

"Here's the thing…" Did she trust him or not? This man who had been her teacher and was becoming her friend?

Carol took a breath and continued, "Jasmine and Doreen didn't just use their magic to protect people, they've also been training people to protect themselves with magic."

Ernesto grew very still, fingers wrapped around his cup, the silver wolf's head of the ring he always wore, gleaming in the morning sun.

The words hung in that room like one of Carol's practice spells.

Shit.

Ernesto stared out one of the tall arched windows, then took a sip of coffee, before setting the cup back down.

"That is outside the bounds of the Association, maga. We aren't allowed to interfere that way."

"I know that. *They* know that. They just don't care anymore." Carol shoved back from the table. The energy had been increasing in the room and she needed to move.

"Why?" he finally said, tracking her progress as she paced from the door to the work benches under the arched windows and back again.

"Because an even bigger battle is coming and they want people to be prepared. Jasmine says they're running out of time up there. Things are getting bad. With the police. And other things, she said. She and Doreen have been trying to get Terrance to help, but he keeps refusing. Doreen's almost ready to fly down here herself." She stopped her pacing. "And I think that's what my visions are about."

"And you've been hiding all this from me," Ernesto said. Carol didn't reply.

Just like you've been hiding your radical Chicano newspapers, Carol thought.

"Sit. Show me what you have," Ernesto said, chair squeaking against the wood floor as he stood up again.

Carol sat again and flipped back through the yellow pad, to try to find the right beginning.

Ernesto leaned over the table, smelling of coffee, Bay Rum after-shave, and damp air.

"It's here," Carol pointed to a series of glyphs she'd found, and the notes from her conversations with Jasmine.

"Let's see what we can learn here," he said. Pulling out a chair and sitting down next to her, he drew the yellow pad toward him, stared at it a moment, then turned to one of the open binders and flipped through that, stopping with a hiss.

"What is this?" Ernesto asked, shoving the binder toward her.

She followed the point of his finger and began reading her own neat letters. "*Let us now make bold to say that a werewolf is nothing else but the sidereal body of a man...*"

Carol looked up, tucking her blond hair behind her ears. "That's Eliphas Levi."

He should know that.

"I know. Keep reading please, maga. The section you copied just after that."

Carol bent her head back to her notes. "*The hurts inflicted on the werewolf do actually wound the sleeping person by an odic and sympathetic congestion of the Astral Light, and by correspondence between the immaterial and material body.*"

Ernesto nodded his head, and stabbed his finger at the book, his wolf's head ring sparking in the sun.

His wolf's head ring. Carol held her breath and pulled her energy in as subtly as she could.

Ernesto shook his head and gave her a distant smile. "No, maga, I'm not some werewolf. The wolf is simply an ally of mine. That's not what I'm seeking in your notes here. What I'm seeking is that phrase about the Astral Light. It's reminding me of something…"

He stood suddenly, shoving his chair backward.

"I think we need to see Rosalia."

Carol found that she was sweating, despite the December cold. He'd gone straight for the werewolves.

Out of all the weird things in that binder, out of all the things she needed him to look at, Ernesto zeroed in on shifters.

And Carol hadn't even told him about the some of the Panthers being shape shifters yet.

She wondered if he already knew.

CHAPTER EIGHT
LIZARD

Now that the sun was up, Lizard could see eddies of dark brown and gray swirling and shifting through the room. It was hard to breathe, but still possible. The gaping wound upstairs was at least still doing the job of drawing the poisons away from them all. Up and out into the smoggy Los Angeles sky.

Even so, his chest ached with the chemicals.

"We need a surrender flag," PeeWee said. "Anyone got one?"

A few of the men gave rueful laughs at that. Like any of them were ever prepared to surrender *shit* to the pigs.

Finally, someone found Peaches a white cloth. A handkerchief. She straightened her skirt and cleared her throat. Lizard watched her chest rise and fall as she fought to take a deep breath. It barely looked like her spindly legs would hold her, but they did.

He'd always thought Peaches was pretty. But she wouldn't look at the likes of him. Not when there were men with more experience in the movement available. Men a few years older than him. Men who swaggered with their guns and camo pants. Their black berets perched on perfect naturals.

The men he wanted to be.

Lizard shook his head. He couldn't bear the thought of surrendering, but now that the booming and constant gunfire had stopped, now that his adrenaline was crashing, he had to admit he didn't want to die. His mom would be happy about that.

When he was in the middle of it all, death was a given. His heart knew he could die anyway. Any day of the damn week. Might as well be on his terms. Head unbowed to the fucking pigs.

But now? Now he just wished he could be home, or hanging with the cats down the street, just an eighteen-year-old having a beer.

But this shit wasn't over yet, even though the bullets was gone and the shooting had stopped.

Lizard's knees hurt from being crouched on the floor for so long, but he wasn't ready to move. Not quite yet.

Peaches walked to the splintered door, white kerchief clutched in one of her bony hands. She pause a minute, took another breath, and raised the white cloth over her head. Then stepped out.

There was something so brave about her, stepping out with a straight spine, to face the police and SWAT team with nothing but that scrap of cloth to protect her. She could have been gunned down in an instant.

They all knew it.

She knew it.

"Hold fire!" A voice cracked out the order in the early morning. Something upstairs creaked and then crashed to the floor. Lizard listened for more movement. Just more refuse shaking itself down. He reached up and took the cigarette filters from his nostrils and tossed them on the floor.

Gas and gunpowder still lingered in the air, but wasn't so bad anymore. He could smell his own sweat, and something stronger. A strange scent. Like the musk of a cat. Shaking his head, Lizard tried to clear his ears.

Several sandbags leaked dirt onto the floors. Dirt from the tunnel they were digging near the back door. The tunnel that was supposed to be their way out, into safety.

They'd never finish that tunnel now. There was no escaping into the sewers and waterways spread out in a grid under the city. It had been a good plan. But all their plans were contingent on "unless the world blows up tomorrow." Or the roof blows off today.

There was no mistaking this attack, though. They all knew something was coming soon, after they'd heard about the shooting in Chicago. They still didn't know where Fred Hampton was. On the loose somewhere. It was a miracle he and Deborah weren't dead, though stories were circulating about that, too.

Strange stories. No one knew what to believe.

His comrades were slowly getting up. Some bare chested, in pants barely pulled back on after sleeping. Lizard never slept in his underwear anymore. These days, Lizard wore his pants to bed and had a jacket always ready, hanging on a chair. Geronimo taught him that.

"Let's go." That was PeeWee. Wayne followed.

Lizard found his voice. "What should we do with Tommye and Roland? They can't walk."

"The pigs will bring stretchers in. But we should carry them between us."

So that's what they did. Gathered them up. Lizard and Wayne carried out Tommye in a cradle made by both of their arms. Lizard didn't see who got Roland. They all filed out, under the "Feed Hungry Children Free Breakfast" sign that spanned the sidewalk, out toward the cops in their flak jackets and vests. The brand new SWAT team, formed to keep the people down. Shotguns and M16s everywhere.

Sniper rifles on the rooftops.

Lizard's mouth filled with the taste of bile. Tommye muttered, "Damn."

He was an enemy of the state now. Official. They all were.

Beyond the phalanx of pigs, crowds of people milled and stood, shoved behind wooden barricades. Black and brown faces stared back at him. One man raised a fist in the air. Others joined him.

"Power to the people!" someone shouted. A lone voice from the crowd.

Not everyone offered their fists in salute. Too many cops around. Cops were like crows, Lizard sometimes thought. They always remembered a person's face.

The pigs were waiting for them with ropes. Not handcuffs. Fucking ropes. Like the Panthers were some sort of animals. Not even worth clicking steel on wrists. Ropes like they were runaway slaves, ready to be bound up in the back of a cart or on the bottom of a boat, being sold down the river.

The cats around him all held their heads high. No one was hiding. Bold as brass, they were. Militant. Disciplined. Just like they'd been trained.

After setting Tommye down against a lamppost, Lizard stood up tall. His whole body ached from the tension of the hours of crouching and shooting, and his muscles were going to cramp up later, he could tell. He didn't care. Lizard set his jaw and lifted his own head higher into the morning sun.

Then a strange scream split the air. What the…?

The crowd started shouting, screaming, pointing. The pigs were backing frantically away, guns leveled, pointed directly at him. *Shitshitshitshit.*

No. They were pointing *past* him. Lizard whipped his body around, crouching down to the oil-stained sidewalk between the known danger and whatever the hell was behind him.

"I am *not* dead!" Roland Freeman was shouting, voice booming across the street.

There was a gray blanket on the ground in a heap. They must've lain Roland on it, or covered him with it because they thought Roland was… Roland was…

Was it actually Roland?

It *was* Roland. Same bullet-shredded camo pants and bullet-shredded white shirt hanging half off his torso. Dark stomach muscles rippling up into pectoral slabs. Roland was bigger than Lizard remembered. And standing now. How the *hell* was that cat standing?

Lizard brought his hands up to rub his ears. Trying to clear them. Make them pop.

There should have been a lot more noise. Walkie-talkies. Pigs talking. People talking smack. His ears should have been ringing still.

Maybe his ears had been damaged by the detonations and the guns fired in close quarters. But no.

It wasn't really no sound, or even muffled sound. It was like Lizard was in a bubble. He *could* hear things, but it was like playing a 45 at 75 rpm speed. Low. Slow. Weird. And everyone was moving real slow, too.

He stayed, still crouched low, not even thinking about the SWAT team at his back anymore. Lizard's mind kept flickering in and out. He kept blinking his sore, tear-gassed eyes. Kept trying to swallow some moisture in his dried-out, cordite-and-bile tasting mouth.

He kept trying to make sense of the whole thing. The whole thing that wasn't making any sense at all.

Lizard tightened up his taint. He was not going to piss all over the damn street, squatting like a dog. He blinked. Hard. Then his blood-shot eyes raked down Roland's arms. Shoulders. Biceps. Strong fore-arms. Hands. No hands. There were not hands at the end of his arms. There were…

Where there used to be hands, there were now big black-furred paws with ivory claws unsheathed and dripping red.

Lizard's mind finally took in the cop with a slashed neck at Roland's feet, blood staining the sidewalk, head lolling to one side, practically severed.

And then Roland's face began to change shape.

"A panther," Lizard whispered. "He's turning into a goddamned, actual panther."

Lizard pissed his pants.

CHAPTER NINE
JASMINE

Every rickety metal folding chair in the church hall was filled. Community members lined up on the walls or sat on the scratched-up wood floors. I'd never seen the room without the neat rows of tables, ready to feed the children who came every morning for breakfast before school.

Maybe I shouldn't have run from Snake Guy. But damn, I just wasn't sure enough in my magic to take someone like that on alone. I really needed to consult with Doreen, but she'd been at work all day, so I had called Carol instead.

And tonight, there was this meeting. Fred Hampton was still in town for a few precious days, and gathering with the Panthers had to take priority.

Even over my safety. And maybe even my sanity.

We risked meeting at Father Neil's church because none of the other Panther meeting places were big enough to hold everyone who was going to want to hear Chairman Fred speak.

Father Neil was down with the program. I just hoped we could keep him safe.

The Panthers tried to keep the event quiet, for security reasons, but even so, word had gotten out. Folks couldn't keep a secret this big. I was wondering how many cops or Feds knew Fred was in California.

Hopefully they were still searching Chicago and hadn't trailed him this far west.

Or they thought he was already gone from Oakland. Which he would be soon enough.

Security was fully strapped tonight. Leather coats, black berets, and rifles, they were stationed on all doors, in and out. Along with those I now knew were shape-shifters.

The shifters were placed strategically around the perimeter. Their musky smell blended with the soft scents of lilac perfume from the grannies and the old skunky marijuana smell rising from the clothes of some of the younger folks in the room.

I was leaning against one of the long side walls in my own long leather coat and green corduroy bell-bottoms. I'd picked my natural out carefully before leaving the house tonight. Maybe it was vanity that made me want to look like a revolutionary. But it was sure nice feeling like I belonged.

Sorcery floated just beneath my skin, like the waters of the bay just beyond the shipyards to the west.

I scanned the crowd. The usual party members were in attendance. There was Tanya, with her two kids in tow. I'd never seen them before. They were cute. She was one dedicated sister, I'd give her that. Impressive. Even though she tried her best to act like she wasn't a threat to anyone, I suspected Tanya was stronger than most.

I gave her a small wave. Jimmy was setting up some chairs and a wooden podium at the front of the room. Drake was there with some friends from school. He was turning into a fighter, that one. He'd gone from a scared kid running from white bullies, eyes wide when I'd used a bit of magic to chase them off, to a young man training others to make spells.

Drake had more magical potential than Doreen or I thought at first, and he certainly had leadership ability.

Doreen sat in a chair near the front, navy pocketbook held neatly on her lap.

Jerrold was absent. He was still under some sort of house arrest until leadership figured out whether he'd been used by magical operatives or he was a willing infiltrator. I was the one who had outed him as the person who'd fired a shot in the middle of a crowded nightclub, putting everyone at danger and calling the cops down on us.

If I hadn't been able to get a shield up in time, we might have all been taken to jail.

Yeah, people were still pissed off at me about Jerrold.

Like I'd been the one to betray the Party.

So be it.

A lot of the people who had stood with us at DeFremary Park were in the buzzing room. Everyone was waiting for the Chairman to come. With Huey still locked up, Fred had become the symbol for us all. A beacon of power and hope, Fred was our visionary, the cat rapping about community, freedom, women's rights, gay rights, and most of all, Black Power.

More importantly, Fred was miraculously alive. Deborah, too. And she was carrying their child, a child of the movement.

That baby could be born any moment now. In the midst of rising chaos, a symbol of survival. Pretty heavy thing to gift a child.

Leaning against that wall, I wondered how many of the folks gathered knew Fred was a shifter, rumored to have survived a rain of bullets, killing two Feds with his own claws.

How many would take that in stride, the way they had acclimated to me and Doreen teaching them how to use pre-loaded spells to protect themselves from the police?

I shook my head. The world was strange even to me, and I'd been raised with sorcery. But I hadn't been raised knowing some people could change into animals, even though it turned out Uncle Hector had been one. And I wasn't used to things being out in the open.

The Uncle Hector thing pissed me off a little, a family secret being kept from me like that. But I was struggling to get over it. There was too much work to be done to coddle my feelings about the past.

It was a brave new world and I was on the front lines of making it all happen.

There was bustling at the side door, and two sets of shifters walked through, followed by men holding handguns at the ready. I could tell who the shifters were now, and was amazed it had taken me so long to figure it out. They had a shine and a swagger to them that even the most powerful humans just didn't share. The cats were graceful, beautiful, and carried the scent of wild magic on the musk that breathed out of their pores.

Just like my Jimmy.

The whole room rose to its feet.

And Fred Hampton walked into the room, straight for the podium, guards fanning out around him, three on each side. The door slammed shut.

Fred raised his right hand, fist in the air.

"All Power to the people!" he shouted.

"All Power to the people!" every voice in the room roared. I shouted it like my life depended on it, snapping my fist out, tears pricking at my eyes. Fred. Chairman Fred.

People sat back down, but no one was relaxed in that room. Everyone leaned in to listen.

"Power anywhere where there's people," Fred said. "A lot of people get the word revolution mixed up and they think revolution's a bad word. Revolution is nothing but like having a sore on your body and then you put something on that sore to cure that infection. And I'm telling you that we're living in an infectious society right now."

People nodded their heads. There were a few "um hums!" rising in the crowd.

"I'm telling you that we're living in a sick society. And anybody that endorses integrating into this sick society before it's cleaned up is a man who's committing a crime against the people."

I never thought I would actually get to see him like this, preaching at a podium in the very church where I served food three days a week. How long did we have with him?

He couldn't be here for long, that was for sure. It was too dangerous. I could see that in the eyes of the security detail guarding him.

And I could feel it in my bones.

But dead or alive, there was a fire inside that man. A fire he was doing his best to impart to the rest of us.

"We got to face some facts. That the masses are poor, that the masses belong to what you call the lower class, and when I talk about the masses, I'm talking about the white masses, I'm talking about the black masses, and the brown masses, and the yellow masses, too."

All of these words that I'd read on mimeographed sheets were now coming from his mouth. The watery spark inside me rose to meet them, twining from me, toward the man at the podium. The man with the soft drawl and the smile, and the steel in his spine.

"We've got to face the fact that some people say you fight fire best with fire, but we say you put fire out best with water. We say you don't fight racism with racism. We're gonna fight racism with solidarity. We say you don't fight capitalism with no black capitalism; you fight capitalism with socialism."

He looked right at me, I swear, his brown eyes flashing amber. The scent of musk grew stronger, and my magic reached out to touch his face. He put a hand to his cheek, and I watched it turn into a soft, black-furred paw.

There was a gasp from the front rows and that paw receded, becoming just a man's brown hand again.

But I had seen it. I had felt it.

Fred wanted me to know that he had seen *me*, too.

CHAPTER TEN
JASMINE

We were back at headquarters, packed into the front room in West Oakland HQ. What was once upon a time a Victorian parlor was now a hodgepodge of chairs, low tables, and a blackboard and the radical Emory Douglas posters that I loved, all bright shapes and proud faces.

Jimmy, Doreen, and I were crammed into the chairs, along with leadership. The fact that they were letting Doreen and I in on a meeting with Fred meant that they were finally taking our magic seriously.

I guess throwing up a people-powered magic shield around the park during a standoff with the cops had made an impression.

The meeting at Father Neil's church was powerful. Fred had talked for more than an hour and people were seriously inspired. As we left the hall, small groups were still talking on the sidewalks, not ready to go home.

The scene reminded me of my arrival in the Bay, when I first saw the Panthers massing on the steps of the Oakland courthouse, all leather coats and berets even in the summer heat. I still felt the way the tears had filled my eyes.

That sight had changed my life, taking me from a nice, middle class black sorcerer from Crenshaw and sprinting toward the radical magician I was becoming.

I was a Panther now, even if I couldn't shift my shape. And I bet half the people in that church auditorium were joining up, in some way or another.

Jimmy held my hand, our shoulders bumping in the close-set wooden chairs. It felt nice, sitting next to him like that. Jimmy calmed me down inside.

Cigarette smoke filled the air, warring with shape-shifter musk and someone's cheap perfume.

My leather coat was in my lap, but the room was heating up. I shifted to drape it across the back of my chair. Leroy, sitting in a row behind, caught my eye and gave me a nod. That was good. It meant maybe he had forgiven me for outing Jerrold as a possible plant.

I still wasn't sure what was going on with that, whether security was…

"Be still, girl," Doreen said. "Conserve yourself."

I sighed. "It's just always so hot in here."

"I think you'd be used to that by now." She looked at me accusingly, reminding me of all the nights I'd lied about where I was. "Besides, the temperature feels just fine to me."

It would. Doreen carried Fire like I was Water. Now that she was back to doing sorcery, Doreen was all on board with lighting things up with her orange-colored fire. Including the Association.

I grinned. I'd heard her shouting on the phone with Terrance multiple times. And she and Helen were cooking up some sort of conspiracy.… I wasn't sure what. And she and I just might be cooking a conspiracy of our own.

Plus, I grinned to myself, Aunt Doreen had gone from a shut-down woman to a possible lesbian in cat eye glasses, almost overnight. Luckily, magical people were used to all kinds. I just hoped the Panthers would be, too. I'd heard Huey Newton was down with gay rights, but you never knew with some other folks.

At any rate, Doreen was *bathing* in Elemental Fire right now, and enjoying every second of it.

Me? I wiped the sheen of sweat from my upper lip and tried to concentrate.

My attention moved toward the edges of the room, checking out the wards. Doreen and I had spent one afternoon putting up protections around the whole building. Huh. The corner between west and north felt cracked already. How in all the Powers had that happened?

"Doreen…" I started to ask, and then Fred Hampton strode into the room, robbing the room of what little air there was.

His presence was mighty. Palpable. The part of me that was half in love with him set up a flutter in my belly. The rest of me sat up at full attention, waiting on his words.

Fred shook Tarika's hand, and nodded Jimmy's way. Someone set a glass of water on a low table near an empty chair for him.

"Thanks, brother." He remained standing, all of us looking up at him, expectant.

"You've been doing well out here, sisters and brothers. And that shit that went down at the park? That was true revolutionary organizing. We need more of that."

He nodded at Doreen, and then me. It sent a jolt down to my feet. He *had* seen me. No mistaking it.

"And the magic your people are bringing to the struggle is just what the struggle needs. We must be militant. We must stay ready."

Fred paused to drink some water, making me wish I had some in the now stifling, smoke-filled room.

"We *are* ready, Chairman," Leroy said. "A bunch of the cats here want to know when we gonna bust Huey out of prison."

Fred listened, nodding. "We need to make a plan to free our brother Huey, and to free the other cats locked up behind bars."

"Isn't that stretching our resources too far?" said a voice. Tanya. Well, that was a surprise. I'd never known Tanya to speak up like that before.

Actually, what was she doing here? She wasn't usually in meetings, either. And I wondered where her kids were.

Fred took another sip of water and looked her dead in the eye. "We have all the resources of the Party, the shifters, and the people, sister. But you are right. First things come first."

Jimmy rose at that. I reached out toward him. He squeezed my hand, then let it go.

"What happens now that the people know about us?" Jimmy said. "Know that we're more than just The Black Panther party? That some of us are shifters, and we have access to magic, too." He glanced at me on those final words.

Multiple voices started buzzing, excited by his words, but I couldn't concentrate on what anyone was saying. The break in the wards kept poking at the back of my head. I leaned as close to Doreen as possible.

"Do you feel that? Northwest corner."

Doreen closed her eyes, seeking. I split my attention between her, the wards, and the room, calling on the waters from the bay to boost my magic.

Fred's voice entered my consciousness again. "But we can't focus too much on the fighting. We got to feed the people. Keep the clinics running. And most importantly, keep up the Freedom Schools."

He continued, "Without education, people will accept anything. Without education, people don't know why they're doing what they're doing, you know what I mean?"

"Um hum, brother."

"Right on."

Doreen's eyes flew open, I felt a huge *push* against the walls, and the wards cracked.

"Hit the floor!" I shouted. The non-shifters did, shoving chairs out of the way and covering each other with their arms. The big cats all stood tall.

"You, too! Idiots!"

I heard growls at that, but didn't have time to explain. Balling up as much ocean as I could muster, I let the blue-tinged fire burst from my hands and toward whatever was coming through the walls.

Cinnamon fire scorched the air around me as Doreen shot off an orange bolt.

"Protection!" she shouted. A request and a command.

I sent a wave of sorcery to hover over the people on the floor, and sent another cresting toward the Panthers still standing.

Then I saw it. A giant, astral snake.

It was heading straight for Chairman Fred.

CHAPTER ELEVEN
DOREEN

Doreen scrambled, magic flying through the smoky air, orange sparks crackling through her fingers. The cinnamon scent grew stronger.

She was aware of a huge snake shape on the edges of her vision, but didn't have time to deal with that. Jasmine was on it, blue water fire and all.

So far, the protection Jasmine had thrown up over the room was holding, though Doreen didn't trust it, not when something this big and nasty had brute-forced its way through their carefully constructed wards.

Feeling for the cracks, she crouched next to two people. The woman was cursing under her breath and the man moaned. Maybe he hit his head on a chair when he went down?

"Can you drag him out of here?" Doreen asked the woman, barely turning her head. She didn't really have time to look at them, either. She needed to focus on the damn cracks in the wards. But the fewer people who were in danger in the crowded room, the easier sealing the wards would become.

"I can't see a clear path," the woman replied.

"Ask a shifter," Doreen said.

She barely heard the woman shouting for Leroy, and felt the air change around her as the giant panther came closer.

Doreen spared a glance and saw the massive cat take the man's collar in its jaws and start dragging him toward the door. The woman crawled behind, stockings shredding beneath her skirt. She had left their coats behind.

Good. More room to work. Less distraction from scared or furious minds.

The cracks in the northwest corner disturbed Doreen. There was no way anything should have breached that magic. When they set the wards, they went over and over the sphere linking the sorcery together. It was seamless. Doreen knew it. Yet something had...attacked that ward. The sphere hadn't been attacked. The anchor wards themselves had been tampered with.

Doreen could feel it now. The shapes and sigils had subtly been shifted, allowing the strange magic to access the building.

Damn. How in the Powers had that happened?

She lowered her center, rooting more deeply, and tapped the core fire at the center of the earth. Casting her vision outward, Doreen visited all six of the wards. The four cardinal directions, plus above and below.

They hadn't set a seventh ward inside the center of the building, because they didn't trust that the people and shifters coming and going wouldn't knock it out of place.

That had been their big mistake.

"Damn it!" Doreen muttered. It was as if she'd never done magic before in her life. Jasmine might not know better yet, but Doreen should have.

They had sealed the edges, but left the center to take care of itself. Which was fine when the protective sphere was around experienced magic workers. But these Panthers? Most of them had never even sniffed this kind of magic until Jasmine and Doreen started up the trainings.

And the shifter's magic was a different flavor. It rose from the panther forms, not from objects like ceremonialists used, or from Elements, like Association sorcery.

Jasmine was struggling behind her, Doreen felt that.

"Jasmine, do you need me?" Doreen called.

Her niece shouted back that Doreen should hold the line. Good thing that, because there was really no way she could help her niece. Not unless she was willing to risk every single person in this house.

Doreen had to fix this thing. It was her own damn fault that Chairman Fred was in danger again. The Party was vulnerable, not from Feds or police this time, but from the same magical force that had been dogging Jasmine's heels.

Strange sigils shimmered over the wards she and Jasmine had set. They were completely unfamiliar. A magic Doreen hadn't seen before. Black and swirling, sharp-edged and dense—she couldn't quite wrap her mind around the shapes.

She sent out a burst of her own protective magic toward the original wards. A black stream grabbed ahold of her energy and began to flow back toward her body.

"No!" she shouted, grappling with the inky substance crawling its way down her cinnamon stream, heading directly toward her hands.

Which formed a pathway to her heart.

"Fire in the earth, protect me! Fire in the sky, rain down upon your faithful child! Fire in my heart and mind, rise up, flow outward, quench the coming night!"

"*Intelligensssssss...*" the magic hissed inside her ears. The feel of the voice cramped up her stomach, and made her want to wretch.

The voice chanted and babbled, a stream of syllables that bounced inside her head. They sullied her with the sort of magic she had hoped to never feel again. The magic she had caught traces of the night her Hector died.

Doreen swallowed the bile back down, then breathed into her aching belly and *pushed* outward with all her might. Pushing the babbling voice out of her head. Pushing the inky sigils back toward the walls. Pushing protection out to follow the sickening, putrid magic. Trying desperately to cleanse herself again, and clear the space around her so she could reset. The. Damn. Wards.

"Don't seal it off, Doreen!" Jasmine's voice broke through the inner clamor.

"I have to!" Doreen replied. She filled herself with roaring until she couldn't hear anything but the quick rushing of elemental Fire. Jasmine may have been shouting; the voice babbled out a string of incantations.

None of it mattered.

What mattered was to capture the damn snake. Doreen needed to trap it so it couldn't get free again.

But Doreen had somehow missed the door. In focusing on the sigils, she hadn't seen the umber-lined rectangle the snake was heading toward.

Damn it!

The power of Water crashed into her Fire. Jasmine. Jasmine fighting the snake. Must be affecting the sigils and the wards somehow.

Doreen couldn't counter that without getting into Jasmine's way. Damn. Damn. Damn. By all the Powers! Damn!

"You will not harm the ones who shelter here! By all the Fire within me, you shall not rise! You shall be vanquished! Banished! Gone!"

Doreen was shouting like some ceremonial weirdo. Words that never would have come from her mouth before. She rode it anyway. Clearly this magic needed it. Something in the air began to respond.

A sizzling. More crackling. Like circuits shorting out. She vaguely heard Jasmine shouting again. Felt a panther roar.

The ocean crashed through Doreen, quenching her Fire. The sorcery ran out of her for a moment, slamming her onto the ground, bashing her shoulder on an overturned chair.

Pain shot through Doreen. She fought to get the magic back. Struggled against the tide.

Just for a moment.

Then she remembered to relax. Let Jasmine's waves cradle her. And found her connection to the fire deep in the earth again. Deep beneath the ocean bed. Fire lived in everything.

Warmth suffused Doreen's skin.

Flames leapt in her hands.

She pushed herself back up, back to her feet.

Opened every inch of herself to Elemental Fire.

And blasted the damn slippery sigils with everything she had.

CHAPTER TWELVE
CAROL

Ernesto's hands gripped the black-leather–covered steering wheel. Hand over hand, he muscled the Mustang into a tight spot between an old tricked-out Impala and a bright white Cadillac, right in front of the blue door with the faded orange hand.

The yellow triangle surrounding the hand seemed brighter than usual today, though the door paint still flaked around it.

They both stepped out of the car, the heavy doors thunking shut.

Was the brightness magic, or a slapdash touch up? Carol couldn't tell. She bit the edges of her mouth. Even though she was getting used to coming to East LA, she was nervous. They were visiting the hechicera, Rosalia. The hechicera always saw Carol too clearly, and Carol was beginning to think Rosalia expected something from her.

What that was, she wasn't sure.

A row of small windows lined the top of the wall above the door. Last time Carol had been to the shop, there hadn't been any windows there. She could swear to it. The shop door opened before Ernesto even put out a hand toward it. Rosalia ushered them in with a bony hand, silver bracelets clacking on her slim dark wrists.

Blinking to adjust her eyes from the winter sun outside, Carol rubbed at the soft yellow sweater covering her arms. She looked around the botánica, taking in the shelves of beads, shells, feathers, and herbs.

The colored jar candles in rows. The long, low glass counter. The statues of saints.

And Rosalia, in her voluminous burgundy velvet skirts, embroidered shawl around her skinny shoulders, citrine eyes peering at Carol as though they were looking at everything Carol had ever been and ever would be.

The shop was all lit with low blue and red lamps, and candles burning on altars. Smoke rose from an abalone shell; scent of copal filled the air.

Something was off, even though it all looked the same.

"Abuela, thank you for seeing us," Ernesto said.

"Have you brought danger to my door today, Ernesto?"

Carol shivered. Why would Rosalia say that?

"There is a sickness in the air around you," the hechicera said. "Miasma. You carry it from that fancy house up on the hill."

Rosalia turned those pale green eyes to Carol, staring around her, as she always did, reading the space Carol occupied, rather than looking at Carol herself.

Carol straightened up to meet her gaze. There was nothing being afraid would get her here, so she might as well start practicing standing tall. Even in front of someone as old and weird as a sorcerer who could hold a person with one gaze.

Rosalia nodded. "Good, maga, good. You have been practicing. Ernesto here could learn some things from you." She sniffed the air.

"But even you have a strange scent around you. Spider silk, and the spaces between stars. These things touched you before, but there is something new here. You carry scents from other places. Other people's worries, perhaps? Or traces of the sickness in my Ernesto's shining body?"

The old woman swished her skirts and headed for the botánica counter. She rummaged in a cabinet set beneath the glass countertop, emerging with a green-silk–wrapped deck of cards.

"Perhaps both," she said. "Ernesto, you shall read for us."

"But Rosalia, there are things we need to…"

"There is too much you do not know. The cards will tell us more than the half questions you both carry through my door." She unwrapped the silk, and set the deck of cards on the counter with a smack. "The cards will show us exactly what you need to tell me, without the fuss and worry distracting you."

"Read for us, Ernesto. The way I taught you to."

Rosalia pulled a padded stool out from the counter, and gestured to it.

Ernesto gave a small sigh, and walked around the glass countertop. He climbed up on the stool and reached for the cards, wolf ring glinting in the colored lights and candle flames.

Closing his eyes, he grew still for a moment. He was centering. Tuning to the cards. Just like he had taught Carol to do. Then he began to shuffle, cards sliding against each other, cracking and snapping as he formed the bridge.

They were regular playing cards, worn with use. Blue patterns swirled around two scallop shells in the center. The scallop shells flashed and covered black and red pips. Clubs. Spades. Hearts. Diamonds. Queens and Jacks peeked out and hid away.

Carol had never seen anyone read playing cards like this before, though she'd heard that people did.

Rosalia smoothed the green silk onto the counter next to Ernesto. Still he shuffled, methodically. Precisely. Over and over the red and black flashed and hid. Finally, his hands grew still. He set the cards onto the silk.

Rosalia split the pack into three piles, then stacked them again, middle pile on the top.

Ernesto picked them up again, and began to set them out into the shape of a fan, snapping the individual cards out to rest on the green silk.

The ace of spades was in the center, like a black, pointed spear, aiming straight for Carol's heart. She stepped to one side. The ace was flanked by clubs on the left: the two and the king. To the right of that black spear was the the king and two of diamonds.

Carol had no idea what this could mean.

Ernesto looked at Rosalia, waiting.

"Speak the words you know are necessary, child," she said.

He took a heaving breath in, as though the air, his Air, his Element, was burning at his lungs.

"Mierda," he whispered, then cleared his throat.

"Okay. There is a rift. A…fragmentation. The worlds that have coexisted, side by side, not touching, are at a crossroads now. Together. Both of them…"

Ernesto ran a hand over his face and raked it back through his hair, wincing as his ring pulled some strands out of his head. He rubbed his hands on his jeans.

"It is hard to see the truth, isn't it, Ernesto? Continue."

Rosalia seemed angry with Ernesto, but Carol couldn't fathom why. And she'd never seen her mentor act this way, like a scared child in front of a disapproving teacher.

Or like a man who was afraid.

"The worlds have to decide now to…I don't know. I can't read these cards."

"You can," Rosalia said, calm as ice. "But you won't. You've been trapped up in that mansion far too long, niño, eating from the rich white man's table."

He sat back. Looked at Carol. There was pain in his eyes, and something else. Anger. He was angry.

"We have to choose," he said. "We have to choose or fail. There is no hiding anymore. The magic ones must meet the ones from the other side…"

Ernesto paused and looked at Carol.

"And you are the one with the answers in this room. You know who those others are, don't you?"

Carol nodded. Air and Fire were at an impasse, that was one sense of the reading. But really, it was about much more than that. There were too many forces that had been arrayed against one another. Not working together. And if they kept themselves apart…too much would be torn asunder.

Her mouth was stuffed with cotton, but Carol opened it anyway, tasting the copal on the back of her tongue.

Then she took a breath and spoke.

"The animal people are rising. The people need our help."

"The werewolves?" Ernesto said, brow furrowed.

"No. No. I don't know if there are any werewolves. I just found that when I was searching Eliphas Levi for...for all the things I can't even remember!" Carol said.

Rosalia reached across the counter, placing a cool hand over Carol's own. "Tell us."

"Jasmine. The Black Panthers. They're real. I mean, they're shifters. They are people who can turn into big cats. Not Jasmine. But some of the others."

Rosalia was nodding. "We have seen these things. Las Manos knew this day would come. We've been preparing. The Animal People lived with us long ago, but went away, retreating into the canyons when it wasn't safe for them in the places of steel and concrete anymore. That they appear now, means big trouble or big power."

Ernesto looked down at the cards.

"Ay, Diosas," he murmured.

"Yeah. Holy shit," Carol replied.

CHAPTER THIRTEEN
SNAKES AND SPIDERS

*T*he room was dim enough that Samuels slid his dark glasses into the breast pocket of his plain black suit.

The Master was in the center of the room, keening magic syllables over the black marks drawn in heavy ink on crisp white paper.

A man knelt in front of the Master, face a rictus of effort and pain. Other operatives ringed the room, waiting.

Samuels didn't want a second tattoo. The work was enough. The magic was enough. The tiny spider tattooed on the web of his right hand was enough.

And the men in this room already had more power than men should ever wield.

And Samuels would never speak those words aloud. Not here. Not anywhere.

The Master wanted to take the initiations up one more level, to increase their power. Samuels was too far up the pyramid to refuse. He had wed himself to this dark, lead-lined room. Married himself to the secret organization inside the secret organization.

A sheen of sweat broke out on his upper lip.

Samuels had already changed his life. Changed his body. Changed his mind.

What was a little ink on the pale underside of his arm, up near the pit, a place few people would ever see?

Just looking at the sigil from a distance made his stomach churn.

The Master spun the the threads out from his stubby fingers, weaving skeins of light. Catching the reflection from the candles in the crystal held in one of the operative's hands.

The operative knelt, white robe pooling around him, scuffed leather soles of his black shoes emerging from the white, and a flash of black from his trousers. His blond hair fell in a lock over his forehead. The man had been holding that crystal up for twenty minutes now.

Samuels' arms ached in sympathy.

Samuels, like all the operatives, was caught by one of the threads, roped into the Master's work. Like he had been for a decade now.

Tolson—the Master's right-hand man and, some suspected, his lover— had met Samuels at some Washington, DC, party. Glitter and brass and just enough champagne. The kind of party a flunky like Samuels was lucky to even attend.

Tolson had given him a slight nudge with his mind, and Samuels' eyes had flown open in surprise.

Tolson just smiled. Mission accomplished.

The recruitment began that day. Samuels had been turned from an everyday psychic and into a ceremonial magician of high rank. He was brought in on the ground floor of the new organization within the organization.

The Solomonic Temple within the Federal Bureau of Investigation. The thing that no one knew about. Because hidden things had power.

They called upon The Intelligence. A crystalized web of power and intention, part egregore, part angel, it was their God and Guide.

COINTELPRO. The cypher to the prayer, the spell that held the entire web together.

The most potent magic Samuels had ever encountered.

But the Master was cracking apart. Asking for more "vitamin shots" than usual. Babbling about The Intelligence in words that made less and less sense. Having operatives walking those damn beagles for him, day and night, dragging the slobbering dogs across the square.

As though the men didn't have better things to do with their time. Especially now.

Samuels couldn't deny that the magic was strong. Whatever it was the Master was working on was affecting the æthers. Samuels' own snake dæmon grew more powerful daily. It spoke to him in dreams. It slithered out from the focus that was his ring, and, with his well trained mind, he could squeeze and crush that which stood before him.

Most of the time.

He could feel the sweat dripping from beneath his arms.

Samuels' discipline was slipping. He fought to keep his hands still. His aura clear. His mind on the task at hand. They were charging up the sigil, the thing that would power this whole operation, giving it more reach than it ever had before. The damn Negro militants and stupid hippies would quake in their sandals and their boots.

Once the sigil was set, the Chosen Ones would get it inked on flesh, creating a direct link between the magic and their blood.

The Master would control them all.

For as long as he lived.

CHAPTER FOURTEEN
LIZARD

Lizard nursed a beer in the shadowed back of the bar two neighborhoods away from his mother's house. He was no longer thinking about the revolution. He just wanted to stay alive.

Two older guys smacked checkers down, a few tables down, in the corner pocket of the bar. They wore short sleeve dress shirts, and their salt-and-pepper hair was cropped close to their heads. If one of them hadn't had a nose that looked like it'd been broken and reset more than once, Lizard wouldn't have been able to tell them apart.

They musta been friends a long time, he guessed.

Lizard had stopped by home only to change underwear and jeans, and to grab a couple of things, leaving his teargassed clothes in a stinking heap on his bedroom floor.

He wished he'd taken a shower, but hadn't wanted to risk the time, or being wet and naked if the pigs broke down the door.

He'd even hesitated over whether or not his daddy's lizard belt marked him. Decided to thread it back through his belt loops all the same. The only thing he had left of Daddy, now the man had passed. It was his luck. His connection to the ancestors.

He needed as much of both as he could get.

Lizard couldn't go home again. Not now. He was scared to go home. Scared to go out on the streets. Scared to call anyone. He hoped his momma would figure out what had happened, and that someone would get her word he was alive.

So yeah. He was in a bar at ten in the morning. Not his usual place or time. He traced the squares on the red-and-white-checked oilcloth over the booth table, shoved up against the back wall so he could see the whole, dim place. Light coming through the dirty windows at the front of the bar showed a few cars parked on the street, and would let him know if the pigs showed. He hoped to make it out the back door if that happened.

Hoped to make it out alive.

Bottles clinked as the bartender unloaded a case into the once-white battered refrigerator between the long, dark wood bar with its taped-up stools, and the little office room behind it, next to the men's room.

Lizard had washed the worst of the smoke, soot, and tear gas from his face at home, doing a second round on his hair and arms in the little men's room sink, drying off with the big blue roller towel.

The bartender hadn't said a word when Lizard walked in. Didn't even ask for ID. Just pulled him a beer and nodded before going about his business. Black men in this neighborhood walked a fine line between avoiding any situation that would bring the cops down on their business, and keeping other black men away from those same cops.

Lizard was grateful to the man for letting him stay despite the lingering scent of tear gas he knew was all over his tender skin.

The beer was crisp and doing its job of calming him down. Well, the first beer had done that job. Lizard had swallowed that one down as soon as it was set in front of him, practically choking on the foam. When he was done, the bartender had silently set down a second, along with the bowl of peanuts Lizard was slowly cracking his way through.

When people say "all hell broke loose," Lizard usually figured they were exaggerating. But that day, crouched on the sidewalk with piss running down his legs and a man who had been his friend and mentor turning into a fucking giant black cat, and pigs ratcheting bullets into chambers, scared out of their minds?

That day, it really felt like all hell *was* breaking loose. They had gone through the fires of purgatory, with gunpowder like brimstone, and cordite and dynamite like flames.

A car still burned down the street. Pontiac, it had looked like it was when he'd skulked by it, walking quick, but not too quick, head down, hoping to not get noticed.

Lizard was barely aware of the sound of it on the street, among all the other sounds, once his hearing had adjusted itself to the rapid beating of his heart and whatever it was that had altered space and time into slow motion when shit got too real and he'd pissed his own pants in front of the roiling mess of 41st and Central.

Now that things were real time again, it felt like time was moving way too fast. It had taken everything he had to not curl up on the sidewalk next to Tommye, holding his head in his hands like a scared child.

Lizard's hands still shook a little from the scene. The firefight, the gas, the roof opening up over his head? The boom of explosives? A man could handle all of that.

It was the other shit that had Lizard wishing he could run back home to his momma.

Roland had full on turned into a panther. Started roaring like a motherfucker and charged straight through the line of pigs. He about knocked Lizard over as he ran by. The street shook as the giant cat bounded onto the tarmac. And Lizard could smell him. That cat scent.

That scent he had smelled inside HQ. It must've started to rise off Roland when he got wounded.

Freaked Lizard right out, but not so much he didn't take advantage of the confusion and bolt himself. He felt bad leaving Tommye behind, but really? Lizard only felt bad about that once he was blocks away. Actually, he had to admit he only thought about Tommye lying there with gunshots in her thighs after he'd downed his first beer.

What the fuck kind of comrade was he?

"An alive one," his momma would say. She would be relieved that he'd gotten out. But she'd also have that shadowy look of disappointment she sometimes got, lips pursed and eyes cast down. Disappointment that he'd become the sort of man who would leave an injured woman behind.

Lizard was disappointed in that, too. But his guns were all dropped in the sandbags on the bottom floor of headquarters. There wasn't one damn thing he could've done to protect Tommye, or anyone else, at that point.

At least, that's what he told himself. He shook his head. Maybe he could've used the distraction Roland was making and dragged Tommye off somewhere.

He should've tried. He knew that. But he'd just been so damn scared when Roland changed, that all the discipline and training left his body, leaving behind the man he really was, he guessed. One scared motherfucker.

Lizard took another pull on the beer. Shit. He had no fucking idea what he was going to do next. How to even hook up with the Panthers again. No idea what or who was even safe.

CHAPTER FIFTEEN
JASMINE

Doreen, most of the panther shifters, and a bunch of people who hadn't been able to get out quickly were still in the meeting room at headquarters. I hoped the other folks had cleared the building.

Chairs and tables were knocked over, and with the people huddled on the ground, the room had become a tricky obstacle course.

I hoped Tanya was safe, but didn't have time to look around to see if she was still in the room. Hopefully she was on her way home to her kids.

I relied on my extra senses as best I could, to keep me upright, safe, and aware, but mostly? I was focused on the damn astral snake.

The snake was huge, half a foot around, and I couldn't tell how long, with bared fangs in its massive mouth.

It was literally flying through the air. I had no idea if anyone but Doreen and I could see it, but damn it, it was *there.*

Dropping the general protections we'd thrown up around the room for just a moment, I screamed, "Move! Out of the room if you can! Everyone else to the edge!"

I heard the door slam open, and people scrambling toward it while those nearest me crawled to the walls, bumping my shins as they passed.

Standing as firm as I could, I drew on more power. The waters of the bay surged through my skin, filling me up so I could pour the power out again. To everyone else, my power looks like blue fire, but believe me, it is the tide. Salt water beaded on my skin, giving me the moisture I was longing for.

"Doreen?"

"I'm trying to repair the wards!"

"No! You'll trap it in."

She snapped her head toward me at that. "That's what I'm trying to do, fool. You want this thing getting away?"

That pissed me off.

"I want these people safe!"

The stink of cat warred with the cinnamon and ocean, and the papery scent of snake. I could feel it in my bones when the animal people started shifting.

Behind me, I felt Fred Hampton roar, the heat of his breath practically on my neck. Tarika and Leroy must have changed, too, because all of a sudden the room felt too small for the humans and the cats.

A big cat bumped against my thigh to let me know it was there. Jimmy. I could taste his scent on my tongue. Amber and musk, undercut by some sweetness I hadn't been able to place. Yet.

"Thanks," I said, taking a big breath of him in. Just his presence steadied me.

There was no way I was keeping that snake off Chairman Fred. It was too slippery. It sliced through the the waves of my protection, fangs bared, heading for Fred's massive throat.

I stepped between them, pushing out my shields. The snake hit my edges first, bouncing back. Then it started ripping at my energy field with those fangs. I was throwing up more protection as quick as I could, at the same time trying to grab the snake somehow.

Damn me forgetting my knife, tonight of all nights. I could slice this astral thing to bits if I had the extra focus for my power.

The snake whipped its body around me and started to squeeze. My organs squished together, and my ribs started to bend. I struggled to breathe, trying to push out.

Reaching out beyond the bay, I drew on the Pacific Ocean. The whole tide flooded through me, almost knocking me over. I held on, planted my feet again, and pushed with every bit of strength I had.

Jimmy roared and started swiping huge paws at the snake. I was terrified he was going to hit me, rip me open.

"Jimmy!"

He was frenzied by now, trying to bump me back and rip at the snake at the same time. I bashed up into another cat. A huge one. Fred?

Doreen was screaming now. "Jasmine, do you need me?"

"Hold the line, Doreen!"

Bracing myself against Fred's body, I gave a mighty push, just as Jimmy got that astral snake inside his mouth and ripped.

The snake split apart, releasing me with a rush that dropped me to my knees.

"Damn!"

The snake was struggling to repair itself, I could see it, even through the sweat dripping past my eyes.

The rest of the room dropped away, the snarling, screaming, shouting, stink of it all a distant echo heard through a large expanse of space.

We were on a different plane now, beyond material time.

"Okay, snake. It's you and me."

We faced one another on the astral, pure energy. Light and shadow. Slither and sheen.

The snake hissed, smaller than before, but still there.

I countered with a wash of blue Water energy from my right hand. Scales flew off the snake's back as my power connected.

"Jasmine!" I heard Doreen shouting from a distance. Out here, in the spaces between space, it was easy to ignore. To focus all my attention on whatever the hell this creature was.

"Who sent you, you bad beast?" I muttered. Then I refocused my eyes, broadening my peripheral vision. It felt like my head was open, molecules floating in and out, sensing for connections, vision, speech.

"Gotcha."

Threads of silver and green trailed off the serpent's tail, twining off toward a dark door limned in ochre light.

I could feel something behind that door, but I couldn't see it yet.

The snake feinted toward me, seeking a place to strike. I sent out a watery wall. I needed to keep it at a distance.

Hands up, manipulating my sorcery, I opened the field of my awareness three-hundred-sixty degrees around me, keeping the snake in that sphere. It wasn't going to sneak up on me that way.

Then I turned my eyes to the door. Reaching with my senses, I tried to taste what was beyond.

With the serpent in my field, it felt like I had a serpent's tongue, tasting the air for scent. And there it was.

A man. A man in a black suit and a white shirt. A man with eyes obscured by darkness.

And beyond that man…was something else. Something else that held the strings of man and snake alike.

That something was so big it could swallow the night with magic. It could change the world.

All the worlds.

A big, bloated, sickly white thing.

That was what we were fighting. Not the cops. Not poverty. Not the Man.

It was this. So clear in my mind. If only I could…

"Jasmine!" Doreen again, so faint. And the roaring of a giant cat. A cat who knew my name. Jimmy.

I caught the love and worry they threw at me, braiding it into the ocean swelling in my belly and my sex.

Taking a huge breath, I snapped my eyes back to focused attention, held out my hands, and shoved that snake back through that door.

The door shattered at the impact, shards of magic hovering in space, then there was a *whoompf*, and the pieces coalesced again, slamming the portal shut.

I couldn't cross it.

But I didn't need to.

I had the vision. I had the scent. I knew just where to find it again.

But first, I needed to get back to my friends. I needed help.

We needed to organize.

And the Association wasn't going to run away again.

Consciousness smacking back into my body, I gasped. Doreen was on her knees in front of me, eyes dark with worry and anger. I was resting against a solid, warm, breathing mass.

"Jimmy," I whispered. "Shit."

Looking around, I saw the broken tables and toppled chairs. The panthers were still shifted, and circled the room, sniffing. Most of the people were gone. That was good. It meant they were all safe.

At least I hoped so.

Putting her hands on her thighs, Doreen pushed herself back up. "Rest a moment, girl. I've got to get these wards back up."

"It's okay for now, Doreen. It's gone."

She looked at me. "I know. You did good. But I've got to do this anyway. We never know what's coming back."

The panthers started to shift back around me; limb by limb, the black cats receded and the human forms emerged.

Fred Hampton stood, a gorgeous man in jeans and a black turtleneck, natural messed up, but otherwise, he looked just…fine.

Then I saw that his hands were still massive paws. Fred flexed his claws. Looked at me.

"Say it, sister," he coughed out, still some of the big cat in his voice. "'I am a revolutionary.'"

I tried to swallow, but my mouth was dry. I moved my weight off Jimmy so he could change.

I finally got enough spit in my mouth to speak. Then I looked Chairman Fred Hampton in the eyes.

"I am a revolutionary."

CHAPTER SIXTEEN
JASMINE

After the encounter with Fred and the snake, I was too keyed up to go home to Doreen's. She'd reluctantly left without me. I made sure Leroy got her a ride, at least, so she didn't have to take the bus alone.

I stayed with Jimmy.

The room smelled of sex, cigarettes, and wine. It was a tiny room in the old Victorian, all high ceilinged, with an orange mandala-patterned Indian bedspread hung over the one, narrow window. A crook neck desk lamp in the corner gave off a yellow light that didn't quite reach the rest of the room.

Jimmy's head was pillowed on my shoulder. I stroked his naked arm, all warm and just a little bit moist, as his breathing slowed down. There was nothing better than being on the double mattress on the floor of this room he rented out in the big communal Panther share in West Oakland.

Nothing better than the fat candle in a dish on the floor next to the bed, or Clarence Carter crooning from the little turntable that took up half of a dresser top across the room.

I wanted to stay the night, but didn't want to freak Doreen out more than she already was. I also had no desire to cross the city by myself in the dead of night. But I also didn't want to go out in the cold air.

The options weighed on me, and even after sex, they weren't the only things causing a pressure on my thoughts.

"I could run you home," Jimmy murmured, breath soft against the swell of my breast. So sweet. Our time together felt even more precious than usual these days. Sex was a gift in the middle of the escalation of violence, the tension in the streets, the terrible, exhilarating news from LA, and even the increase in my magic.

The increase in magic that was showing up in freaky ways that I couldn't even comprehend yet. I was doing things I never even knew I could before. Stuff I hadn't really been taught, either. It made me wonder what was coming.

And the more violence and the more magic there was around me, the more sex my body craved.

But I craved this, too. This intimacy. These quiet moments. The sense of being cared for. Loved, even. They were a balm to my soul.

But I could do without all of those, it seemed, as long as I had sex and coffee. For now, at any rate. But there was no telling what tomorrow would look like anyway.

The Panthers who were married? Frankly, I wasn't quite sure how they did it. How did they keep from tearing one another to shreds with the intensity of it all?

I ran my hand down the curve of Jimmy's arm.

It was a relief not to have to sneak around Aunt Doreen anymore, but there were still house rules to abide by. They chafed more and more every single day, the less time I spent at school. The more hours and days I spent out in the streets.

The more my consciousness was raised, the less I wanted to be held down by rules of my aunt's house, or the rules set down by the Association for the proper use of magic.

Doreen and I had been bending those rules for quite a while. And breaking more of them all the time.

"You have to know the rules first, girl. Then you can decide whether or not to rearrange them." Doreen always said that.

And she was right. But that chafed, too, when there was so much at stake these days.

Jimmy kissed the side of my breast, then nuzzled at my shoulder with his forehead. Like a cat.

"How you doin', babe? You need to leave, or you gonna stay tonight?"

"I don't know yet," I said, whispering into his hair. "I want to stay, but I don't want to freak Doreen. Give me a few minutes." Wriggling further down into the bed, I adjusted his head on my shoulder. "Just like this."

I wanted time. I needed time. There was no time.

I had finals to study for. Magic to make. Trainings to do. It was all too damn much. There was no freedom when you joined the Movement. Tarika and Barbara had warned me about that, when I first started coming around. It had sounded romantic. Exciting. And it was all of that, still. But it was also a bit of a grind.

Clarence was singing on, as the needle ground its way around the grooves, asking his sweetheart if she could slip away. Jimmy started crooning along with him. "How sweet it is…" His hands started moving over my skin as he sang.

"Oh Jimmy." I could feel the ocean rising underneath me, rising toward his lips and fingers.

Then I pulled it back. Consolidating it into my core. Keeping the blue fires at bay.

Jimmy rolled up onto his elbows, and looked at me with those golden brown eyes of his.

"Teach me some of your magic, baby."

I batted him away. "Go on with yourself, Jimmy."

"I'm serious. Think of it, baby. Think of panther juju mixing with your witchy shit."

Smacking his solid bicep, I growled. "Witchy shit? Witchy shit? Come on now."

Suddenly, he was on top of me, biting at my lips. Kissing me. "Show me your sorcery, baby. Come on. Teach me."

His hips were grinding into mine and I could feel him growing hard again. I was still pulsing from our last round, wasn't quite ready…and then he rubbed up against that exact spot.

As I came for what felt like the twentieth time that night, the blue fire, the watery scent, the power of the whole damn ocean rolled out of me, and over him. I heard a gasp in my ear as the waves caught him up, carried him. Then he was inside of me, and we were both thrashing and rolling with the waves of energy.

I looked up at him, and his eyes were glowing gold. The planes of his face shifted slightly. Flattening. Just a trace. He was the one growling now. I grabbed the sides of his head and stared into those eyes, sending every bit of my ocean energy into and around his body. He started thrashing harder, trying to get away from me, as I tightened my thighs and my hands. He was also starting to whine and groan, like part of him wanted to stay.

The whole room was incandescent blue mixed in with gold. It smelled like the deepest ocean and the muskiest cat. The candle on the floor by the bed toppled and began licking at the sheets. As soon as the scent of smoke reached me, I quelled the fire with the thought of ocean, sending the power of salt water across the still-dry floor.

There was pounding on the door. Shouting.

We came together, screaming, as the door burst open on its hinges.

"What the fuck is happening! It felt like the walls were bending out and all the lights started flicking off and on! You 'bout to call the pigs down on the house, or something worse. They're patrolling outside right now."

I burst out laughing. Jimmy too. He rolled off me. That stuff I didn't know I could do? Guess it included moving walls.

"Sorry, man. Jasmine here was just teaching me some magic."

I finally looked at who was standing in the door, pissed-off, startled look on his face. It was Leroy himself. Shit.

Leroy was shaking his head. "You two do that magic shit more controlled from now on. Or at least warn us some shit's about to go down. We didn't know *what* you cats were up to."

We had covered ourselves up with a sheet by this time. I was staring up at Leroy. A position I never thought I'd be occupying. What was he doing here anyway? He didn't live in Jimmy's house.

"Jimmy, we need you for a conference. Be in the kitchen in five."

Jimmy nodded, still trying to catch his breath.

As Leroy turned to go, Jimmy looked at me, then back toward the door. "Can you hold it a minute, man?" Leroy paused.

"You staying?" he asked me.

"I need to go…"

"Hey Leroy, I need to run my woman home right quick. Can you give me twenty minutes?"

Leroy turned, face hardening.

"That's okay, Jimmy. I can make it home."

He looked at me with a question in those gold-brown eyes. I could tell he didn't like it. But he didn't want to be on Leroy's list, either. And if he was on Leroy's list, I would be, too.

Jimmy rooted through his discarded jeans on the floor, thrusting a tangle of sharp keys at me.

"Take the car," he said, then scrambled into the jeans, kissed me hard, grabbed a T-shirt, and walked out the bedroom door.

If I'd realized it was our last night together for a while, I might have stayed.

CHAPTER SEVENTEEN
DOREEN

The streets of Chinatown were busy for the middle of the week. Jasmine had a break in her finals so Doreen dragged her shopping for dinner. They needed a break from magic, too, after the week's events.

A clump of women clogged the sidewalk ahead with baby strollers. Jasmine clicked her tongue impatiently at that.

"We need to cross anyway; I see persimmons over there." Doreen pointed to a shop across the street whose wooden carts out front were piled with orange globes of fruit and the long green stalks of vegetables. There were even some of the strange lemons with reaching tentacles that looked they belonged in the sea.

Bells chiming, two men rode bicycles past them. As soon as they were clear, Jasmine stepped out onto the street, boots thumping, bell-bottoms just skirting the tarmac. Her brocade coat belled around her legs in the December breeze.

Doreen was glad to see that coat. No leather trench today meant that Jasmine was truly taking the day off, Panthers and all.

Speaking of sea creatures, Doreen wanted a fresh fish, but they'd buy that last, only venturing down to the stinky end of the street after filling her string bag with pok choy and persimmons.

Jasmine picked through the squat orange globes of the winter fruit. Her slender hands were a beautiful contrast to the fruit. Perfect for working magic.

Doreen glanced down at her softer, older fingers and shook her head. She wasn't old yet, and there was no use feeling so. But sometimes being next to a nineteen-year-old made her feel her every bit of her forty-three years, including that decade of grief that had aged her like nothing else.

Especially a young woman as vibrant as Jasmine. The girl lit up the sidewalk everywhere they went, without even noticing.

Humph. Well, now that Doreen had her magic back, she'd just see who was young and who was old. The magic gave her what the kids called a "groovy feeling." That was just right. She was getting back in the groove. She was coming back to life.

She smiled, thinking of Patrice and her luscious lips.

Doreen felt the smooth skin of the persimmon. These were the small, firm kind, the ones she liked to just cut and eat. The larger, soft persimmons were better for pudding, though.

"How'd you learn about this stuff?" Jasmine asked.

Doreen moved on to the next bin for the soft, hachiya persimmons. Deeper orange, they were just starting to squish a little. Perfect.

"How did I learn to make persimmon pudding?" Doreen asked.

"All of this." Jasmine gestured to the stand, with its small peppers, woody stalks of ginger, bitter lemons, and what Doreen called apple-pears. She never could recall their proper name.

"Get some of those firm persimmons, while I sort through these," Doreen said. "Living on the edge of Chinatown for the past seven years, I'd be a fool not to. I ask the folks who run the stands. Checked out a book from the library for awhile. Saw a couple episodes on a PBS cooking show…you know. I just picked it up."

"Huh. That's cool, I guess," Jasmine responded, slipping five of the firm, orange fruits into the string bag. Doreen put her own persimmons in a small paper bag first, to keep the fruit from squishing over everything else in the bag.

As a woman in a flower-patterned smock counted out Doreen's change, Jasmine went very still beside her.

Okay. Something was happening and Doreen didn't know what.

"Thank you!" Doreen said to the woman, then slipped the bag of fruit over her arm.

"Have very nice day!" the woman called out as Doreen steered Jasmine out of the shop and toward a tiny restaurant across the street. Bells clanged over the door and a small white ceramic cat waved a paw next to the register. A series of round tables topped with white oilcloth waited in orderly rows, most of them empty despite the bustle going on outside.

"Let's get you a cup of soup, girl."

Jasmine's face looked a little ashy above her red turtleneck, like a gray pallor covering her gorgeous skin. Her eyes were still bright, though, which calmed Doreen's worry.

Doreen ordered soup and tea when the waitress came. Jasmine was running her fingertips across the white oilskin tablecloth. Silent. She'd talk soon enough, or Doreen would make her.

After the pot of jasmine tea was sitting, fat and steaming on the table, Doreen poured and waited for Jasmine's slender fingers to wrap around the delicate flute of the cheap porcelain cup. The warmth would do her good. Sure enough, two sips in, and some of the color was already returning to her face.

"Are you going to tell me what just happened?" Doreen asked, blowing across the fragrant tea. The warmth felt good under her fingers. She'd grown to love jasmine tea since moving to Oakland, though she kept it as a treat for eating out, not stocking it for her own pantry. The coffee percolator still ruled at home.

Jasmine sipped more tea, a hint of ocean wafting across the table. Her magic was so close to the surface, it made Doreen wonder why she hadn't also felt whatever it was that turned Jasmine this way.

"I can't quite explain it," Jasmine said. "It was spooky. Like a spiderweb brushed across the back of my neck. But it was more than that, too."

Doreen's spine stiffened. She'd felt that spider before, for sure. She'd seen webs in her dreams and felt stray touches across her cheekbones sometimes when she arranged flowers at the shop. But every time she tried to trace it, nothing.

"I've seen those spiders, girl."

Jasmine looked up, startled, dark eyes wide.

"They've come in my dreams. And I've felt the spiderweb feeling, too. At work."

Jasmine took another sip of tea, avoiding Doreen's eyes.

"Jasmine?"

"There's more." She exhaled. "You know how the snakes showed up at HQ the other night? Well, I think I saw the man who sent them."

Doreen froze.

"What do you mean? When?"

"I saw him in a vision while we were fighting…but I've seen him before, too. At school. Before the big meeting at the church. I meant to tell you, but didn't have time, with all the stuff happening with Fred, and… Plus, I think I messed up."

"What happened?"

As Jasmine told her, Doreen flashed on the image of a black-suited man, standing under a streetlight, the day Helen's car got shot through. That man had been there, and disappeared. Jasmine had been keeping information from Doreen, but Doreen had kept some things from her niece, too.

"I know that man, girl. He was there when Helen and I got shot up in that crowd. It was either him, or someone exactly like him."

"I don't understand. Why spiders and snakes all of a sudden? And why us? Why me?" she asked, eyes imploring Doreen to answer her.

That was the question, wasn't it? What was crawling out from under the rocks and why? Why anything, though?

When they'd always hidden before, why were Animal People now roaming the streets, feeding people, operating clinics and food pantries, and facing down police with guns?

Why did Watts catch on fire? Why were police gassing and beating students in parks?

Why was her husband killed by Los Angeles County sheriffs? Doreen didn't have any answers.

"Do you think I did this to us, Auntie? Called this stuff?"

Doreen had never seen Jasmine look so worried, so afraid. Certainly not since she'd been hanging with the Panthers, haring off to meetings and that church kitchen, and walking down the streets, bold as brass.

"I don't see how…" Doreen replied.

Jasmine shook her head a little, and sipped at the jasmine tea. She looked out the big plate glass window toward the street, big hoop earrings almost brushing her thin shoulders.

The waitress came toward them with a giant bowl of steaming soup. The scents of chicken, scallions, and ginger wreathed the table. Doreen's stomach growled, reminding her that she'd skipped lunch and it was now three in the afternoon.

"You think you did this? Called the spiders and whatever that weird snake is we've been battling? Called up a scary man in a black suit? I don't see how," Doreen said.

Jasmine stared down at her cup of soup as though it was the saddest thing in the world. Her long fingers toyed with the porcelain spoon.

"Because I'm with the Panthers. I think I called bad magic because of that."

"Like retribution? We don't believe that way, Jasmine." Doreen set her own spoon down and lowered her voice. "You *know* that! You think our Ancestors want us to look the other way when people need help? You think the Powers want to punish us for standing up for ourselves?"

Jasmine looked at her again, lips tight and thin. "No, Aunt Doreen." She leaned across the oilcloth and the soup. "I don't think that."

Jasmine put her hands over Doreen's. "But I do think the government is attacking us."

Well, Powers be damned.

CHAPTER EIGHTEEN
CAROL

"Both of you knew about this? About the Animal People?" Ernesto asked.

Rosalia walked to the altar at the end of the glass counter and threw some more copal onto the charcoal. Choosing a fresh orange candle, she brought it over to where Carol and Ernesto stood looking at the fan of playing cards and shooed Ernesto off the stool.

"Jasmine finally told me," Carol said. "And I don't think she's known that long herself. A few days, at most."

"I mean, I'd heard the legends, like everyone else," Ernesto said, "but Rosalia, you never told me such things were real."

Rosalia sat straight as a fence post and scratched at the top of the orange candle with a pin, inscribing symbols in the wax, ignoring Ernesto's distress.

"Get the High John oil, maga."

Carol looked around, bewildered.

"It's in one of the drawers back here," Rosalia said.

Carol scurried back behind the counter, pulling on old wooden drawers that stuck in the warped cabinet. High John the Conqueror, the oil for justice, for necessary battles with authority. The oil you needed when you needed to win. She'd been taught that much, though Association sorcerers didn't tend to do that sort of magic.

One drawer held papers pressed with flowers, scraped vellum, and tissue-thin papers in red and black. In the second drawer she yanked open, jars and vials rattled together. Searching through them, she found a small bottle half filled with viscous, golden oil, labeled *John de Conquer* in neat letters on a white label.

"Why High John?" Ernesto asked, as Carol handed the hechicera the oil.

Tipping some of the oil onto her fingers, Rosalia began to rub it on the wick, from top to bottom, and over the scratched impressions in the wax, sending the heady scent of it into the air.

"If we are to win against the spear that would divide us, we must forge every alliance under the great sun in the sky."

Ernesto paced through the shop. Carol could feel the tension radiating from his body, ringing on the wood every time his boot heels struck the floor. She wanted to go to him, but held herself still, waiting for Rosalia to speak.

It was strange. Somehow, seeing her former teacher acting human like this made Carol feel as though she might have a chance with him. Even though now was not the time.

"Rosalia," Carol began, "I know we need to talk about the shifters and the alliances and whatever magic you're doing now, but…"

Rosalia struck a match, sulphur sparking, and held it to the wick. A glowing flame spiked up, three inches high, before subsiding to a warm glow.

"But you have holes in your thoughts these days, and you want to know why," Rosalia said.

She took a yellow jar candle from the shelf and handed it to Carol. The glass was cool under her hands.

Looking into Rosalia's citrine eyes, Carol found she couldn't speak.

"I know, maga. I know. The visions take a toll on us sometimes. And the mind refuses to comprehend the truth that rings like a bell in the plano astral."

Ernesto came back over and stared down at the cards. "We need to discuss Carol's training. But we also need to talk about this," he said, hands gesturing toward the black spear flanked by clubs and diamonds. Signs of strength, money, power and, perhaps, war.

"We do, mijo. We do." Rosalia patted his hand. "But not everything is urgent, even important things. For us to do what we must, Carolina needs to be as clear as glass. Right now, she is muddy with too many things."

A strange pressure was building up in Carol's head. The image of a spider flashed behind her eyes. Then another. The white spider and the brown. The two creatures she had seen battling in her visions. The two spiders Ernesto had killed with his own hands, as they fought and struggled, cracking the panes of glass at the end of the temple hall.

The spiders had invaded the Mansion. They had entered her dreams and made her spout strange visions of apocalypse and betrayal.

And she thought they had visited Terrance as well. Visions had entered the Mansion in a way that rocked the Association. In a way that Carol hadn't seen in her five years there.

Trouble had come.

"What is it, maga?"

"The spiders. They're here."

Rosalia handed Carol a porcupine quill. "Scratch onto the wax your sigils for memory."

Carol sent a breath into her belly, dropping her attention, sinking deep into her Element, the Earth. She took in huge draughts into her lungs, linking to Air. Ernesto had been training her to use the second Element, overlaid on top of Earth, ever since the visions came.

She scanned her thoughts for what she had been taught. The runes. The Theban alphabet. Hebrew letters. What was the right symbol for memory?

It was none of these. The image of a key floated just between her eyes.

That was it. To recall, she just needed the right key.

Breathing across the deep brown and ivory quill, Carol scratch a rude key into the yellow wax. The wax curled as the quill pushed at the wax. Three tines to the key, and an open space at the base. An old-fashioned–looking thing, this key. Just the thing to unlock memory.

"You must burn this every night, and call the memories back to you. You may also burn it while you study," Rosalia said, handing her a vial of oil. Carol opened the small bottle. Rosemary. Remembrance.

She began rubbing the oil onto the wax and the wick, drawing the oil toward her body, calling the magic to her.

The hechicera watched her before speaking again. "Tell the candle you want help, maga. Keep it clear in your mind, what your intention is."

A strange knocking started in the walls, and a hissing noise came through the vents. The blue-painted door rattled its hinges.

Ernesto stopped studying the cards and held up his hands, ready to raise the winds.

"Silencio!" Rosalia said to the walls. The knocking and hissing subsided.

"The spirits want to speak to you, maga. Not all of them have your best interests in mind. Some do. Some do not. It is your job to know them, to sense them. To know the differences between one and the other. And to know which ones are both. Like the laurel seeds I showed you the first time you came. Beauty and poison. Healing and death."

Carol looked down and found that her hands were shaking, still gripped around the yellow candle. She tried to steady her breath. Ernesto put a warm hand on her shoulder.

"Your fear is getting in the way," he said. "That is why you can't remember things."

"I'm not supposed to be afraid of spiders in my head, visions of disaster, and weird knocking in the walls?"

Rosalia laughed. Ernesto shot the hechicera a look. The old sorcerer just shook her head and shrugged.

"Of course these things scare us. They scare anyone with sense." He looked at Rosalia again. Carol was shocked that he was challenging her that way. "But the trouble is that you let the fear shut you down."

"I don't…"

"What Ernesto means, maga, is that even when we are afraid, we do our work. Your mind, it protects you too much. And your heart gets in the way."

Carol set the candle on the counter, shoulders slumping.

"I don't know what to do."

"That's Terrance Sterling talking," Ernesto said. "And Helen. And every damn rich person in the Association."

He gripped Carol's shoulders. "They have made you believe your magic isn't strong, just because of who they are. They did it to me, too."

"And Jasmine?"

Ernesto's hands dropped, and he smiled. "No. They were never able to get to her that way. Her family is too strong, and so's that personality of hers."

"People like us, though, have to learn to take our power and use it. We can't wait for their permission."

Rosalia just nodded, arms crossed over her chest.

"Pay attention to those spiders, maga. But first, pay attention to yourself. Intiendes?"

"Yes," Carol said.

She still had too many questions, but she was damn tired now, and just wanted to go home.

CHAPTER NINETEEN
LIZARD

Lizard had been changing bars and coffee shops since the shootout. Different place each day.

He wasn't quite willing to leave Los Angeles altogether, not until he found out what Geronimo, Roland, and the others were planning, but he was staying as far underground as he could, without being under house arrest somewhere. Lizard couldn't stand being cooped up. Never had. He couldn't even explore the sewers leading up to Panther HQ for long, even though he'd been part of the reconnaissance team looking for a safe tunnel out.

Not that they'd had time to use any tunnel, despite all the digging out they'd done in shifts, by the back door.

The bar Lizard was in that day was nothing special, for sure. Different set of old dudes in the corner, playing dominoes this time. Middle-aged cat at the bar, paper spread out now, heavy framed glasses perched on the end of his nose, reading the racing news.

This place had those windows patterned like the bottoms of gold glass bottles, and the sun slanting through turned the whole place amber, even the ratty green barstools and the crappy, carved-up table he was at along the wall. Never would sit at the bar these days.

Probably never would again.

He drank his beer and sat. Waited. Waited on what, he wasn't exactly sure. Word? A shift in the wind? Another explosion?

Things on the streets were not calming down. Lotta shit still going down around here, and Lizard hoped he was a small enough fish that they might not bother with him for awhile. So he'd been taking his chances, and chance had found him, sooner than expected.

Angela Davis and some others had been organizing sit-ins, which kept most of the pigs busy. Masses of people were in the streets, emboldened by the Panthers' success and pissed off at the pigs. More and more brothers were out on the streets packing heat.

Pigs shoulda been preoccupied, with no time for a foot soldier like Lizard. The pigs should be scared as fuck.

Shit, *he* was scared. This made him a bad soldier, hiding out, drinking cheap draft, but real panthers were roaming around LA. Or men who could turn into beasts. Lizard had no idea what to call them. Animal people? Shape-shifters? And he sure as hell had no idea what to think of it all.

So he just kept drinking beer, even though all the training told him not to. Told him it wasn't safe. But if Lizard thought about what he'd seen that morning, he might crack all the way apart. Better unsafe with a fairly quiet mind than in a psych ward somewhere, strapped down to a bed. Or dead from clawing his own eyes out from the terror of it.

"Give me pigs with guns over men who can change into fucking actual panthers," he muttered.

His mind kept sliding off the image of Roland with those weird paw things at the end of his arms, every time he tried to figure it out. Lizard didn't even want to remember the rest of it. Roland changing into an actual huge panther, running through the crowd. How was that even possible? Like some Lon Chaney movie.

"It's some Hollywood shit, for sure," he mumbled again.

"What's that?" called the bartender.

Shaking his head, Lizard waved a hand at the bartender to tell him never mind. The big, light-skinned man shook his own head and went back to rattling bottles onto refrigerator shelves.

More than the bombs and bullets and fires, the panther shit shook him to the core. Had him crawling into bottle after bottle of cheap beer.

Good thing bars were as good a place to hang out as any other.

Then the Man walked through the door.

The Feeb had pasty skin, and he shaved close. Clipped dark hair under a trilby that he took off and set on the chair next to him. He had one of those white-movie-star waves on top. How the hair didn't get crushed by the hat was a mystery. Maybe it was magic.

The man wore a straight black suit, and a starched white shirt that screamed "FBI." He'd found Lizard in a bar, just as Lizard figured some-one like him would.

When the Feeb swung the bent wood chair out from the table and sat across from him, Lizard wasn't surprised. He almost sagged with relief that the waiting was over.

Lizard wasn't the most patient brother in the world. But he also didn't want to have to make whatever damn fool choice Mr. Black Suit was about to set on the table.

"Dave Perkins?" the white man asked.

"Depends."

The man slid his dark glasses into a breast pocket, wincing a little, like it was bright in the dim bar.

He brought out a crumpled pack of Chesterfields. Striking a match, the man looked at Lizard the whole time with these weird, blinking, ice-blue eyes. He just stared as the gray smoke writhed up through the gold, glass-bottle tinted air. Offered Lizard the pack.

Lizard shook his head. Even though he don't have much patience, he also didn't mind waiting this one out. A pig is a pig. Even one in a suit, about to cut some sort of deal. Or take a man in.

"You were at 4145 South Central?"

Lizard took a sip of beer. It tasted a little sour all of a sudden. "Depends."

The man's pale lips pursed at that. Lips were kinda thick for a white man. Made Lizard wonder if he had some Sicilian or something in the mix. He took another drag off the cigarette.

"You a member of the Black Panther Party?"

Man, if Lizard had been a real panther, he'd a swiped that cigarette right outta the man's hands. Ask him a question or two, like "You ever beat a black man for no reason? You pistol whip a woman before raping her? You get paid well to do that shit, or you just like it?"

Lizard held his tongue like his momma taught him, and drank more beer.

It was just the bartender left in the place right then. The dominoes game had walked out around the time Mr. Feeb lit his cigarette. Lizard had no idea when the man at the bar had checked out. Likely the minute the suit's ass hit the chair.

Then Lizard saw it. A small tattoo in the webbing between the man's thumb and pointer finger. It was a spider. That seemed like a strange thing for a federal employee to have. Sent a shiver down Lizard's spine, like a ghost had walked over his grave.

His momma always told Lizard to listen to that. "Trust your instincts, boy." His instinct said there was something worse than sitting across the table from a Feeb, and that was not knowing exactly whether the Feeb was some weird shit besides an agent. Nothing about the situation seemed all right anymore.

Weird shit piled on top of weird shit. It was like the whole world was on a bad trip.

His instinct said the man across from him had something stranger going on than just working for the government. But Lizard had no idea what that something was.

What the hell was he going to do about that? Nothing in his eighteen years had prepared Lizard for this. It hadn't prepped him for dealing with men turning into big black cats, and it hadn't prepped him for some Feeb to not just be a spy kind of spook, but a real sort of spook. Like, you know, spooky. Voodoo-hoodoo shit. Whatever people called it. His own family were Baptists, so Lizard didn't really know.

And right then? Lizard's instinct said he should walk the hell away.

Shoving his chair back from the table, Lizard spoke. "I have another appointment."

The man's hand shot out and grabbed Lizard's wrist.

"I don't think you do."

"What you gonna do about it, pig? You have a warrant for my arrest? Papers saying you got a right to detain me?"

The pressure from the man's hand increased and he moved his fingers, grinding against Lizard's wrist bones. A strange sort of heat started to rise from the man's hand, like the kind you got from rubbing rough pieces of steel together.

Lizard could almost hear the sound of it inside his skull. His skin started to singe, with a faint scent of cooking meat.

Sweat popped out on Lizard's forehead. The Feeb still looked cool as can be. Like a damn snake.

"Just because you're in a suit…" Lizard gritted his teeth, and looked straight into those icy eyes. "Doesn't mean you're not still a pig."

All Geronimo Pratt's training was kicking in now, even through the beer haze.

The Feeb let go, flinging Lizard's wrist away. Good. He'd pissed the man off. Seemed like the least he could do. Power to the fucking people.

Lizard stood and backed away. Pausing at the bar on his way out, he kept the Feeb in his sights.

"Can I get some ice, man?"

The bartender unfolded a paper napkin and scooped some ice in. Handing the cold package over, he said, "Don't be coming back in here. Right?"

"Right."

Lizard walked out the door, ice held to his blistered wrist.

Then he ran like a motherfucker, boots smacking pavement fit to wake the dead.

Chapter Twenty
Jasmine

The sun peeked in and out of a bank of clouds, just over the hills. Basketball hoops sported chain nets that swung and creaked, waiting for a game. But we weren't out to play.

Not today.

The blacktop felt springy under my boots, just a little give from the tar, despite the cold morning air. Anything was better than concrete. Right arm up. Block. Jab. Two steps back. Double jab forward again.

Punching at the air felt surprisingly good.

My body moved in formation on the blacktop of the old playground, breath huffing a white mist in front of my face. I'd pulled on my old combat boots before I left the house, lacing them tight around my ankles. I needed all the support I could get.

Leadership had me out there, when otherwise I woulda been at Father Neil's, stirring up oatmeal. The new rules were, if I was training people in *magical* combat and self-defense, then *I* had to train in *physical* combat and self-defense.

Even though I protested at first, it was right. As Chairman Fred said, "Peace to you, if you're willing to fight for it."

Well, I needed to learn a lot of different ways to keep the peace. Snakes and spiders coming at us; cops shooting our comrades down or locking our people up. Federal agents stalking us.

Learning how to punch wasn't a bad idea.

I knew that magically, practicing offense meant you were less likely to have to use it. There was something about the swagger of just knowing that you could. Changed a person's energy field from prey to predator, and that made people leave you alone.

Or at least think twice before striking.

Huh. Doreen and I needed to step it up fast.

When I'd arrived at the lot next to the old boarded-up market, I'd dropped my big fringed bag and started to shuck off my leather coat.

Leroy stepped forward to stop me. "You gonna stop and take off your coat when someone comes at you?"

"No," I said.

"Then train with it on."

He was the boss. He was also right, but I was regretting not showing up in a sweatshirt like some of the cats here. The coat wasn't bulky, but it pulled under my arms every time I blocked or punched. My body moved through the unfamiliar motions, boots sure beneath me, moving forward, leather coat swinging around my knees, then to the side, then back, then forward again.

A dozen other bodies moved with me, mostly men, though two other women had come out to train. Since this was my first class, I wasn't sparring yet. Leroy had taught me three basic steps and punches and told me to keep going through them. Getting my muscles used to moving like I knew what I was doing. Practicing.

Just like I practiced letting the power of the bay fill up my veins and move out through my skin.

I couldn't harness that into a ball of blue fire energy to hurl toward an opponent, or to weave a dome of protection for a whole city block if every bit of me hadn't trained to make it happen. And every bit of me *hadn't* trained for that, not yet. But now that the revolution was here, I aimed to keep on.

Well, Doreen's jaw had dropped when I told her my suspicions. About the Feds, the watch lists, and all the rest of it.

"I should have suspected this was true, after what happened to my Hector," Doreen said. My uncle, shot down by sheriffs in the Los Angeles hills. Turned out he was a big cat, a golden California mountain lion. Had his head chopped off with a machete.

And just how had the sheriffs known they needed to do that? That chopping off a shifter's head was the one sure way to make sure they were dead?

"I never thought about it," Doreen said as we sat sipping chicken soup in her favorite Chinese restaurant. "I was too sunk in my grief to even notice all the things that just weren't right about it."

All the things that chased her up the coast to land in Oakland and locked her magic away in the attic of the tiny bungalow we shared.

Considering I'd just barely found out about Uncle Hector being a big cat, damned if I could figure this shit out. But we were gonna have to.

Especially since it turned out we were surrounded by actual cats. Including my boyfriend.

That made me smile, as always. Jimmy was special in more ways than one. I needed to open up to him more. He was always right there for me so far, no matter what.

My arms were getting tired from punching air and a sheen of sweat covered my face. Damn. Clearly I needed the practice. Fighting was my nature; the Mansion taught me that. But this kind of fighting? I didn't know how to do it yet. I didn't really want to know how to do it.

And my body most surely didn't want to do it. Even my calves were starting to scream from the effort, and the pits of my arms leaked sweat under the layers of turtleneck and leather. I looked over at Leroy, who was correcting two of the men who'd been sparring.

That was one dedicated cat. Seemed like Leroy had a hand in every Party program. A full-time revolutionary. Speaking of which, I realized I had no idea how he made any money.

Leroy leaned his body into the punches, back foot pivoting as he swung. He was paying me no mind at all.

I smiled at myself. It was like I was a kid in school waiting to see if my teacher was gonna call me out.

I stopped moving, and shook out my hands. Wished I had some water. Leroy glanced over at me and just nodded as I went over to the cyclone fence and started stretching out my calves.

But yeah, this fighting shit…there wasn't any avoiding it anymore. The cops had brought the battle to our door.

Chairman Fred talked about the need, not just for self defense, but that sometimes we were going to have to attack our oppressors. I had enough white-picket fence left in me that I wasn't quite comfortable with that, yet.

"I am the people; I'm not the pig. You got to make a distinction. And the people are going to have to stand up against the pigs," Fred said. "That's what the Panthers are doing, that's what the Panthers are doing all over the world."

My breath wasn't making white clouds in front of my face anymore. It must have warmed up without my noticing, or my body had. The sun was just up now, and it was almost time for me to get to school. But I felt like I should wait, check in with Leroy before I left.

Standing up against the pigs? Doreen would say we shouldn't call anyone something that they weren't. That creating monsters meant we made beings with no responsibility for their actions.

"Our words have power, Jasmine girl. That's why we use them in our magic. Be careful of the words you use. You just might create something you don't want."

I didn't want to attack. I wanted to defend. And for now, I'd keep calling them cops, instead of pigs.

But the day was coming fast where that might change. We were being pushed too much. Plenty of brothers were off fighting the war in Vietnam and here we were, in the middle of a war at home.

Assassination attempts and shoot-outs, Little Bobby Hutton shot dead in the street, plus all the harassment, and some of our best people in jail.

And a bunch of Panthers facing a bunch of men in uniform. Who might as well be pigs.

I was trying to work that out, for Aunt Doreen's sake, and for mine. But adding it all up, I wasn't sure how. I didn't think we were making monsters.

The monsters made themselves.

CHAPTER TWENTY-ONE
JASMINE

School was next to impossible. Surrounded by white kids in love beads, the scent of marijuana oozing off their skin, or by the close-clipped squares who tried their best to ignore us all.

I guessed UC Berkeley was more integrated than some school in white-bread Iowa, but there were still a lot fewer black and brown people than I'd grown to prefer.

Funny, despite hanging with plenty of white people growing up, since moving north, I'd grown used to being around black brothers and sisters more and more.

Black Liberation felt real to me now. It was something I'd never even thought of before. Life in the Association meant that magic was the focus, not my skin. That was all right as far as it went. But the reality of it all was, black and brown people had always had plenty of magic, and the Association was still mostly rich and white.

Why was that? Well. I was starting to get some answers.

My scalp itched with the sense that the snakey man was out there, somewhere. My fingers pricked with barely contained sorcery. There was so damn much to *do*.

But here I sat, in the tipped bowl of a university auditorium, half-way up the half-full room, trying to pay attention to some white man's words. A nice white man, to be sure, but a white man all the same.

Professor Glanville. Chalk marks smudged the edges of his green tweed sport coat. He was always grabbing his lapels and pacing, like he was doing now.

Utilitarianism. Dewey. Mill.

"…actions are right if they are useful or if they benefit the majority."

Yeah, it was that last bit that was the problem. What about the minority?

I exhaled in a huff, and tried to straighten up in the hard wooden chair. Slumping wasn't going to help me pay attention. And Black Panther Party members didn't slump.

Huey Newton and Bobby Seale probably hadn't failed their classes, either, even while they were founding the Panthers. If I didn't get this final paper in, I'd be lucky if I got out with a C.

My combat boots hit the back of the chair in front of me. The straggly bearded white dude who occupied it jumped and half turned in his seat.

"Sorry," I whispered.

He nodded and turned back.

But what use were statistics and philosophy? My mind could barely wrap around them anymore. Thank all the Powers the semester was almost over. I'd have to make some serious decisions about whether or not I was coming back.

And wouldn't my parents freak at that?

Professor Glanville was off on a tangent again. The old dude was amazing, though: he always managed to find his way back to the original point.

I struggled to listen, to pay attention to the white marks scribbled on the big black board. Today's talk was heavy on Dewey—Glanville's favorite Utilitarian.

Smirking, I wondered what would happen if I scrapped the final paper I'd been working on and actually talked about some of my favorite Utilitarians. Weave in some Franz Fanon. Or Fred Hampton Jr.

Or if I lit up the auditorium with blue ocean fire.

Chairman Fred was gone. Back into hiding. I didn't have the clearance to know where he and Deborah were. The Feds were sure to be sniffing around soon.

I just hoped they both stayed safe long enough for the baby to be born.

HQ was still buzzing about who the plant was. Word was that it was William O'Neal. A brother everyone had trusted.

How could a black man turn another black man's life over as a sacrifice? Especially to a government hell-bent on killing us all?

Jury was still out on Jerrold, the man I had put under suspicion. Doreen and I still needed to figure out if there was a way to test him for magical residue. To test whether or not he'd been manipulated by that snake, or if he had acted willingly.

Jerrold had insisted he was clean, but was locked out of meetings for now. Couldn't even come to the house.

Lotta people pissed at me for that. They knew Jerrold had a beef with me. He never trusted me, and let people know. I wondered now if he didn't trust me 'cuz he could sense the magic on me.

Damn. Doreen and I might have to go the Association for help around all this. And I surely didn't want to.

"Your final papers are due in my office mailbox by Tuesday. Have a great break," Dr. Glanville said.

The sound of twenty students packing up filled the room. Books slamming, book bags zipping. I slid my notebook into my giant fringed leather bag and started up the stairs. I needed to get back to Doreen and Drake. Keep the magical training on point.

"Miss Jones?" Dr. Glanville's voice chased after me.

I turned, and he raised a hand to beckon me down.

"Miss Jones," Dr. Glanville started, "you've been distracted these past few weeks and I just wanted to make sure you were on track with your final paper. I'd like to give you the A you deserve from your earlier work..."

He paused, expecting a response from me. What was I going to tell him? That I found out my uncle was a mountain lion killed by sheriffs, my boyfriend was an actual shape-shifting panther, and I'd been battling snakes and spiders while holding off police with magic?

I must have been staring, gobsmacked, because he raised an eyebrow at me then.

"Miss Jones?"

"I'm sorry. Yes. There's been a lot going on lately. But I've got my paper mostly written and will have it in on time."

He turned toward his own stacks of notes and books on the podium. "I'm glad to hear that, Miss Jones. You are a very promising thinker."

"Thank you, sir," I said, then turned to head back up the steps to the door.

"Miss Jones?"

What now? I turned again.

Dr. Glanville peered at me behind his gold-rimmed glasses. "I know that things are hard right now, for everyone, and it sometimes seems that the life of the mind is useless against reality. But it isn't." He swallowed, as if this was hard for him to say. "It isn't. What we study matters, not just inside this room. I hope you write about that."

"I...okay. Thank you, Dr. Glanville." I nodded at him. "Thanks a lot."

Huh. So the old white man wasn't off in the clouds after all. And he'd pretty much just given me permission to call on Fanon or Chairman Fred.

My boot heels clomped up the linoleum-covered steps, and I pushed my way out the heavy door.

People clumped in conversation or hurried down the long hallway toward the glass doors that led outside.

A few sisters nodded at me as I walked by. One of them, natural picked out five inches around her head, like a glowing halo under the fluorescent lights, raised a fist up to her shoulder, giving me the salute.

I raised my fist back. Her bead-covered boyfriend pulled her to his side, looked at me from under a newsboy's cap, and smiled.

"Black is beautiful, baby," he said.

Yes. Yes it was. But was it enough to turn the tide?

Chapter Twenty-Two
Carol

Cecelia and Carol walked the pathway that curved through the manicured lawns of the Mansion grounds. Low-heeled pumps and granny-boot heels made small thocking sounds on the cement as they rounded the copse of flowers and manzanita where Carol's favorite marijuana-smoking bench sat in the shade.

Jasmine's mother was formidable. Her Earth power was so different than Carol's. It was smooth and even, built and perfected over the course of many years. Carol wondered what it would be like to train with her. Or do battle.

Mrs. Jones, Cecelia, was neatly dressed as always, a green wool jacket over a trim, cream-colored dress that set off her dark brown skin.

The sound of the riding mower buzzed from the distance. The never-ending labor of the Mansion gardener. Cut grass overpowered every other smell.

Carol had felt a little uncomfortable even calling Cecelia, but things with Terrance Sterling had gotten so bad, she needed outside help.

And it wasn't going to come from Helen Price, or even Ernesto. They were still too entrenched in the Association power structure, in the running of the Mansion, the training of the students, the politics of it all.

Helen, Carol understood. She was Terrance's right hand.

But Ernesto? He was ticking her off a little. Or maybe it was just the desire to kiss him that was coming up more and more lately, and getting under her skin. Carol was having a hard time shoving that away.

It was irritating.

"So, you and my daughter think you're going to change the world with magic?" Cecelia's tone was light, and mildly skeptical.

Just great. Carol was going to have to convince her, too. And why hadn't Jasmine's Aunt Doreen done that work already?

Carol knew the answer: they'd been too busy.

"What else is our sorcery for?" Carol grumbled.

Cecelia laughed at that.

"It's for a lot of things." She looked at Carol then, stopping on the path. "I don't want you to think I'm unwilling to help. But we need to figure out what we can *actually* do, and how and why. Sorcery of the sort you're talking about needs to be strategic."

Okay. That wasn't so different from what Ernesto had said. But Carol still wasn't sure if that meant she should listen, or if these people were just too old to convince.

Not that Ernesto was old, but at twenty-seven, he sometimes he acted like it.

They continued walking.

"Mrs. Jones…"

"Cecelia, please. You aren't a girl anymore."

"Cecelia. Things are happening now, in the world, that can only be affected by magic. You have to feel that!"

A row of orange and yellow marigolds were still blooming on the edges of this stretch of lawn. The mower sound cut out and Carol could hear the distant traffic from the freeway.

"What do you mean?" Cecelia asked.

"Look. I've been having visions. Things are looking bad. But that's not all. There are weird things happening. Spiders, and, and sigils and…"

"Snakes." Cecelia said.

Carol stopped this time. "Can we sit down?" She gestured to the bench near the manzanita.

They sat on the concrete bench, Cecelia smoothing her cream skirt over her thighs.

"Yes, the snakes. Jasmine told you, then."

Cecelia just nodded, waiting for her to go on.

Looking toward the big, white plaster walls and the red-tiled roof of the Mansion, Carol blinked at the blue December sky.

"The attacks on the Black Panther Party by the police are connected."

"To the snakes? And these spiders?" Cecelia asked.

"Yes."

"Cecelia!" Terrance Sterling's voice called across the lawn.

Damn it. Carol had thought he was still away from the Mansion.

He walked toward them, a smile plastered on his face that was all white teeth. His silver-gray hair was in place like normal, and his bespoke suit was charcoal gray today, set off by a burgundy silk paisley tie.

"What brings you to the Mansion?" he asked. "Did I know you were coming?"

The implication was clear: why hadn't she made an appointment? And why was she talking with someone who wasn't him?

Carol and Cecelia both stood as he approached. It was reflex, Carol realized. People didn't sit if there wasn't also a chair for Terrance Sterling.

She shook her head. When had she become so programmed? *The minute your thirteen-year-old self got off the plane from Minnesota and stepped through the Mansion doors,* her own voice replied.

"I was just checking in with my daughter's friend," Cecelia replied, calm as could be, as she held out her hand.

"I bet you were," Terrance replied, smile leaving his face.

"Are you in on this little plot?" he asked.

"What plot is that, Terrance?" Cecelia asked. Her voice was still calm, but Carol could feel the force of Earth gathering around the woman's body.

"The plot to drag the Association into the goings-on of that damned Panther party."

"Hmmm…" was all Cecelia said.

Carol could feel all of the Elements rising around Terrance now. The man was angry.

"You are! You want to throw your lot in with those unwashed *radicals!*"

"Better than not doing a damn thing with our sorcery," Carol replied. "Better than just using it to shore up your bank accounts!"

Her own Earth was growing underneath her skin now, ready to push green fire out from her fingertips.

"How dare you! I didn't become head of the Association in order to get schooled by a girl." Terrance spat out.

"Carol," Cecelia said, calmly, placing a hand on Carol's arm.

Carol throttled down her own anger and stared at the head of the Association.

"I pledged to use my sorcery to help people, Terrance. I believe that you did, too," Cecelia said.

"You know that's not what we're talking about here! And plotting against the Association is a breach of your magical contracts."

"Isn't it what we're talking about?" Cecelia replied. "I think you know it is."

The manzanita leaves shook a little, rustling behind them. Was that her, or Cecelia? Carol couldn't tell. All she knew was there wasn't any breeze.

Cecelia spoke again. "How long have you known me, Terrance?"

That stopped him short.

Carol watched the anger and confusion cross his lean face.

"Twenty-five years."

"Have you ever known me to put the Association in any kind of danger?" Cecelia spoke clearly, voice pitched low. "Have you ever known me to act in a foolhardy way? Or do anything that would threaten my vows?"

"No."

"Then you'd best not start accusing me of it now." Cecelia held out her hand again. Confused, Terrance reached out. She shook his hand.

"Good day, Terrance."

"What are you talking about? We are *not* finished."

"I have another appointment and just stopped by to see Carol for a moment. So I'm afraid I really do need to leave now." Cecelia's voice was dry as California hills in August.

"Walk me to my car, Carol?"

Carol looked from Cecelia to Terrance, and then nodded and began walking toward the front of the Mansion, where Carol assumed her car was parked.

"This conversation isn't over!" Terrance said. "I know you're planning something, and the Committee is going to hear about this."

Carol watched, amazed, as Cecelia just lifted her hand and gave a little wave. As though Terrance Sterling hadn't said anything at all.

Once they rounded the corner of the building, Cecelia spoke.

"We need to get Jasmine down here."

"Wait," Carol said, "you think we're right? What changed your mind?"

"Oh, I've been noticing some things of my own lately. But mostly? I didn't like what I saw in Terrance's eyes just now. Or what I didn't see."

Cecelia stopped at the car parked on the big roundabout driveway and snapped open her purse, looking for her keys.

"You're both right. There's something off about him. I haven't been paying enough attention."

Jasmine's mother looked at Carol. "I'm sorry for that. You know, it's easy to get used to things running the same way, year after year. I just assumed I didn't much like Terrance, and was better off letting Helen deal with it all. Stay out of the politics."

She unlocked the door.

"But I see now I was wrong. You young people are right. There's a fight here. I don't know yet what I'm going to do about it, but I'll be making some calls."

"Thank you," Carol said.

Cecelia nodded and slid into the leather driver's seat.

"Call my daughter. I think she needs to come down. If this is as serious as you all say it is, and Terrance's behavior makes me think so, then this Association needs to get it together and get these people some help."

Carol thought so too.

"But…"

"I know there's more to talk about, but I wasn't lying to Terrance. Well, not one hundred percent." A smile curved on Cecelia's face. "I really do have an appointment. But I promise we'll talk soon."

"Thank you," Carol said.

She walked back toward the big carved wooden front door of the Mansion as Cecelia started up the car and drove away.

Maybe Jasmine could help her figure out how to convince Ernesto this was serious.

And how to get him to kiss her, too.

CHAPTER TWENTY-THREE
SNAKES AND SPIDERS

*H*e paced his cell.

Not a prison cell. A bedroom. A monk's cell. A place of meditation. Discipline. Clarity. Order. Rest.

The small room was comfortable enough. A very nice double bed with a navy comforter. A sink with a mirror where he knotted his tie each morning, and smoothed the dark wave of hair from his pale face.

A few books on a small, wood bookcase with two shelves, the top of which held a crystal pyramid, two pewter candlesticks twined with serpents, and a brass pendulum. Samuels' snake ring rested there the rare moments it was not next to his skin.

A jewel-toned rug on the floor was the one real concession to beauty and comfort. The bed had to be firm, but comfortable enough for him to rest.

Samuels never brought anyone here and never would. Sex was something done on occasion. Like taking medicine or jogging down along the Potomac River, it kept the body healthy and the mind clear.

As long as you didn't allow yourself too much of it. Then it became a drug. A weakness. A liability to the cause.

No man or woman was supposed to get that close to them. The warriors in their dark glasses were to be Stoic in mind, body, and heart. No drugs but those to help them fly when needed. No sex except when the body demanded.

Sure, there were whispers about Tolson and the Master. And those "vita-min shots"? The weakness of an old man trying to boost his energy again. The methamphetamines were a sign the Master needed to be watched now.

But Samuels would never let anyone else know.

He grunted in displeasure. His mind was wandering today and it shouldn't be. He needed to be focused. Stay on task.

But that Panther bitch was a distraction. A cancer growing in his gut.

He was dreaming of her at night. Those dark eyes. The cloud of hair. Slim hips.

And the stink of powerful magic on her skin.

They could be the joining of opposites and raise more magic than the Master ever could. The purist. Not wanting to sully himself with women at all, let alone a Negro woman. Let alone a revolutionary.

"Stop it!" Samuels said out loud, pausing in his pacing. Damn it. He had come back to his room only for a wash, a shave, and some meditation.

Instead, here he was, preoccupied by a woman he had permission to kill, who was part of an organization he was in charge of taking apart.

Samuels was beginning to hate her. She was too clever. Too powerful.

She wasn't going to run away and hide. She seemed to be gaining momentum instead. Not backing down.

The bitch.

Funny, Samuels had been trained to be dispassionate. Cold. To calcu-late risk and action. To just do his damn job, and do it well.

He wasn't sure if the Master's mania was rubbing off on him, or if the magic was growing too complicated, or if it was something else entirely.

The damn new tattoo itched under his arm. He knew that was part of the healing process, the annoyance of a bad sunburn, the flaking. The itch that could not be scratched for fear of tearing some of the layers of ink away.

He wondered if he shouldn't tear some of those layers off. But the thought of altering the magic sent a cold finger of paranoia up his spine.

Samuels just wasn't sure enough about the magic that had gone into the sigil to know how to alter it properly. He could change things for the worse. He could unleash who knew what horrors.

Taking out the Panthers and the damn radical hippies? Who cared? They deserved it. Order must be restored to the Temple. The Obelisk must rise like a beacon of lawfulness and strength. The Pentagon must remain the heart of magic, its five sides bringing just enough chaos into the area marked by the four corners set by the Founders.

Four. Stability.

Five. Change.

Six. Restoration of the Temple. The building of the altar of blood and stone.

Samuels knew all of this. Felt it crawling in his bloodstream, whispering in his mind.

The ants would build but the snakes and spiders would weave and protect.

That Panther bitch?

She was getting in the way.

CHAPTER TWENTY-FOUR
JASMINE

Well, Carol got me down to Los Angeles all right, and on the Association's dime. My first airplane ride. It was hard to enjoy it, though, considering how pissed off I was feeling.

And that wasn't half as pissed as I was going to get.

I'd worked overtime to get my final papers turned in before heading south. If I wasn't giving up school for sure, I still had to make an effort. Besides, Doreen hounded me about it. Even Jimmy refused to see me until finals were done. And now I was in LA, and didn't know *when* I'd see him.

So yeah, I was extra pissed off, and feeling extra revolutionary right about now.

Fuck this fancy-ass restaurant with its white wicker tables on its fancy covered outdoor deck. Potted palms and climbing jasmine trellises. Who ate breakfast at these places? Excuse, me. Brunch.

Who ate perfect, fluffy eggs scrambled with cream? With strawberries? Who had slender white flour crepes wrapped around ricotta cheese and cherry jam?

White people. Rich people.

Rich. White. People.

People with stock portfolios and trust funds. The people sitting at round tables all around us, laughing softly, discussing last night's opera and next week's fundraiser for the hospital downtown. Women with hairdresser-coiffed coils arranged artfully on top of their heads. Men with gleaming, manicured fingernails and heavy gold watches peeking out from beneath their starched cuffs.

And my dark-skinned mother, Cecelia, in her respectable, slim purple dress, looking well as always, next to her dark-skinned daughter in a tweed mini above black knee boots, leather coat flung over the back of my chair. It was a bit too warm for the coat, but I carried it like a talisman of the revolution.

It was a little piece of Oakland. Berkeley. The Panthers. I needed that, sitting across the table from Terrance Sterling and Helen Price as they flashed their perfect teeth at us and sipped their cups of tea, brewed exactly for two and a half minutes each.

Everything about those two was perfect. Terrance's perfectly styled silver hair, hundred-dollar gold-rimmed glasses perched precisely on his nose. Helen's chestnut-brown hair in a subtle Jackie O bouffant, sweeping toward sharp points that framed her jaw.

Doreen was lucky she had stayed in Oakland.

Waiters flitted around in black slacks and white shirts, black aprons tied around their slim hips. They were all white, too. Which seemed strange to me. I bet the kitchen staff were black and brown. Washing dishes. Scrubbing pots. Hosing off floor mats. Chopping onions. You'd never see a brown face out on this floor, though. That was the thing about California. The racism was all tucked away.

No shucking and jiving Uncle Tom waiters in gleaming tuxedos here. Not in liberal LA. That sort of behavior was relegated to "the South," to Birmingham, Atlanta, New Orleans. To those people who killed that Dr. King. Who'd been so nice until he insisted on getting everyone riled up like that. They liked his speeches, though. He should have stayed with oration. Clearly gifted.

The fury built inside me, barely contained by politeness.

My mother and I sipped at our coffee, lightened with cream and sugar. We were waiting for our omelets and toast. Excuse me. Brioche.

This place didn't have something as prosaic as sliced wheat bread. Gods, I'd forgotten all this stuff after not very long away, this ridiculous charade of the endless parade of money. Comfort. Greased wheels.

Moments before, holding the heavy menu, I had commented that the Panthers could feed one hundred kids breakfast for what this one was going to cost us. My mother had placed her hand on mine and murmured, "Stop." And Terrance had remarked that as he was the one paying, what did it matter?

I had shut myself up, for a while, but I wouldn't for much longer. As soon as we got some of the fancy food down our throats, I was going to speak. Terrance, all sharp in his navy suit and purple tie, and Helen in her tasteful green dress, thought they were going to control this conversation, I was sure. Well, they were in for a big surprise.

Little Jasmine had stopped being so docile and accommodating. Not that I was ever really that way inside. And not that I'd never had my flare-ups at the Mansion. I had. But I had also stopped needing their approval and really didn't give a fuck if I rocked their precious boat.

"So Jasmine," Helen asked, placing her china cup back in its saucer without even the slightest clink. How did a person do that? "How are your studies?"

"Which ones?" I asked.

Mother sent out a soothing waft of Earth my way. I ignored it, pretending I hadn't felt a thing. But I had to admit it felt good. That was one thing coming down here had showed me: I actually missed home.

Cecelia and William. My magical mother and my loving, lovely, ordinary father. Dinner with them last night had been a joy, even with them giving me the third degree about the Panthers, and Jimmy, and Doreen. I'd forgotten the ease we had together. Things up north were always so damn tense. Exciting, but not restful.

Helen looked confused, slight lines marring her perfect brow. "School. UC Berkeley! Aren't you studying…?"

Sipping my perfect cup of coffee, I smiled at her. I was enjoying this. I suppose that was mean. I'd actually always liked Helen, but all of this wealth and nicety was grating on my nerves. I was anxious to get down to business.

We were interrupted by a waiter, carrying plates stacked on both his arms. "The red pepper omelet?" he asked. "And the artichoke frittata?" He set those down in front of my mother and Helen.

"The ham and scrambled eggs? And the strata." Yeah. Ham and eggs were mine. I had no idea what strata was.

"Yes. Berkeley. I wasn't sure if you meant my studies with Aunt Doreen, or the Marxist studies I've been doing with the Panthers."

Helen looked slightly ill at that and Terrance cleared his throat.

"Berkeley is good," I continued. "I have some great professors, but it's hard to keep up with all of that and everything else on my plate. And sometimes I wonder if it's worth it."

"What do you mean, sweetheart?" Cecelia asked, looking worried.

Shit. I'd been goading Terrance and Helen, and forgotten Mom was listening, too. Of course she would wonder. Both my parents would wonder. They were paying good money for me to go to school. My family was well off for black folks, but we weren't the kind of middle class that didn't sometimes wake up sweating when there were too many extra bills one month. And school gave them plenty of sleepless nights, I'm sure.

I looked at Cecelia's beautiful face, so out of place in this restaurant, the only other dark face in a sea of peach, white, and beige. She was like an orchid in a field of daisies. So beautiful. But orchids don't grow in fields of daisies. And out of their environment, orchids don't fare very well.

"It's nothing, Mom. I just feel for all the people in the world who need help, is all. And some days it feels like the world is burning up around me, and what I'm doing is sitting around, reading books."

The eggs were good, I'd give the place that. Creamy, just the right amount of cooked. And the brioche from the basket the waiter had set down was flaky and delicious. I wouldn't admit that to anyone at the table, though.

My mother nodded at my response. "Well, I think you'll help more people if you stay in school."

"That's right! We need more young people like you getting an education!" Terrance barked. He must be nervous. Terrance never barked.

He must know I was about to bring up why we were there. Any minute now.

I'd slept amazingly the night before, and woke up feeling pretty good, which was the only reason I hadn't ripped Terrance's throat out already. If we'd been in the privacy of the Mansion, believe me, it already would have happened. Wily man. We were meeting on this fancy back deck of a sun-soaked winter Los Angeles restaurant with its tinkling fountain, clinking forks and knives, and light, genteel laughter for a reason.

Places like this were buffers for the rich. As good a protective shield as any magic any one of us at this round, glass-topped wicker table could throw up at a moment's notice.

If Terrance thought strata and tea and white cloth napkins would protect him, he was going to be very surprised.

As soon as I ate some more of these creamy eggs and perfectly seared ham.

And had a second cup of coffee.

Damned if I was going to choke on food this good by mixing it with my rage.

CHAPTER TWENTY-FIVE
JASMINE

That second cup of coffee was sitting wrong in my stomach. Like I'd drunk a cup of acid. Two hours later and we were still at the damn restaurant, having moved on to sipping water with delicate rounds of lemon floating on top of the ice.

I recrossed my legs under the tweed mini, the zippers of my black leather boots catching slightly on each other. It was taking everything in me to keep the salt ocean magic rushing in my veins quiet. Even Cecelia was less sanguine now. I could sniff the scent of turned earth rising from her armpits as she fought her magic down. The potted palm closest to us was reaching toward her and beginning to vibrate at the tips of its leaves.

The brunch rush was done by this time. We were one of three tables left sitting in the whole covered porch area. It was a good thing the place was almost deserted. Even I wouldn't go too far in a packed house. Terrance had gambled on that with this meeting. He just hadn't bargained on my waiting him out.

The waiters were avoiding our table by this point, whether by some subtle rich-person signal from Terrance and Helen, or because they could feel the barely contained heat beginning to wind itself around us all. Helen and Terrance were keeping themselves in check, of course. They didn't have as much to lose. But I could lay a bet that any moment we'd start to rattle the glass-topped wicker table from the floor between the four of us.

At this point, I didn't much care for white, bourgeois propriety. This fancy restaurant with its covered outdoor patio could burn to the ground for all I cared.

"Terrance, what use is the Association if it won't actually do what's necessary to *help* people?" I felt like I was spitting glass through my teeth with every word. Holding back the full force of the blue ocean fire within me grew harder every second. "This is not what I signed up for."

He smiled at that, showing his perfect, straight teeth for just one moment, blue eyes sparking under his round gold glasses frames.

"I don't believe you 'signed up' for anything. I believe you were born to this task, Jasmine, and I would like to remind you of the responsibility you bear to the Association. You took oaths, just over a year ago now, yes?" He looked at Helen for confirmation. She nodded.

She had administered the oath herself, in the grand hall with the ornate altar in the center of the gleaming wood room. Light had streamed through the tall windows that day. I'd felt good. Like I was becoming an adult. Ready to do something.

Ready to do something, like right goddamned now.

"I believe you took oaths too, sir. Was that so long ago you've forgotten what they are? You took an oath to 'Serve the light and seek the truth resting in darkness. To aid those in need, to the utmost of your power. To learn the avenues of magic and to protect the secrets of the Order whenever possible. To risk your own life before putting the life of another in danger.'"

I stared right back into his eyes. He wasn't smiling anymore. Bingo. "Do you need me to go on?"

Terrance raised his hand to signal for the check. Cecelia reached out and slowly forced it down. A waiter hesitated, hovering on the edges, taking one step forward and then freezing in place. Finally, Helen turned toward the poor man and shook her head. He backed away again.

I was starting to wish I'd taken Carol up on her offer to join us. Even though she wasn't invited, she'd been willing to push her way into this brunch as backup. I'd refused, thinking it would start Terrance off too angry, and make any negotiation impossible. But that may have been a miscalculation on my part. The man needed to know that people opposed his decisions, that there were rumblings in the Association.

And that we were willing to organize.

"You know people are noticing the Association's immobility, right?"

"Because of you," he said. "With your whisper campaigns and complaints. Pushing your childish agenda."

Cecelia stiffened beside me and started to raise her hand again. The plant leaves started rustling. I don't even think she realized it. Terrance did, though. So did Helen, who quickly said, "Surely we can continue to discuss this in a civil manner. Wouldn't we do better to go back to the Mansion and get this out of public?"

My mother, may all the Gods bless her, said, "That might be wise, because I'm having the hardest time remaining civil at this point."

The rustling stopped.

I leaned across the round table and the detritus of the brioche basket, butter melting in little ceramic dishes, water glasses sweating, tea and coffee cups empty. The breakfast plates had long been cleared away.

"You're not getting away from this so soon," I said.

Terrance held up a hand as if to stop me.

"Don't." I said. "I will speak my mind."

The other two tables got some subtle signal from one of our party, some nudge that said, "Aren't you done here? Isn't it time for a walk in the park? Or some shopping?" They seemed to all stand at once, filing out the gate leading to the parking lot.

As soon as they were gone, I stood.

"You, Terrance, are a coward, and if I must, I will call the Association against your leadership. You have not kept your oaths to the Association or the People. The people are in need and we have the ability to help."

He clenched his teeth. "You are not being reasonable! If we act now, we will expose ourselves. You already put us in grave danger with that stunt you pulled in the park up there. You and Doreen, who should know better."

My mother threw her napkin on the table and snorted at that. "There are actual panthers running in the streets of Los Angeles, Terrance. You think people don't know something's going on? You think we can hide our sorcery anymore? Wake up! Our country is on fire and has been for years now. It's time the Association took a stand for good."

Helen finally spoke. "Terrance, I think we at least need to call a session. It's been too long and there are things we need to discuss with a quorum."

He started to object.

"You can't do this, Terrance," I said. "Members have legitimate concerns that directly question your authority. This is out of your hands now."

I sat back down, reined the ocean back in.

Terrance looked deflated; a bit of luster had left his glasses and cufflinks and the rim of his heavy watch. His eyes remained sharp, though. Terrance Sterling was no fool. He would keep his power, whether he remained head of the Association or not. He hadn't magicked his way to the top without having real power, even if some of his influence had waned.

And that was still in question. Just because a young upstart like me challenged his power didn't mean anyone else actually would.

"So witnessed," said Cecelia. Right on, Mother. Place a seal on that shit. Make it real.

Terrance pushed up from the table. "I'll pay the check now. Follow me out when you're ready."

The leather soles of his shoes slapped softly on the flagstone floor. The fountain burbled. Huh. Funny. I'd been so focused, I had forgotten about the fountain. That was likely a good thing, or I might have started drawing on it for help. I looked at the sculpture, liquid cascading down its sides, and noticed that the flagstones around the shallow pool were dark with water. Maybe I'd been affecting the fountain after all.

"I'm not yet sure if I agree with you, Jasmine, but you have my word that we will go about this in the proper way." Helen paused. "If the Association decides that helping you isn't the right thing to do, will you abide by their decision?"

I pushed my chair out again, grabbing my long leather coat as I stood.

"No."

Then I made my way through the glass-topped tables, boots clacking on the flagstones, announcing to the world that I was there.

CHAPTER TWENTY-SIX
DOREEN

Jasmine had been right about Drake. The boy she'd helped when he was being attacked by two white boys had turned into a strong young man, burgeoning with adolescent pride.

But today, Drake looked at Doreen like he thought she was crazy, but was too polite to say it. He just tugged at his rumpled plaid shirt collar peeking out of the maroon sweater he'd thrown on over his jeans. He'd tossed his ratty brown jacket on top of a battered Army surplus book bag on the wide planks of the attic floor.

Thirteen years old, with a close-cut natural, button nose, and a broad mouth, and he already knew too much about the world. But that was the way for black boys. They couldn't be children for long. No black child could these days. Seems like everyone was out to get them.

It was the end of the school day, and Doreen's day off from the florist shop. They were up in the attic, among the watching statues of old Egyptian Gods, the books waiting to be shelved, the ancestor mask from Angola, and jars and jars of herbs. She'd asked Drake if he didn't need to be at the library, studying, and he'd just rolled his eyes at her before catching himself.

"No ma'am. I don't got any schoolwork left to do."

Doreen figured he was fibbing, but wasn't going to push it just yet. So she'd made them both hot chocolate, and poured it into a plaid, red-topped Thermos before leading the boy out the kitchen door and up the rickety back stairs to the attic.

The scent of chocolate mingled with old frankincense and the dried herb jars Doreen had opened on the long wood table under the umber-shaded central bulb. The two of them worked quietly, lost in their work.

The winter light filtering in from the small dormer windows wasn't strong enough to see by, but the overhead light in its amber sconce cast a warm glow over the room. It assuaged some of the sense that the world was breathing down her neck.

Drake sipped at his chocolate in between stitches. She'd taught him how to hand sew little cloth spell bags. The standoff at the park had used up their resources, as had the protection bundles they'd gotten to everyone who had wanted them the first round.

After news spread about the magic in the park, more and more people from all over the city wanted protection for their homes. With Jasmine in Los Angeles, Doreen and Drake were barely keeping up. They were going to have to train some others, soon.

Luckily, folks didn't need much magic to put together bags of herbs, twigs, and stones. They just needed magic to charge them once they were done.

What they did need was some focused understanding of what they were doing and why. Drake had that. Ever since Jasmine had saved him from bullies by using her magic, he'd been a stalwart presence, learning everything he could shove into his quick mind.

Every stitch in every cloth bag was something serious to him, like it was life or death. And it was. Even though the damned Association didn't want to see it that way.

Doreen should have been down in Los Angeles, backing up Jasmine, but there was too much work to be done up here in Oakland.

Doreen nodded her approval at the boy, then went back to sorting out herbs and picking through small tumbled stones.

"We're going to need more bags and bundles, Drake," she said. "Do you have any friends who might want to help?"

The boy frowned a little, creases lining his forehead before smoothing out again. "I don't know, ma'am. A lot of the kids still scared, you know? They scared of the cops, but they scared of you, too."

"Scared of me?"

"You got the magic, ma'am. And that's a scary thing."

Doreen picked up her mug of chocolate and took a swallow. Then she sighed.

"I suppose it is, Drake. I suppose it is."

It was funny: some of the adults were willing to train, but the kids were spooked. Maybe it was because the kids saw more. Felt more.

Huh.

Doreen laid more piles of herbs out, readying them for the bags. Every time Drake sewed up four or six bags, they would pause and fill them together, herbs slipping between their fingers, perfuming the air with wolfsbane, acacia, and anise seed. She shook out some cloves onto a dish as well. Cloves were always good for courage.

"Drake, you know you have the shine yourself. Did you ever want to get some more training?"

"What are we doing here, ma'am?" He kept his head bent, carefully stitching the blue cloth with red thread, but Doreen felt the way he strained toward her, wanting to know exactly what she meant.

"Well, you are helping me, and I'm teaching you some about herbs. That's a form of magic. And you've gotten good at the energy work we're teaching folks in the playground…. But I meant your other skills, son."

Drake's needle paused mid stitch, but he didn't raise his head. "What other skills?"

"Drake. Look at me, son."

He did, for a scant few seconds, before dipping his head again, staring at the chocolate in his cup. Drake made a show of picking up the cup and drinking before looking at Doreen's eyes again. He could barely hold her gaze.

"I know you see things sometimes." Doreen spoke as gently as she could, but she wanted him to hear this. "I could help you with that. Help make it stronger. Help you to focus better."

He whispered something at his cup of hot chocolate.

"I can't hear you, son. What did you say?"

He looked at her, eyes wide, chocolate milk pooled in the creases of his mouth. Drake licked his lips. Ran a hand over his close-cropped hair.

"I don't like what I see, ma'am," he said. "I don't know I want to see more."

Doreen exhaled, then reached out across the table. Drake paused a moment, then held out his hand. His skin was dry in the palm of her hand.

"You don't have to talk about it, Drake, but I would very much like to hear what you've seen if you want to tell me. Sometimes talking helps."

He nodded, then pulled his hand away. "I'm done with these bags, Mrs. Doreen."

Doreen nodded. "All right then. It's likely time for you to be getting home. Will you ask your parents if you can come by again? Maybe Saturday?"

Drake shoved the chair back and picked up his jacket and Army surplus bag.

"Yes ma'am. I will."

Drake paused at the door and spoke, half to the night outside, and half to Doreen. "I been seeing snakes, ma'am. And a giant white spider. It makes me scared."

"They scare me, too, Drake." She paused. "But we've been battling them all the same. I want you to know that. And we'll learn how to win."

Drake looked up at that, staring at the jackal-headed statue of Anubis on the table behind Doreen. He still couldn't look directly at her.

"With magic?"

"Yes. We aren't sure exactly what kind yet, Drake. But Jasmine and I? We'd be proud to have you there to help us."

Drake stared at that statue like it was going to start speaking any minute. Then, with a quick nod to Doreen, he was out the door, closing it carefully behind him.

He clattered down the back stairs, leaving Doreen alone, a sorcerer under a ceiling light, surrounded by small cloth bags and jars of herbs.

She wondered exactly what was in those images of snakes and spiders Drake saw. It couldn't be good, him seeing the very things that were preying on both the Panthers and the Association.

It couldn't be good at all.

CHAPTER TWENTY-SEVEN
LIZARD

Lizard ran, sidewalk jarring his shins as his boots smacked the concrete. "Watch out, brother!" a man yelled as he went by. Lizard couldn't pause long enough to shout a "sorry" back. Barely even registered that he'd slammed the big man's shoulder.

A car was still smoldering, blocks away. Lizard could smell it, and could have sworn he smelled traces of tear gas, which should have been long gone, held by the same pressure force that trapped the lead and stench from all the cars in the LA basin.

You live in Los Angeles, you get used to the air.

Snniiiick!

"Huh-*whoof!*" The breath left Lizard's lungs and he stumbled, almost crashing into a woman dragging a squeaking shopping trolly down the sidewalk.

His left shoulder blade was on fire, his eyes almost blind with pain. Lizard tried to keep going, but something tugged on his back, right where the nexus of pain radiated outward.

"Shit!"

Lizard fell for real this time, collapsing against the folded-up metal gate of a bakery, hands and knees scrabbling on the poured concrete.

He saw a smashed pink-frosted donut near his head, before pain blinded him again.

Then the pain was gone. Just like that, leaving Lizard gasping and choking. He shoved his back up against the metal, trying to get purchase beneath his boots again so he could stand.

Black trousers and high-shine shoes stopped in front of him. White shirt cuffs. Just a hint of Brut teased Lizard's nose, winding through the scent of car exhaust, baked goods, and things burning.

Then came the sense of *something* slithering up Lizard's calves, squeezing and releasing. Sweat popped out on his forehead and a low whine escaped his throat. Lizard had been scared in his life—what boy hadn't? But he'd never felt absolutely terrified before today.

He was scared during the shootout, but was busy keeping himself in the fray and helping his comrades. His comrades…who he'd left behind to deal with pigs and roaring shifters.

This. This was not fear. This was terror. Some *thing* squeezing up his legs, wrapping itself around his torso. Pressing the air out from his lungs. A giant, unseen boa constrictor had a grip on him.

Lizard was caught. And caught good.

He caught sight of the silver serpent coiled around the white man's finger. And that tattooed spider in the webbing near his thumb.

"Fuck."

"Let me help you," the man said, in that calm, cold voice of his. He crouched down. Lizard's terrified face reflected in his black glasses. He could see each comb line in the man's wavy, movie-star hair.

Lizard was terrified. But no way was he letting a white man scare the piss out of him. He clenched, gritting his teeth, as the Feeb tucked his hands in Lizard's armpits and hauled him up off the ground.

Those hands were not kind.

People walking toward them either stepped off the sidewalk and took their chances on the street, turned around, or ducked into open shops along the way.

No one down here wanted to mess with the Feds. Not when a firefight had just happened. No matter how much they hated the Man, people loved their lives more. And who was Lizard? No one on this block knew his name. Not that they would've helped him even then. The power of the black suit and starched white shirt was strong enough that folks might spit, but if they were smart? They'd always walk away.

Lizard couldn't blame them, but he sure as shit wished Roland Freeman was around right now, or even some of the other cats with guns.

The pressure around Lizard eased up enough so he could breathe easier, but enough remained to let him know the man still had him tethered.

"What'd you hit me with, man?" Lizard croaked out.

The man gave a half smile that did nothing to animate his face. "Magic."

Shit. Didn't that just take the cake?

CHAPTER TWENTY-EIGHT
JASMINE

I was already regretting the orange turtleneck layered under the long black Panther leather coat, and the black beret. It was cool out for Los Angeles, but warming up by the minute.

And walking down the sidewalk of East Los Angeles, I could only wish I was in South Central, instead.

I wanted to get down to 41st and Central, but my parents would freak. Not that I would let that stop me. Mostly, I knew my energy needed to focus on the Association. Getting shot at by the LAPD wasn't going to help the movement, not short term or long.

I hated that I even had to think in those terms, but one thing I was learning from Jimmy and the Panthers was strategy. Other folks were holding it down in front of headquarters down here. Angela Davis and Ericka Huggins didn't need my body down there.

It disappointed me, for sure. To come all this way and not meet some of the heroes of the revolution. But my Panther discipline was intact. The folks coming to rely on us for magical protection needed everything I had.

We had to start training people down here, too. As soon as we got the Association's head out of its ass. If not, Cecelia was on board anyway, which meant Carol and Ernesto would have backup.

Carol and Ernesto were just ahead of me on the sidewalk. What was up with those two anyway? Carol insisted nothing was happening, but it sure didn't smell that way to me. Their bodies leaned toward each other as they walked, blond hair and black, bare inches apart, listening to more than the words they were exchanging.

I could tell Ernesto was stopping himself from touching Carol, from sliding an arm around the rust-colored leather coat cinched around her slim waist. Her blond head was bare, and a navy corduroy skirt swished between the coat and almost matching rust-colored knee boots.

Of course Carol was in denial. She'd had a crush on Ernesto Alvarez practically since the day she arrived from Minnesota.

Huh. Must be a trip to find out your schoolgirl dreams could come true, like some romance novel. Like the novels Carol thought I didn't know about, shoved under the twin bed of her room in the Mansion.

That girl needed to deal. She also needed to move out of the Mansion someday. The sooner, the better, as far as I was concerned.

I hadn't been in East LA in a long time, but it looked exactly the same. Fruit stands, piled-up vegetables, the tire stores, hardware, little craft shops and bakeries. And the piñata sellers. I guessed those never went out of season.

The scents were what I loved best about East LA. Exhaust fumes, of course. They were a constant undercurrent, building the smog-filled air, leaving the biting taste of lead way back in my molars. But that was layered over by palo santo, rubber, burnt sugar, coffee, cigarettes, and oranges. Occasionally I'd catch a whiff of fresh tortillas, or everything would get overpowered by the greasy stench of fried pork skin.

Different smells than Oakland Chinatown. But the two neighborhoods weren't so different in my mind. Working class people making a living, selling a variety of goods to one another. And acknowledging that food was life. It kept communities together.

Carol looked over her shoulder, eyes alight under her round wire frames. "We're almost there," she said.

When did Carol get so confident? I mean, she was weird about the Ernesto thing, but striding through the barrio? And, apparently, standing up to Terrance Sterling?

Sweat trickled down the small of my back under my orange turtle-neck. I shouldn't have worn the leather coat, but in the last few weeks, it had become my armor. It also let people know what was what. A few folks on the street today had given me the nod. A couple of others backed away. One Brown Beret raised a fist in salute. I saluted back.

"Power to the people, brother," I said.

"Power to the people!" he said back.

That felt good.

See, if the Panthers could get folks down with the revolution like that, no matter who they were, the Association could do the same with magic.

We were an arsenal being used for petty shit. What a waste. So today, instead of another tiresome meeting with Terrance and Helen, we were going directly to folks Ernesto said would help us.

The woman who'd been training Carol out from under Terrance's nose.

Yeah. Carol was definitely not the mousy girl I'd left behind. That made me grin. Lost in my thoughts for a moment, I wasn't paying attention and almost crashed into Ernesto's back.

Dumb of me. I shouldn't be woolgathering on the street. Too dangerous.

They had stopped in front of a chipped and faded turquoise door. A yellow triangle surrounded an orange hand, facing palm out, like it was warding off danger.

Or protecting against something evil.

Small windows were set near the top of the wall. There weren't any windows a person could see into from the street. Definitely a well-protected space.

Carol knocked three times and turned the simple brass knob, shoving open the door.

I braced myself and followed Ernesto in. The smell of his hair cream was comforting somehow. A touchstone to a time when things felt simpler. Easier.

Like there was less at stake.

The inside of the shop smelled like incense, candles, and herbs. Frankincense, copal, myrrh. Dandelion root. Bay. Lavender. The stink of valerian causing my tongue to curl. I closed my eyes for a moment, letting the varied scents swirl around me, letting my eyes adjust to the dim room.

The magic felt like soft fingers on my face and hands. Something brushed the back of my neck, ruffling the wisps of fine hair tendriling out from my natural.

Opening my eyes, I saw rows of jars stuffed with materials any decent witch would need. Turning, I saw pieces of pressed tin nailed all over the walls. Hearts. Lungs. Legs. Arms. Torsos.

Milagros, I knew they were called. This shop did a big business praying for the sick, then.

There was a jingling of metal behind me, and a tiny woman with skin the color of madrone bark pushed through a burgundy curtain that must have led to a storage room.

Her eyes were citrine green, set in a hawklike face. A long, green velvet skirt swirled around her legs as she walked toward me. Bracelets stacked themselves up her thin arms, over the long sleeved black jersey shirt she wore. She was staring through me. Pinning me to my spot like I was a mouse and she was a hungry owl.

Shit. Carol trained with this woman? No wonder she'd had to grow a spine.

"Rosal…" Ernesto started to speak, but the woman waved one hand for silence.

Then she raised her hands toward my face, cupping my cheeks. Her hands were smooth and cool. I was so hot all of a sudden, like my sorcery came from flames instead of ocean. What was she? Something else, that was for sure. Something I'd never felt before.

"You have come just in time. Los Manos saw you, long ago, when you were just a tiny drop of water. You are heir to the mighty Beatriz. She saw many things. She told us you were coming before she died."

Momma Beatrice. My grandmother.

"But, how…I never even met her," I said.

"Sssh, hechicera. Let me look at you. Open up your mind."

Part of my brain scrambled to get away from her. My body wanted to run. But I took a breath and found my center.

My center trusted her. Trusted her with my life and my soul. I was just frightened of her power. That was okay. I could deal with that.

So I took as big a breath as my tense chest and belly would allow, and sought out the water in the room. There was a small font near the door. Right. Ernesto had blessed himself when we came in. I'd seen that, but not really noticed. And there was Florida water, and other blessing and cleansing potions in bottles on a lower shelf.

All the liquid in the room said that this space was safe. So the woman who made them must be safe, too.

I called on the Powers to protect me just in case, whispering a prayer inside my mind.

Then I opened up and let the old magic lady in.

CHAPTER TWENTY-NINE
JASMINE

The sorcerer's hands on my temples were all I felt for awhile. The shop, Carol, Ernesto, the candles, the frankincense, the tin milagros…they all winked out.

She and I—Rosalia, Ernesto and Carol called her, though we hadn't really been introduced—were floating in a field of stars.

Rosalia released my head and stepped back, then took my hand.

"Come, hechicera." She led me, walking—how were we walking?—through the stars. It was as if they were a glimmering field of flowers. My brain knew that stars were massive and would burn us alive if we touched them. It also knew that space would crush us.

So that meant…

"We are in the plano astral," Rosalia said. "You have not been there before?"

Huh.

There was a faint scent of burning metal, rum, and raspberries. It made me feel slightly ill. Like the time I'd shoved a handful of raspberries in my mouth and discovered one of them was moldy.

"I've been on the astral, sure. But it looked all misty. Gray. Not like this." And it sure hadn't smelled this weird. I didn't remember it smelling like anything at all.

I could feel her smiling next to me. And how I could feel that, I didn't know. So I pulled my eyes away from the winking, shimmering field of gold, purple, and turquoise blue and looked at her face. Sure enough, she was smiling.

"You have not yet learned to trust your sight, hechicera. That in you which is afraid contains the space so it looks pale to you. Washed out. We must train ourselves to be able to see all the colors. Hear every single sound. Beatriz knew such things. It is too bad she is not here to pass them on."

A sudden pounding gripped my chest, *BoomBoomBoomBoomBoom!*, before settling back into its ordinary rhythm as I forced breath into my lungs. This was almost too much. I had a hell of a lot more respect for Carol now.

"If you opened up my head, how come we're here? I don't know this place. And why do you keep calling me *hechicera*?"

"Because you are like me, mija. You are a sorcerer who is meant to lead other sorcerers. You have a mind like steel and a heart filled with anger and knowing." She paused to consider. "And love. Great love. But your power outstrips the others. You need to learn to accept it."

No. No way was I letting this shit in.

"Lead people like Terrance, you mean?"

The stars hummed around us. Singing. A slow, up-and-down cadence. So soft I hadn't heard it until now. My ears must be growing used to it.

Rosalia laughed, sharp and loud, her voice cracking across the plane. Two of the star flowers shattered and drifted outward in a spiral of color and light.

"Nothing like Terrance. He is a tin pot general. What power he had is now twisted by fear and doing things that look right to others."

She turned toward me then, stopping me with those warm hands.

"To have power, true power, you cannot care so much what others think, hechicera. You have to listen, *feel*." One hand clenched into a fist and pressed firmly against my abdomen. "You feel the power, down here, and you know, then, what you *must* do."

"No matter what people think," I whispered to the thin air.

"You do what is right." She shrugged. Like it was so simple. Like she'd never made any mistakes.

I missed Jimmy all of a sudden. I missed his lips on mine. I missed his big panther head butting up against my hip. I missed his musky, familiar scent. I needed that grounding right about now.

I was so out of my depth.

Rosalia looked at me, those citrine eyes glimmering like the field of stars.

"I did not answer your other question, hechicera. We are here because you *do* know this place. You have just not reached deep enough into your power to recognize it yet. You are the one with the keys. You can do anything you want."

Tears pricked my eyes and sick bile crawled up the back of my throat. I felt hopeful and terrified. The feelings crashed inside, rolling over me like a giant wave, and I blacked out.

Waking up seconds later with her strong, bony, manzanita hands cradling my back.

We flew through the air then. Projected around us were scenes of people starving, children with distended bellies, cauldrons flaming, buried land mines exploding under soldiers' feet, flowers opening from bud to bloom and dropping petals on hard ground. A woman screamed and pushed, belly swollen with child, sweat streaming down her body; an old woman closed her eyes and rattled out a final breath; a bayonet speared a child; two men kissed; a woman stroked ochre paint across a canvas; a lamb struggled to stand.

"All of this is power, hechicera, feel it. Take it in."

My body fought against her arms and my mind fought to keep the images out. They were coming too fast.

"I. Can't," I grunted out through gritted teeth. I just wanted it to stop. All of it. Right now.

"I need to stop. I. Can't."

"You need to *see*!" she shouted in my ear. "You need to *feel*!"

"Get me out of here!"

"No!" she roared. "Call on Beatriz! Call your ancestors. They will help you!"

Fuck her!

Still flailing, limbs knocking wildly into Rosalia's bony arms and legs holding me tight, I found a part of myself that somehow knew what she was talking about.

I called the Powers. I drew up the image of the photograph of Momma Beatrice from my mother's dresser top. I held it in my mind.

And relaxed.

And breathed.

The images slowed just a little. But mostly I…felt them now. Tasted them. Could feel the life pulsing through it all.

"Initiation," I said out loud.

"Yes."

"And Jimmy?" Why I asked that, I didn't even know. But there was some question there that needed answering.

"The Animal People are part of this, too, hechicera. They are part of the power that calls to you. Part of the power you hold," Rosalia spoke into my ear.

I shook my head.

Rosalia untangled herself from me. "I can bring you back now. Prepare. Your eyes can close, if that feels better. But I think you should see."

And the images faded, becoming a backdrop to the field of stars and then we were dropping, falling, descending from the stars. The air rushed through us, not around us, and then *pop* we were in the shop before I could even think to close my eyes.

Ernesto and Carol were staring at us. Carol was white faced with fear. Guess her spine hadn't grown to include this shit yet. Ernesto just nodded and disappeared behind the burgundy curtain. I heard water running into metal. There must be a kitchen back there. Sounded like he was making tea.

Carol grabbed me and static shot between us. She stumbled away, shaking out her hands. It felt like my hair was two sizes larger, standing out around my head. I patted at it gingerly. Yep. Bigger.

"Are you okay?" my friend asked, eyes huge.

"I need to sit down," I said.

Rosalia led me to one of the stools behind the long counter. Carol followed, making sure to not touch me again.

I climbed up on shaking legs. I needed to soak in a tub with a glass of wine. Or curl up with Jimmy.

Or eat a steak.

Or all of the above.

"What the fuck just happened?" I said to no one.

"You got a taste of your power, hechicera. For the first time in your life." Rosalia boosted her frame onto the stool next to mine. The scent of space still clung to her.

I sniffed my own wrist. Raspberries and burning steel.

My stomach growled.

"I'm hungry."

Rosalia smiled.

"Power needs to be fed," she said. "Welcome home."

I wasn't sure what she meant, but had a feeling that it was going to become way too clear.

Too soon.

CHAPTER THIRTY
DOREEN

D oreen stepped through the big doors to the church hall. It was just as she remembered it from the night young Fred Hampton spoke. Except instead of rows of chairs, long tables were set up throughout the hall, a chair at each place. Pitchers of chalky milk and clear apple juice were on each table.

A young man was setting out napkins. He wore a patched denim jacket over his broad shoulders, and denim bell-bottomed pants. His natural had a reddish tint to it, down to his thick sideburns. Leroy, Doreen recalled his name was.

He looked up as the door slammed shut.

"Hello, ma'am." He smiled, cheeks rounding on his pleasant face. "Jasmine with you?"

He always seemed like such a nice young man.

"Good morning, Leroy."

A burst of laughter came from behind a big swinging door. The kitchen. The comforting, earthy scent of oatmeal and raisins mingled with the smells of worn wood and cool morning.

Doreen tucked her navy pocketbook more firmly under her arm and walked further into the room, the heels of her sensible shoes making quiet tocking noises on the scarred-up plank wood floors. Those floors had seen generations of dances, socials, and meetings, she was sure.

And now the Black Panther Party served breakfast to schoolchildren here. Close to two hundred children every day, Jasmine said. It was quite a remarkable feat for a bunch of college-aged men and women to pull off. Plus running a free clinic and their "school," such as it was. Jasmine spoke of the school in glowing terms. Doreen wasn't so sure about that yet.

But the clinic, food giveaways, and the breakfast program? Only a fool would think those were bad. Though the government had tried to change people's minds about that. Going into black neighborhoods and asking folks, "Do you know the Black Panther Party are socialists?"

Well, the people had the right answer to that: "If free food means they're socialists, that's all right by me."

"Ma'am?" Leroy asked again. "May I help you?" He'd stopped what he was doing and was right next to Doreen. She must have been woolgathering. Had walked right to him without really noticing.

That wasn't good. These days, she needed to pay attention to everything. Just like she'd been training the people. Protection magic started by noticing what was around you. Not by floating off into unnecessary thoughts.

"I'm sorry," she said. "To answer your first question, Jasmine is in Los Angeles right now. Family business." Which was true, as much as the Association could be considered family.

Leroy looked at her, clearly waiting for an explanation. Doreen just looked around the room. Long scratched tables, very clean. High windows set into the tall walls. A podium tucked into one corner. Stack of Bibles and handbills on a table near the wall. A long, white cloth banner, carefully sewn, proclaimed *God is Love* in red letters.

"Did you come to volunteer?"

Doreen looked at Leroy.

"In a manner of speaking," Doreen said. "But I'm not here to serve food."

"Do you mind if I keep setting up while we talk? The children should be arriving any minute."

Leroy pointed to a pile of cheap cutlery on one of the tables, next to a stack of paper napkins.

Doreen grabbed some of the rough white paper and a clattering stack of spoons and forks.

"What's for breakfast today?" she asked.

"Eggs and oatmeal. Milk and juice," Leroy replied from across the long table. "So, what did you want to talk about, ma'am?"

Doreen hid a smile. If white folks only knew how polite these young men and women were. Leroy had clearly been raised right.

"You were at DeFremary Park. When it all happened."

He paused in setting out the napkins, a strange look on his ruddy face. His eyes grew sharp. Wary.

Afraid.

"Yeah. I was at the standoff with the pigs." Leroy stood tall, hooking his thumbs in the brass-buckled belt holding up his bell-bottomed jeans.

Okay. So this wasn't going to be easy. None of this was easy.

Doreen straightened up herself, fixing him with a straight gaze. Her fire rose. With a breath, she diffused the power along her skin, raising traces of cinnamon scent that mingled with the oatmeal and raisins, and the smell of cooking eggs.

"Then you saw what Jasmine and I did. And all the neighborhood people. You saw the dome we raised around the park. The police bullets bouncing off it."

Leroy shifted uncomfortably. "Yes, ma'am." He shook his head, and spoke more softly, "There was no damn way to miss it."

He looked at her again, eyes shifting to pleading, like a boy asking an uncle for protection. Or to keep the monsters away.

In that moment, Doreen wasn't sure if she was the monster or the protector. Or both. And that was the reality she had to shoulder now. The thing she'd avoided in her years of grief.

She was a sorcerer. And while that power included the ability to protect life, she was clear in this moment, that this young, broad-shouldered man—who likely knew how to protect his own body and community with guns or fists—he knew that Doreen had the power to kill.

Doreen closed her eyes for a moment. Damn it. This conversation wasn't supposed to be going this way. She was supposed to come in and talk about protecting the children, not having a deep realization about her powers.

Taking a breath, she opened her eyes again.

"Leroy. We need to protect these precious children, and we need to teach them how to do it themselves. We need to get their parents to agree to the project."

She watched as his shoulder muscles tensed, and then relaxed. Just a little. But enough.

"You plan to teach the children magic." A statement. Not a question.

"That I do. But we need everyone to come together on it. Whether that means I meet with leadership and then the children's parents, or whether that means you speak on my behalf. I only know that people've been having visions. Bad ones. It isn't pretty out there. And it is only likely to get worse."

Leroy picked up the napkins and his pile of forks and spoons, and started setting the table again.

Doreen followed suit. She'd give them both some time to deal with the weight of what she'd just said.

As Jasmine's Jimmy would say, "That's heavy." The thing was, with the fire running through Doreen like it was, with this new realization that she had to accept, deeply, her ability to kill if necessary to protect the children she could hear approaching the door, she knew she could handle the heaviness.

At least right now.

The outside doors squeaked open, a little girl dragging against the weight of the wood with all her might, smile on her precious face, hair scraped back into a puffy pigtail topped by a yellow bow.

Other children crowded in behind her. Boys and girls with book bags and sweaters, white knee socks, plain dresses, dark slacks. Sleepy-eyed, scowling, smiling. Smelling of morning.

Possibility.

Tears flooded Doreen's eyes, and she quickly wiped them away with one of the rough napkins.

"Good morning, brothers and sisters!" Leroy said, voice booming against the walls of the church hall.

"Black is beautiful!"

"Black is beautiful!" the children shouted back.

"Find your places," Leroy said. "Rafael, no pushing. You are children of Africa. Disciplined and strong."

Chairs scraped on the floor, jackets and book bags hanging from the backs. The children chattered with each other as though they didn't have a care in the world.

Doreen knew that wasn't true, but she hoped they could believe it anyway.

"Pour yourselves some milk and juice." Leroy nodded at Doreen, inclining his head toward the tables. He picked up a pitcher and poured for the younger children. Doreen understood the gesture.

Get to work. These children need to feel welcomed here. Cared for.

There would be time for talk of magic once empty stomachs were full.

Chapter Thirty-One
Doreen

"Here's the thing," Leroy said. He paused in the middle of scrubbing down the big twelve-burner stove to scratch at his sideburns. He stacked cast iron burners to one side as he worked his way down, making sure the globs of oats and eggs got cleaned off before they hardened into mortar.

"We saw what you all did at Bobby Hutton Park. But talking to parents about arming their kids with magic? I'm not sure they're gonna be down with that."

He clattered two of the big burners back on the cleaned portion of stove before stacking the next two, working his way down the scratched old behemoth. The thing looked almost as old as Doreen, though she knew it wasn't. The big stove and its ovens had just seen hard use over the last twenty years.

Doreen, Tanya, Leroy, and a woman named Leticia were all in the big industrial kitchen off the main church hall. The children were already off to school.

Leticia and Leroy had dragged the big black rubber mats to the side and Leticia was running a soapy string mop over the big rust-colored tiles. Doreen hoped the shoes she wore under her jeans had good soles. Those tiles looked slippery.

Tanya ran a rag down one of the long steel kitchen counters. Doreen could smell the bleach in the water and was glad the girl was wearing yellow rubber gloves.

Though she shouldn't call Tanya a girl. She was a grown woman with two children and a job downtown. Jasmine always spoke of her with respect.

Doreen perched on a Naugahyde-covered kitchen stool. She'd offered to help, but they said they had their routine down and would get through it quickly. *With her out of the way* was implied, but not said. The Panthers were nothing if not polite to their elders.

Even if their elders were only in their early forties.

Doreen sighed. At least Patrice made her feel young.

This was the only time they were all going to be able to talk with Doreen that morning, before Tanya left for her bank teller's job. Tanya didn't quite fit in with the rest of the crew, with her neatly pressed hair, A-line skirt that skimmed her knees, and brown boots.

Leticia and Leroy both looked like revolutionaries. Afros picked out in ovals, Leroy with his sideburns, both of them wearing bell-bottom jeans and turtleneck sweaters.

And then there was Doreen, not old by any standard except the standards of extreme youth. But these were no kids in front of her. They were adult people with adult minds.

And adult concerns. Like getting shot down in the street. Or kids going hungry. Or any number of things on the ten point program Jasmine made her read. Every bit of that program made sense to Doreen. She was here to help them make it real.

She just had to convince them that magic was as useful as food, medicine, or guns, the way she and Jasmine had convinced leadership. Convincing the people the parents trusted was the only way to get the children safe. So here she was, pocketbook resting on her lap, waiting for them to agree.

"I don't see how teaching children physical self defense is any different than the magic. Drake is assisting us. He's proof that it all works."

Tanya kept wiping down the counters in a rhythm she'd clearly gotten down over many month's time. Her pink-and-blue–flowered apron clashed with the business clothes.

"The thing is, ma'am, parents trust what they know, and mistrust what they don't know. We're still struggling ourselves with figuring out that some of leadership are actual panthers." The young woman stopped at that, wringing out her rag over a small bucket of bleach water. Her face was serious.

"Some people feel betrayed, or scared. Other folks want to use the power of leadership to move on some of our issues right away. Other folks are counseling patience," Tanya said.

"So you see why we're not so hot to try some other new thing right now. Dig?" Leticia said, staring down at the floor as she swept the mop in arcs from side to side.

Doreen knew now was the time. There was never going to be another opening like this. Sending a brief apology to Jasmine in her mind, she drew on a little bit of fire and spoke.

"My husband was a mountain lion."

All motion in the room stopped.

"What?" Leroy asked.

"My husband, Hector, was a mountain lion. He was killed by the Los Angeles County Sheriff's Department. In the mountains two miles from our home. They shot him twelve times. Chopped his head off."

"Damn," Leroy said.

"It's why I came up to Oakland. I gave up my magic. I severed connection with family and friends. I needed to get away."

Tanya stripped off the yellow gloves and came to stand next to Doreen. Her eyes were so kind. Her nails were perfect pale pink ovals on the tips of her brown fingers as she took Doreen's hands in her own.

Why did Doreen notice that?

"I'm sorry," Tanya said.

"Thank you. It was years ago. I'm only telling you this… It's because of you that I'm doing magic again. Because of the Panthers. You offer a sense of strength, and hope. You all give so much. I see that now. I used to have the opportunity to give, too. I left it behind."

Leticia wrang the mop out in the big wringer on the top of the rolling metal wash bucket.

"I'm still not getting it. What does this have to do with training up the kids?" she said.

Doreen looked at the younger woman, ankh earrings dangling from full lobed ears, broad, beautiful nose, gap teeth flashing from between her lips. Leticia looked every inch of a proud black woman, and Doreen wanted to keep it that way.

"Because I never want anyone else to feel the rage, and pain, and hopelessness I felt. Because I want every parent and husband and wife and sister to feel like they can do something to protect what they love. And that if they can't be there, the people they love have a way of protecting themselves."

Leticia rolled the yellow bucket toward one of the big sinks and took the wringer mechanism off.

"Leroy?" she asked. He came forward, and together Leticia and Leroy hoisted the bucket up to dump it in the deep steel sink.

Tanya just waited. Silent.

Once the bucket was empty, Leticia thumped it back onto the tiled floor.

"Tanya?" Leticia asked. "You got kids. What do you think about all this?"

Tanya looked at Doreen to answer. "I think we hear what Doreen has to say. And I think we give our children as many chances as we can so they survive."

Leroy nodded.

"Okay, Doreen, if you and Drake come up with a plan to train the children, we'll see to it that it gets added to the training," he said. "The parents will either be convinced, or they just won't bring their kids. As long as the kids get fed every day, we don't care as much about the rest."

He started to drag the big black rubber mats back in front of the sinks and stove. Leticia helped him wrestle them in place.

"The sooner Drake and I can get started, the better," Doreen said. "And if any of you ever want to talk about what it's like living with shifters, I'd be happy to."

Tanya slid her skinny arms into a patchwork leather jacket. "It can't be easy for you, coming here like this, Doreen. I appreciate it. We'll get some parents on board, I promise you that."

The young woman got her bag out of the kitchen closet; it was a large, brown leather affair.

Tanya continued, "But as for the rest, if it takes people turning into giant cats to help the revolution, I'm down with it."

"Magic, shape-shifters, oatmeal…whatever it takes," Leroy said. "We'll get used to it."

He leveled his gaze at Doreen.

"We have no choice but to get used to it. As Fanon said, 'Colonization and decolonization is simply a question of relative strength.' If you're offering us another way to get strong? We'd be fools not to take it."

CHAPTER THIRTY-TWO
CAROL

Seeing Jasmine like that terrified Carol. And sent jealousy shooting through her body like a grass fire.

Here Carol thought she was finally catching up with her friend, only to have Jasmine outstrip her, as always.

Once again, Jasmine Jones was the center of attention, the shining star, the one everyone wanted to be around. The one everyone listened to, as though every word was worthy of notice.

And it probably was. But just for once, Carol wanted to be the one people looked at. She was finally ready for it. Ready for Ernesto to *see* her. Ready for someone to acknowledge what Carol had found out about Terrance, and how there was something seriously fishy going on with him.

And the fact that *Carol* was the one seeing the sigils and the spiders and the visions.

But did anyone care?

Not now that Jasmine was back.

And here Carol thought they were doing well. That their friendship was going to be more equal from now on.

Guess not. Carol was just the skinny white girl from Minnesota, who, yeah, they'd say was worth more than just a magical babysitter, but who still shouldn't get too far above her station.

She was so sick of it.

Looking at Jasmine, perched on that stool behind Rosalia's counter like she belonged there…

That was the stool Carol had sat on, stuffing spell bags and reading cards, bent close to Ernesto. The one she sat on when Rosalia walked her through the visions, or asked her help with the sigil that one customer brought in.

The sigil *Carol* had seen. The one she'd drawn over and over in her magical notebook. The one they still hadn't figured out the meaning of. But that was clearly connected to the wild magic floating around.

Carol had been valuable. She knew it. Or she thought so.

And it was all swept away.

Standing in front of the statue of the Virgin of Guadalupe with her red and gold rays spiking out in a halo around her blue cloak, Carol looked into the small eyes painted black on the kind brown face.

Candles lit up the space around the statue. It was almost the Virgin's feast day, so extra care was taken with the statue at this time. There were shrines set up all along the sidewalks of East Los Angeles, dedicated to the Virgin of Guadalupe, still known to some as the Goddess Tonantzin.

Carol almost prayed. Prayed for guidance. Help. But Tonantzin was not her Goddess, despite what Rosalia said. That the Virgin listened to anyone who asked of her.

Carol huffed out a breath, causing the candle flames to flicker.

The burgundy curtain leading to the back room swept back, taking Carol's eyes from the statue for a moment.

Ernesto brought a cup of steaming lavender tea out from the back room. One cup. For Jasmine.

Sure, she needed it. Carol knew that. But she hated that he wasn't bringing tea for her.

Carol reached out and grabbed several chunks of pale gold copal incense, gripping them between her fingers, trying to bring herself back from the anger and jealousy. To feel what was real. What was important.

The magic was important. The danger they were all in—including Jasmine—was important. Carol's feelings? Not so important. At least, she needed to convince herself that was true.

She threw the fragrant resin on the charcoal that burned in an abalone shell. Smoke rose up, wreathing the statue, dancing in the candlelight.

Carol breathed deeply, and opened her feet to the earth far below the layers of building, plumbing, and concrete. There was soil there, rich with tar. It comforted her, steadied her inside.

"Maga?" Rosalia's hand touched Carol's shoulder.

"I'm here," Carol said.

"Come, Ernesto will make some more tea." The hechicera steered Carol back toward the long counter where Jasmine sat huddled, clutching at the cup of tea. Rosalia jerked her head at Ernesto, who nodded and went back through the curtain.

Great. Rosalia knew she was a jealous child.

She looked at her friend. Jasmine looked hollowed out and incandescent all at once. Like she was still halfway gone.

"You okay, Jaz?" Carol asked.

Jasmine nodded once. "The tea's helping. I need some food, though."

"We'll send Ernesto out soon. He'll bring us back some meat. You need that, I think, hechicera," Rosalia said.

Hechicera. Sorcerer. That was what Rosalia was. She called Carol "maga." Magician. Why was that?

"Some things are simple, maga." Rosalia trained her citrine eyes on Carol's face.

Shit. Carol was still thinking too loudly. She froze. Stiff. Embarrassed and pissed off all at once. Well, she had a right to be. Carol raised her chin and stared right back.

"Simple?" Carol felt the Earth moving up through her feet, growing in her belly like a cypress, strengthening her spine.

Rosalia continued, "You think I insult you. I do not. Being a maga is very important. You have a way of tasting the world that Jasmine and I do not. You have not come fully into your power yet."

The hechicera hoisted herself up onto the stool next to Jasmine.

"Once you fully accept the power, you shall know what I mean. In that moment, you will know whether you are to remain a maga or shift into an hechicera. But you will also know that one has no more power than the other."

"I don't get it. I feel like everyone is just always trying to make me feel better about being the runt of the litter. And I'm tired of it. I thought you were different. That you *saw* me."

Ernesto came back with a tray of cups and a whole pot of tea. He'd mixed spearmint in with the lavender this time, smelled like.

"Carol," he said, setting the tray on the counter, "believe me, we see you. We just think you don't yet see yourself."

Ernesto reached a hand out, and touched her face. It was such a gentle gesture, filled with…something. Love? But…

She backed away with a sharp jerk of her head, getting herself far away from his touch. She couldn't bear it. Not right now. Not when she felt angry and discarded. Not when the person who was supposed to be her best friend had swooped back into town and become the center of everything again.

"Carol, please?" Jasmine croaked out. "The Panthers need you. The people in this neighborhood need you. The whole damn Association needs you if they'd be smart enough to own up. But I need you, too."

"Right." Carol ran her hands through her straight blond hair. She grabbed her rust-colored leather coat from one of the stools. "Why don't I go get some food? You all seem to have this under control."

"Sit down!" Rosalia commanded.

Carol froze, hand gripping leather, lips tight. She could feel a flush starting on her neck, but couldn't have told anyone whether it was fear, embarrassment, or anger.

"Carol, you will sit, please," Rosalia said more gently, but with steel still in her voice.

Carol did, sitting on top of the coat she'd been about to put on.

"Drink some tea," Ernesto said, sliding a cup across the counter, shoving it between her hands.

She picked up the heavy blue ceramic, warmed from the hot liquid. The first sip rolled in a wave over her tongue. Honey. Spearmint. Lavender. Thyme. It was almost too hot. She drank it anyway, fighting back tears.

Ernesto leaned over the counter, too close. She could smell cinnamon gum on his breath. He was trying to catch her eyes, but she stared down at the golden-green tea in the blue cup.

"Carol, I'm sorry," he said.

What? That made her look up, just for a moment. His deep brown eyes looked sad behind the tortoiseshell frames. Carol looked back down, running her thumb over the ceramic cup.

"I'm sorry the Association made you feel like you weren't worth as much as you are. I'm sorry I didn't do more to show you how talented you are."

Shit. She was so going to cry. Her throat was tight with it and her nose was starting to run. Damn it. Damn the Powers for not making her more steady. She'd rather be pissed off than this.

"Just. Stop," she said.

She could feel Jasmine on the stool next to her, reaching out a watery wave toward her. The smell of ocean was so familiar, and so good. Carol wanted to lean into it.

She also wanted to get as far away from it as possible.

"I don't want pity," she said.

Jasmine spoke then. "We aren't offering you pity, girl. We're trying to tell you that we've all messed up."

Jasmine was tugging at Carol's shoulder then, trying to get her to turn on the stool and face her.

"Seriously. Be pissed off. Frankly, I think you should've gotten angry long ago. The Association deserves it. Hell, maybe I do, too. But don't feel sorry for yourself."

"What do you know about it? Why shouldn't I feel sorry for myself?"

"Because," Jasmine said, "you're at least as powerful as anyone in this room, except Rosalia, and we can't be mad at her for that. And

Powers know we need you now, dig? All hands on fucking deck, Carol. Use that Earth of yours to grow a spine."

Carol's hand swung out to smack Jasmine's face. Jasmine's hand shot up just as quickly and stopped her.

"I'm not the one you need to fight," Jasmine said.

CHAPTER THIRTY-THREE
JASMINE

Oakland. What a relief it was to smell the waters of the San Francisco Bay.

That shit with Rosalia still had me shook. And things with Carol still felt uneasy. I didn't like that, but she really needed to step up now, and stop being afraid of her own power.

I couldn't coddle her anymore.

But that didn't mean it felt good. To be fighting with my best friend.

At least Jimmy felt good. We were in the parlor of Doreen's bungalow. He was lying on the rug at my stockinged feet. I was getting used to his panther form.

Now that I knew he was a shifter, he started turning more and more. Said it was relaxing, hanging out as a cat.

When I thought about it, it made sense. Cats were either completely wired or totally relaxed. Ready to strike, or ready to sleep.

A cup of mint tea steamed at my elbow on a little wood side table under the glowing lamp shade.

I kind of wished it was a glass of wine. But there was too much to do these days to check out. And I might need my sorcery at any moment, the way things were going.

Jimmy, Doreen, and Leroy had been meeting in my absence. Making plans to get people more training in basic magic. Especially the kids.

It was a good idea, and one I just hoped I had the time for. Thank the Powers I was done with finals.

Jimmy rested his large head on my lap. I stroked the black fur that swept back from the bones around his eyes. The bones of Jimmy's face were heavy. Solid. He looked up at me with one large, gold-tinged eye. The other remained closed. Content.

Those eyes were the same as the man I loved.

Yeah. Had to admit that now. I loved Jimmy. And that alone made it feel like whatever the hell we were facing was gonna become possible to bear.

I'd shoved the coffee table off to the side so his massive body would fit. It's funny, he wasn't that much larger in panther form, but seemed heavier and bigger than when he was a man. Maybe it was just the bones, or maybe the fact that he was 160 pounds of cat instead of man. I think the weight was less noticeable upright.

The mountain lion painting looked down us. The television was quiet in its cabinet.

That's why we were here, instead of Jimmy's bedroom. We both needed a little quiet right about now. Rank and file were adjusting to having leadership be shifters, but frankly, things were still buzzing too much.

Doreen and Patrice were laughing in her bedroom. It was a joyful, homey sound. I relaxed into the cushions of the couch, and scratched at Jimmy's ears. He gave a huge yawn, which was frankly a little intimidating still, and kind of strange.

But not too strange.

Who knew I could feel this content with anyone? Who knew that adjusting to a shifter boyfriend was going to feel so easy?

At least for now…the little voice in the back of my head warned.

But frankly, that voice could shut up. Compared to being the biggest, baddest sorcerer of my generation, or whatever it was Rosalia's little journey showed me, and compared to battling snakes and spiders and frankly, police in the streets?

A boyfriend who was also a giant panther wasn't such a bad thing.

For the first time in awhile I felt safe. Comfortable in my bones. This thing with me and Jimmy? It was just right. Kind of like how I remembered Doreen and Uncle Hector, even when I didn't know Hector was a mountain lion.

"You are one handsome cat, Jimmy Rollins."

His chest rumbled with a growling purr, and the musky, earthy smell increased.

"But much as it's nice sitting here relaxing with you, I need to figure some shit out. Powers know, now is not the time to take a break."

Jimmy raised his head then, and looked at me with both of his gold-rimmed eyes. He shook his head a little, and very eloquently laid that big skull back down on my lap, closing both eyes.

Something crashed in Doreen's bedroom, followed by huge, surprised laughter, immediately shushed.

Shaking my head, I grinned. By all the Powers, who knew Doreen had it in her? Good for her.

"Right," I said to Jimmy. "You think we need rest. And we probably do. But I also…that trip Rosalia took me on still has me kind of weirded out."

"You should have already known all that."

Oh shit.

"You can talk inside my head like this?"

A growling laugh filled my mind.

"I guess I can. The other shifters all talk this way. Never tried it with a non-shifter before. Never had to."

"Well, far out. That'll make life easier."

It meant I could talk to Jimmy about what was bothering me. But it also meant I could communicate with the shifters mind-to-mind when we were dealing with the cops. Or in other situations.

Like when that bar was getting shot up and I figured out one of the party members—Jerrold—was a possible government plant.

"You think I can talk to the other shifters like this? And we can talk like this when you're in human form?"

"That's how it works with the other cats. We talk mind to mind all the time."

Huh. There was so much I didn't know about the Black Panther Party, it turned out. And so much I didn't know about how magic worked, either.

Like, why the hell didn't sorcerers talk this way? We sent images sometimes, and the Air sorcerers could read thoughts if they felt like being intrusive, but we didn't try to carry on conversations in our heads like this.

At least, no one ever taught me that we did. Besides, emotions were always my specialty. Our psychic skills overlapped, but pretty much broke along our Elemental lines.

Water was good at sensing emotional states. Air picked up on thoughts. Fire tracked energy. Earth got information through the body. And most of us could do at least a little bit of some of the others.

But to be able to hear words spoken so clearly in my head? I'd never had that before.

"Maybe it's because we're lovers, baby. Ever think of that? We're already half inside each other all the time. No matter how much we try to keep from one another."

"You're right," I said. "And I'm starting to think we're stupid to keep as much from each other as we do. I mean, I get it, dig? You've got Panther security to think about. It's engrained. And I've got the same thing from the Association, though I'm starting to think a lot of that is bourgeois shit."

A loud moan came from down the hallway. Oh my ancestors and Powers. I was happy for my aunt, but didn't really...and more loud moaning. Right.

"Jimmy, I need to talk to you about what I saw, and what the plan is going forward. I mean, we really need to talk. But I'm a little distracted right now."

He nuzzled his big head into my thigh, opened his mouth and gently grabbed the meat of my leg through my jeans. I could feel the slight pressure of his teeth on my thigh, and feel his breath through the denim.

"Damn, Jimmy. You aren't helping."

"Didn't mean to. Let's go back to your bedroom. I'll shift back and distract you some more."

I let my head flop backwards on the couch for a minute. Then took a big breath in.

What the hell? Even sorcerers need to refuel sometimes. And the easiest way to recharge for me was making love to Jimmy.

The snakes and cops and spiders and whatever other evil shit was around would still be there tomorrow.

Shoving against the black fur of his muscled shoulder, I heaved him away and stood.

He stood next to me, head at my waist, looking up at me.

"Let's go to bed."

A big "oh, yeah!" shattered the hallway. That was definitely Patrice's voice. You go, Aunt Doreen.

"Seems like we won't even need to be quiet."

"That's a good thing. I intend to make you scream tonight. Maybe even get you to bend the walls again."

"You're on," I said.

I was so ready to be in his arms. So ready to not think about my problems for a while. So ready to leave behind the tightness coiled in my belly, and the sense of doom looking over my right shoulder.

I was also afraid to not pay attention to it all. To take my mind off of it at all.

"Momma Beatrice, watch over us tonight, okay?" I sent the prayer out, hoping she was there, listening, like Doreen said she was.

Then Jimmy bumped his head into my hip and walked out the sitting room door.

I shook off the sense of dread, and followed the musky smell of lust instead.

CHAPTER THIRTY-FOUR
JASMINE

Making love with Jimmy was the best part of all this. And now he could admit he was a shifter, things had opened up between us. Grown more powerful.

This was what Doreen must have had with Hector. A blending of wild, animal magic with the Elemental force moving through.

Jimmy said I made him feel stronger. My own magic was increasing, for sure.

"This part of the revolution?" I asked him quietly, when we paused to catch our breath.

"It is now." He grinned.

He had started as a panther, nuzzling my breasts and between my legs. Careful, but strong. His massive head caressing me with bristling soft fur. His tongue offering a few, careful strokes…before he changed into a man, looking up at me with gold-rimmed eyes, so full of love and lust I didn't know whether to scream or cry.

"Sometimes I wish we could make love before you change," I confessed into the darkened room, lit only by the streetlight outside the sheer white lace curtains.

"It's too dangerous, Jaz," his sex-rough voice replied. "I could hurt you, really badly. Even with my tongue."

I knew that. I knew it all too well. But I wanted the danger. My whole body sang with it. I wanted dark fur against my skin. Rough tongue washing my breasts. A roaring in my ear.

"Maybe someday," I said.

He rolled over on top of me, soft and warm, muscles hard against my chest. Then he looked at me, tracing the planes of my face with his eyes.

"Jasmine Jones, I want nothing more than to be with you, for as long as I can, in as many ways as I can."

I sighed, and every part of me relaxed. That was what I needed. To hear those words.

"Thank you," I whispered.

He kissed me, long and slow, then rolled back to my side, and yanked the blankets and the purple Indian bedspread over our naked, sweating bodies, before the chill of the room took hold.

"But much as I like lying here with you, we got some talking to do, too."

"You mean, what are we going to do about Fred Hampton? Or that snake?"

He exhaled, a big sigh. His stomach rumbled.

"Hungry?" I asked.

"Yeah. But time for that soon enough."

Jimmy propped his head up on his right hand, staring at me again. I turned my head to meet his gaze.

"That shit that came through HQ? That gonna happen again?"

I smoothed some stray hairs off my forehead.

"Doreen re-sealed the building pretty good. And I sent that snake off somewhere, though I can't tell exactly where."

The conversation was making me feel restless. And I needed food now, too.

Swinging my feet off the side of the narrow bed, I shivered. Maybe I should turn the furnace up. I reached into the closet for a robe, and tied the soft flannel around my bare skin. Then I reached in again and grabbed a long dashiki from a hanger, holding it up to Jimmy.

He nodded and grabbed it, pulling the green-and-orange–patterned cloth over his head. The robe was slightly short on him, but it would do.

"Let's go get some food. I can't stay relaxed and talk about this stuff, so we may as well go eat."

Opening the door, I saw that the kitchen light was already on, and heard low voices.

Turning to Jimmy, I smiled. "Sounds like we aren't the only ones who made ourselves hungry tonight."

He leaned in and whispered in my ear, "With the noises they were making, I bet they clear out the whole damn fridge."

"Hey Aunt Doreen, Patrice."

The women sitting at the red kitchen table looked up in surprise, then burst out laughing.

"Mind if we join you?" Jimmy asked.

The table was covered with sandwich makings. Sliced cold ham. Swiss cheese. Spicy mustard. Bread. A jar of cucumbers pickled in dill.

My tongue contracted and saliva filled my mouth. Jimmy's stomach gave a loud gurgle.

That set off a fresh round of laughter from Patrice.

"Sit down," Doreen said. "We're just having a midnight snack, and it sounds like you need one yourselves."

I grabbed two plates and pulled out one of the red padded chairs.

"We need to talk magic," I said.

Jimmy slathered mustard on some bread for us and started piling ham and cheese on top.

Doreen sighed, and looked at Patrice. "I should have known our little break couldn't even last one night."

Patrice reached out a hand, her manicured orange fingernails such a strange contrast to Doreen's own blunt, plain hands, slightly cracked and ashy from working at the flower shop. It was clear Patrice was falling for Doreen. Hard.

That was a good thing. Doreen needed it, after all these years.

Jimmy took a huge bite of sandwich and gestured at me with the meat-and-cheese–stacked bread.

"Right. Guess I'll dive in. Snakes. Feds. Spiders. The cracks in the wards. We need to figure out what the hell is going on. And what to do about it."

"That's a tall order," said Patrice. "We've already got our hands full protecting the community. More people want charms and spells than we even thought. Which is good, but Drake and I don't have the experience you two do. We can only do so much for folks. You all need to up the trainings."

The sandwich was so good. I really wished we could just sit and eat, drink some wine, and talk about something nice for a change. But no. Instead there was a pot of tea on the table and we were talking offensive and defensive magic.

Guess it was what I signed up for, the minute I walked through the Panther Party doors.

Doreen grabbed white cups from the cupboard and poured us all some tea. Spearmint, smelled like.

"First off, what the hell happened with that snake?"

"I sent it through the doorway," I said. Then paused for another bite of sandwich.

Doreen just waited, sipping her tea.

"Actually, I didn't send it anywhere. It got away. Why were you trying to trap it? I don't get it."

Doreen shook her head. One of those *oh girl, you have so much to learn* things that folks her age like to do to folks my age.

"If we had been able to keep it in the room, we had a chance to get its signature." She held up one finger. "To keep it from attacking anyone else." Finger number two. "And more importantly, maybe even to dismantle it entirely." Three fingers were in the air now. Every one of them felt like an accusation.

It must have shown on my face, because she shook her head again.

"I'm not saying it's your fault. You did the best you could, and frankly, did pretty well given the circumstances. But we could have done a lot better, if we'd been prepared."

"I did get a signature, but you're right. We could've dismantled it, I guess."

Jimmy was done with his sandwich and wiped his mouth on a paper napkin.

"And how exactly were we supposed to prepare for a snake busting through the walls you said were safe?" he asked, looking from Doreen to me.

Yeah. That.

"You gonna tell him, or shall I?" Doreen asked.

I cleared my throat. Damn it. Why couldn't I just have a boyfriend and go to college like everyone else my age? Well, except the hippies getting their heads bashed in, and the sad dudes in Vietnam. Oh, and the kids getting shot up in the streets. Face it, Jasmine Jones. Nothing is normal.

"Jimmy, you know I've seen that snake before."

"What you mean?" His fingers tensed around the white cup of tea.

I gripped my own cup, sandwich forgotten, fingers seeking warmth.

"That snake has attacked me before. It's what attacked me in the yard at HQ. The thing you all couldn't see. And it's attached to a man we think is a Fed. He attacked Doreen and Helen."

Jimmy's face grew stern. Angry.

"That day you drove up in that shot-up town car?" he asked Doreen. She nodded.

"And you all didn't bother to tell me? Tell leadership what we were up against? That this thing is growing strong enough so we can all *see* it now? And that Feebs are...what? Doing magic?"

"We didn't know," I said. "Not really. We've just been putting pieces together, bit by bit."

Jimmy stood. Carefully placed his sandwich plate on the counter. His back toward us all, he braced himself, shoulders hunching, against the porcelain sink. I could hear him breathing.

Finally, he spoke.

"We have to tell leadership about this."

Then he turned. I could tell he was still angry. His eyes kept darting away from mine.

That hurt my stomach. Chased the playful sex and kisses right out of the room.

"We don't have to do it tonight," Doreen said. "We have other things to talk about. Like getting more people on board with protecting themselves now we know what this magic can do."

"We need to talk to leadership about *all* of this, Jimmy. I agree. But I want to come to them with a plan. We can figure out what to do, now that we know."

"All of us?" he asked.

"All of us," I said.

"Better put some coffee on," said Patrice. "I think this is going to take a while."

CHAPTER THIRTY-FIVE
CAROL

Jasmine had gone back to Oakland. Things between the two friends still weren't really okay.

Carol decided that, rather than licking her wounds, she would strike out on her own.

She needed to grow a spine? That stung. But it also pissed Carol off enough that she decided to do something about it. Whether Jasmine was right or wrong, the surest way to prove Carol's backbone was by doing some sorcery she hadn't already been told to do.

She was going to find out what the hell was going on with those sigils if it killed her.

Carol eased herself out the back door of the mansion, walking as quietly as she could across the terra-cotta tiles toward the dark garden just beyond.

She was wrapped up in clothing. Navy blue bell-bottom cords. Teal turtleneck. Sweater. Jacket. Her Minnesota parents would scoff at all the layers. It couldn't be lower than forty-eight degrees out, but Carol's blood was thinner now. And besides, sorcery could be draining. She'd seen it before: after some of the adepts used heavy magic, they were left shaking with cold.

Her boots shushed across the manicured grass, behind the Mansion that loomed white in the gathering dark. The Spanish tile roof hunched over the sheer plastered walls, cresting upward into peaks, a fortress in the darkness.

Some of the upstairs windows glowed golden yellow. Bedrooms. All the lower windows facing the patio were dark, except the library. A dim light showed, far from the panes of glass. A lamp on one of the tables for a sole studier.

Terrance's office windows were dark, small panes blank under the curved arches that led to the patio. Funny, she thought of him as Terrance now. All traces of Mr. Sterling had vanished over the past few weeks.

Carol wasn't sure if it was a matter of seeing his flaws so amplified, or if she was coming into her own, despite Jasmine's opinion. She gave a slight shrug. The why didn't really matter. What mattered was that she didn't feel so cowed all the time anymore.

The moon was waning, just past full. It wasn't ideal for Carol's purposes, but she'd make do. She wanted it *dark*. She wanted to travel on the darkness. She wanted to see what it was that needed to be seen. But the work she needed to do wouldn't wait for the dark of the moon.

Carol started practicing scrying when the visions had come on. Ernesto wanted to figure out whether or not her visionary streak was trainable, or just the haphazard, frightening mess that had come on so suddenly a month before.

One by one, they were trying different methods. Candle gazing. Smoke reading. Crystal ball. Mirror. And the method she was going to use tonight, a black bowl filled with water and a few drops of juniper oil.

She just hadn't told Ernesto she was off hunting sigils. Or that she wasn't safely inside in the warded workroom.

The bag slung over her right shoulder was heavy, tugging at her skinny shoulder. That was another change since she'd moved to the Mansion. No chores meant less physical exercise. She supposed she should do something about that, but there was always too much studying to be done.

The cloth bag was weighted with a jar of water, a black bowl for scrying, a small vial of oil, two candles, a matchbook, and a piece of oilcloth to set it all on. Carol would have liked some incense, too, but didn't want to get ahead of herself.

"Keep it simple. Keep it focused." She whispered Ernesto's words to the air.

Night blooming jasmine and grass wet from the sprinklers mingled with a whiff of skunk. Underneath that was the smell of something rotting. A dead squirrel, maybe. Carol just hoped the carcass wasn't where she was heading.

No way to tell until she got there.

Her straight blond hair lifted out from her head, and the back of her neck pricked with the change of atmosphere.

"What the—?"

BOOM! A charge cracked the air in front of Carol, splitting her skull, knocking her back with a whoosh. Her tailbone hit the grass, hard, jarring all the way up her spine, and snapping her teeth together. The bottle clanked against the bowl and something cracked.

All of a sudden, the damp, manicured grass just ahead of where she'd landed was on fire. How was that even possible? And what had knocked her down?

There was no lightning, just that sonic boom.

Skull ringing, half blinded with the pain, Carol scrambled, boots slipping, hands grasping at chopped-off blades of grass, trying to right herself, trying to figure out what was going on. She flung the bag off her shoulder and got herself into a crouch.

Yes. There it was. A ring of grass was on fire, a tracery of yellow-white flames that danced around the bench set underneath the manzanita tree. The place Carol had been headed before she fell on her ass.

The flames whooshed large, then died down to a low crackle, bare inches above the grass.

What the hell was going on?

In the middle of the circle, a snake coiled and writhed, scales lit by the sickly yellow flames. There was no heat to the fire; Carol could sense it. Heart hammering, she crawled toward the circle, everything in her wanting to just run away.

But she couldn't. If she was going to help Jasmine, she was going to have to learn some courage. That moment might as well be this one.

"Shit." Her head was killing her and the right lens of her glasses had a large scratch running through it.

Carol forced herself to keep moving toward the weird flickering, sore tailbone and splitting skull be damned. She could hear the flames now, crackling and spitting. The snake was silent, twining around itself, again and again. It wasn't just one snake. It was two. No. Three.

The shapes kept moving and shifting, resolving themselves from strange symbols into the strange vision of serpents who might have been astral, or might have been real, but who nevertheless were here, on the Mansion grounds.

They'd gotten through the property wards, just like those spiders she'd seen in the Temple hallway. The ones Ernesto had crushed under his robes.

This wasn't good.

The three snakes writhed in a circle, braiding themselves together and squeezing at something Carol couldn't see. She crawled closer still, hands and knees wet from the grass, until she could almost feel the flames.

How were those fires still lit, with the grass as damp as it was? Why weren't they spreading? Why wasn't the manzanita tree on fire?

Peering through the moonlight and wavering fire, and the writhing, gripping, shapes, Carol searched out the object in the center of it all.

She stopped cold.

The snakes were squeezing a man. A black man around her age. He looked so solid. Around five eight. Powerful looking, despite his lack of height. Broad shoulders sculpted by fine muscles. A man with a strong nose and tapered jaw, whose eyes stared straight at Carol, mouth opening and closing, like he was trying to speak.

She crawled a few lengths closer.

The serpents squeezed and squeezed, tighter and tighter. The more tightly they wound themselves around him, the less substantial the man appeared, until he was a pale wraith of a figure in the midst of the squeezing shapes who grew more solid as she watched.

Carol cursed her glasses. The fire catching the lenses showed scratches, small etchings, all refracting and distorting the light, making it hard to see.

The man was still there, eyes staring right at Carol, as if he could make her understand what he needed through sheer force of will. As if he was trying to cast an idea from his head into her own. His lips continued to make shapes shapes in the night, lit only by the flames dancing over the grass.

Carol could finally decipher the words.

Over and over, the man was repeating a litany that shot her through the heart.

"Help me. Help me. Help me."

"Who are you?" she shouted over the flames.

His brow furrowed, then cleared. "Lizard," he mouthed.

At least that's what she thought he said.

The man was so patient. Not shouting. Not fighting. But trying his best to communicate to Carol. Trying his best to get her to see.

To see.

All of a sudden, she did see. But she still wasn't sure what to do.

Chapter Thirty-Six
Lizard

Lizard was stretched out on his bed, on top of the ratty green flowered comforter his mother had bought years ago.

Lizard had finally risked a shower. Damn. It felt good to be clean, and in clean jeans and his favorite, soft, navy T-shirt.

When he'd rushed out days before, he'd left the clothes he'd been gassed in piled in a heap in the corner. They'd stunk up the room, so before showering, Lizard bundled them all up into a garbage bag and set it on the little back porch. He didn't know if he should try washing them, or just throw them all away.

The torn window shade banged against the window as a breeze came through. He had to open all the windows in the back of the house. Try to clear the toxic stink out.

The house was quiet. Just the refrigerator groaning from the kitchen, and the tap, tap of water from the bathroom faucet across the hall. He was supposed to have changed the washer on it weeks ago. Yeah. Some other shit happened instead.

Grunting, Lizard punched his pillow into shape behind his neck.

He couldn't relax. But he needed to. Needed to slow his mind down, the way Geronimo Pratt had trained him and the other Panthers to do.

Lizard needed to think.

Sirens whooped by outside, and with the lingering tang of tear gas in the air and the banging shade, relaxing felt impossible.

But mostly, it was remembering that man. The Feeb. His dead blue eyes when he'd taken off his glasses in the dim bar.

Eyes like a snake.

That the goddam snake was coiled around Lizard's body now. Tugging at him. Pressing on his ribcage. Squeezing Lizard so it was hard to even breathe regular.

Lizard couldn't take a shit without the man knowing. And he couldn't drink to escape. The Feeb had made sure of that, somehow. After his shower, Lizard had opened the round-fronted refrigerator and tried downing a beer. He almost puked.

The white man told Lizard to find out where Roland, Geronimo, and the others were. To make them think Lizard was safe. Had gotten away.

The Feeb told Lizard not to worry over the pigs anymore. Lizard didn't know whether to trust that or not, but he was already tired of running. Besides, what more did he have to lose?

The man—Samuels, he said his name was—told Lizard to look for Cotton. Give Cotton a sign if he could, but not to worry if Lizard couldn't.

Damn, man. It turned out Cotton was a snitch. Worse than that. He was an informer and always had been. Was never even a real Party member.

Not like Lizard.

Not like Lizard being fucking held captive in his own body by some weird snake magic-man. Who was gonna be forced to turn in comrades now. The men who trained him. The women who organized with him.

Lizard just hoped the kids who depended on them all were safe, and would have food tomorrow. And that the bags of food would still get filled and handed out next week. And the newspapers would make it out on time.

Damn. In the firefight and running after, Lizard hadn't even had time to think about everything they would all lose if shit kept going down.

The Panthers were all Lizard loved, besides his momma. They'd taken him in when he was feeling at his most aimless. Trained him. Become his family.

And not only had Lizard run away from his comrades, seemed he was now gonna be forced to infiltrate in the worst possible ways. They were gonna kill him.

Someone was, anyway. The Feds or the Panthers. Didn't really matter.

Unless Lizard killed himself first.

Tears leaked out, hot trails from the corners of his eyes, making them burn and sting all over again.

Man, when he thought of Roland turning into an actual big cat? And what this pasty black-suited honky was asking Lizard to do now?

His blood ran cold.

But he didn't know what to do.

CHAPTER THIRTY-SEVEN
DOREEN

The magic filled her blood, spreading the scent of toasted cinnamon throughout the attic. Doreen "heard" Drake thinking about cinnamon rolls and smiled. She would have to bake for the boy when all of this was done. He liked the kind with icing.

The attic was warm. They had turned off the light overhead, and placed candles on every safe surface. Jar candles, small votives, and on the main altar, the one Doreen and Patrice had dedicated to the ancestors, two tapers flickered on either side of Momma's large, quartz crystal ball.

Shadows snuck through the corners. The bottom bookcase shelves rested in darkness, hiding books and jars of herbs, loose crystals, and Tarot cards.

The warm light reflected off Patrice's red lipstick and Drake's cheekbones, turning both their faces into pieces of art. Oil paintings, rich with color and hidden detail.

Doreen refocused her thoughts, drawing strength from the presence of Patrice and Drake, and from the ancestors whose spirits rapidly gathered at the big altar table, resplendent with the red and black Chokwe mask from Angola, the old sepia photographs, a small pot of marigolds, the crystal ball and candles.

She took Drake and Patrice's hands, wanting to solidify their connection before the working began. The easiest way was through physical touch.

"To do this magic, and to start teaching the children, we need to get a blessing from the ancestors. We can't reach the descendants unless the ancestors are honored, and asked."

"What if they don't agree?" Patrice asked. Doreen could tell she was a little nervous. Doreen squeezed her lover's hand.

Doreen let out a little laugh.

"Well, then we listen to the ancestors. And if they don't have *very* good reasons, we tell them we respectfully disagree."

Drake's eyes got wide at that.

"You can do that?" he asked.

Doreen looked at the boy. The collar of his plaid wool shirt was turned half inside out and the red acrylic sweater he wore over it was pilled all down the arms. She was glad his parents trusted her—and him—enough to let him help her with the magic.

She hoped they still felt that way when they found out she was sleeping with Patrice, and had been, ever since the standoff at the park.

"You can tell the ancestors anything, Drake. They're just family. And just because people are dead, doesn't mean they're always right."

"Cool," he said.

The charcoal had finally stopped outgassing and glowed red. Doreen dropped Drake's and Patrice's hands, and nodded at Patrice, who threw some frankincense and dried rosemary onto the glowing disc.

Doreen sat in the wooden folding chair in front of the crystal ball. The mask was on a cloth-covered riser behind the ball, pillar candles at the base. Doreen stared at the white-rimmed eyes of the mask, breathing in the incense. The candle flames on either side of the crystal wavered, sputtered for a second, and then steadied once again.

"Pour some water in the goblet, Drake. And say the words I told you."

She felt the boy move beside her, grabbing the pitcher he'd carefully carried up the attic stairs.

The water cascaded from the plain glass pitcher, swirling into the fine crystal cup that Beatrice used to serve red wine in. The faceted diamond cuts were as interesting to Doreen now as the striations in the crystal ball.

"Ancestors, please accept this offering. Quench your thirst. We honor you, and thank you for giving life to our line. Ashé."

"Ashé," Patrice and Doreen echoed.

"Slow your breath down, and center yourselves," Doreen said. "Help keep me steady. You're my anchor to this world. Okay?"

She felt Drake nod, and heard her lover murmur, "Yes."

Then Doreen dropped her awareness down her spinal column, deep into her own center. Her breath slowed down as though time itself was running backward. As though she was in some vast chamber, where everything was perfectly still, and the only thing she heard was breath, the only thing she saw was blackness.

Forcing her eyes open, she saw the red and white eyes of the mask staring back at her, sockets empty of everything but space and blackness. The three pillar candles—black, red, and golden yellow—sat at the base of the riser the mask rested on, calling the ancestors from Angola with their light.

Doreen's gaze drifted downward toward the crystal sphere and the diamond-patterned cloth beneath it. A small brown shell and seed pod rested near the stand that held the sphere stable.

The brown shell and the seed pod from Angola. The objects that returned from her vision. She hadn't been able to get any more information from them.

Yet.

The only sounds were a dog barking far away, and the herbs and resins hissing as they burned. And the soft breathing of the three humans in the room.

The crystal, which looked so clear and clean in full light, was filled with moving shadows now. The candles caught at every imperfection, creating gullies and peaks, hidden places and swift, bright lines.

"Show me," Doreen whispered.

The shapes churned and swirled, forming and reforming. Doreen softened her gaze and unfocused her eyes. They kept snapping back, trying to find focus again. She had to unfocus her gaze four times, breathing deeply in between, before her eyes adjusted.

The reminder to practice more slid through her mind. She let the thought go.

Ivory tusks. Clusters of berries. A full gardenia bloom. A live oak. The fender of an old car. A large, brown spider, weaving a vast web.

Doreen softened even more, and let her spirit open around the edges of her aura. Her fire was banked into a bed of coals, resting in her belly and the soles of her feet. She let the diffuse warmth rise and open, blending with the candle flames.

And there it was. A woman's face, half in shadow. Unclear. The cheeks were round, soft. The nose and forehead were broad.

"Who are you?" Doreen whispered.

She could feel Drake and Patrice on either side, humming softly. Some old song.

"Show me?" she asked again.

The face formed itself more clearly. Wide smile. That thinner top lip. The dimple in the right cheek. The purple pansies on her favorite pillbox hat.

"Momma?"

The woman smiled, then faded again.

The spider emerged, large and round. A deep brown, with markings like a mottled cowrie shell down its back. Its legs were striped and sturdy. The spider wove a mighty orb, shot through with stars, even and round, with cross threads gently sagging in between the strong warp.

Sweat broke out on Doreen's forehead. On another breath, she willed her fire to dim.

"What's happening?" Drake's voice, slightly elevated.

"Ssh. We don't know. Leave her be." Patrice's voice. Answering.

Doreen dipped back into the vision. Momma's face again. Her mouth was moving, but Doreen couldn't make out the words.

"Tell me," she said. Momma's brow furrowed. Her eyes grew bright with the same stars that had dotted the spider's web. Mouth still forming words.

"I can't..."

Inside the crystal, Beatrice's face grew still.

Heat flared off Doreen's body and a red line cracked the crystal orb. Doreen jerked, Drake shouted, and Patrice placed both her hands on Doreen's shoulders.

"Hands on her feet! Hold her down!"

Doreen felt Drake's hands wrap around her shoes. She took a shuddering breath.

And looked again.

The spider and Momma's face shared the crystal now. Superimposed, layer over layer, hidden in the striations and occlusions of the crystal. Where there hadn't been a line before, a dark slash crossed through the center of the sphere.

"See this." Momma's voice, inside her head. "I have come to help. Grasp the web. Hold tight. I will not let you go."

And then the crystal was just that. A crystal. A piece of quartz, milled into a sphere, and polished until the edges were completely smooth.

Doreen's chest heaved.

"Water," she said.

"Quick, boy." Patrice's voice, still speaking softly, which was good. Doreen could not take a loud noise right now. Or brightness. Even the candles were too bright.

"Patrice…"

"Yes, baby?"

Doreen gestured weakly to the tapers on either side of the crystal ball. Patrice licked her fingers and snuffed them, spit on her fingers hitting the wicks with one hiss, then two. The smoke spiraled upward.

Drake pressed a cup of water into Doreen's shaking hands. Nothing had tasted so sweet before. She drank it down. All of it.

Then exhaled.

"Looks like the ancestors are on our side."

The red, black, and gold candles flared up, then subsided.

"And my mother wants to help."

CHAPTER THIRTY-EIGHT
SNAKES AND SPIDERS

Samuels mopped his brow with a scratchy white towel. He had to keep in condition, so sit-ups and push-ups in the Los Angeles hotel room were a discipline he couldn't let slide.

The battle was getting harder than he was used to, and the Master was coming unhinged.

Chicago had been an outright failure, and Oakland was proving too resistant. Samuels needed another approach.

But he had hopes for Los Angeles. The raid at 41st and Central had been a moderate success, and the coordinated murders of Black Panthers Bunchy Carter and John Huggins had sown much-needed discord between Karenga's US group and the Black Panthers. That part of the plan was working well.

The Master was wise on that point: get like factions warring with each other, and all of them were easier to discredit and control.

And Samuels was taking the necessary next steps. Planning carefully. Building the trap like one would build a magical operation. Now that he had another contact inside, and this one more magically bound, there was nothing that should get in the way of his success.

The serpents were squeezing the prey, turning the lizard into an ally, not a quivering piece of meat.

Samuels had locked a sigil around the man's ankles that would rise up and squeeze the man like a constrictor pressing the life from a coyote or a hare.

At least, the young man named Lizard would think that was happening.

Temple magic was a powerful thing to inflict upon an untrained mind. The painstaking energies built over years of ceremony, honed by hundreds of minds and voices over time? There was little out there that could stop it.

And for the unprepared? It was a juggernaut of light and sound.

Samuels could crush a man's mind and will in thirty seconds if he needed to.

He was needing to more and more these days.

He just wished the damn tattoo under his arm didn't itch so badly. It made him suspicious of the magic.

And suspicion wasn't a thing he wanted the Master to notice.

Samuels couldn't become a target now.

There was too damn much at stake.

At the Master's bidding, he had set the counter-sigils upon the protective wards the sorcerers in Northern California had surrounded the Black Panthers with.

That damn girl. The one with too much power.

How Association sorcerers came to be working with the terrorists, Samuels still didn't know. It made no sense. The Association had never involved themselves before, preferring to stay on the fringes, keeping to themselves, and taking care of their own.

But, like everything right now, things were changing. And the Master worked overtime to get his combatants up to speed.

When he wasn't tripping out of his damn mind.

Samuels sneered. Then locked his own thoughts down again. The Master may be going crazy, but he could still kill Samuels with the flick of a finger, or the striking of a match.

Especially now, with the damn sigil inscribed under his arm. If there had been any way to avoid it… But there hadn't been. Not and stay alive.

Oh, he might not have been killed outright. Perhaps the Master would have just stripped Samuels of his magic. But for a man like Samuels? Altered to live off magic? Altered to see better in the dark? There was no turning back. For a man like him, death came either quick or slowly. But it would come all the same.

Unless he kept doing what the Master wanted.

Like placing informants inside dissident walls.

And sending his serpents through the sigils, straight into the Panther's lair.

CHAPTER THIRTY-NINE
JASMINE

It felt good to be back in the big church hall. I could smell the ghosts of oatmeal and raisins, along with the slightly sour scent of spilled milk.

The meeting with leadership had gone okay, though there was still some distrust coming at me because I'd waited this long to tell them that a Fed was on my tail. It wasn't clear whether I'd heightened the risk to HQ by not talking about it.

Jimmy was still a little ticked off at me about the whole thing, but it seemed like I'd be able to work it out with him, at least. Regaining everyone else's trust was something else.

But luckily, everyone agreed, with things so hot right now, the children needed extra protection.

Father Neil was still uneasy about sorcery being done on church grounds, but he was a pragmatic man. If it actually stood to help the community, he was going to allow it.

The church hall was cleared, tables stacked and leaning against the long side wall closest to the swinging kitchen door. Leroy, Tanya, Jimmy, and I had set up concentric circles of chairs in a half moon, and the community was just starting to arrive.

The big *God is Love* banner graced the long wall above where Doreen was standing, watching Drake and Patrice lay magic supplies out on a long table.

Folks needed all the love they could get.

I was standing with Jimmy near the kitchen door, watching the people trickling into the church meeting hall.

"Glad to be here?" he asked.

Looking at his gold-rimmed eyes, I nodded, wondering if he was glad to be here with *me*. He reached out and squeezed my hand, as if he'd heard me.

He probably had.

I returned my gaze to the folks finding seats, collaring their kids, taking off coats and hats.

The people were dedicated, that was for sure. Working two jobs, some of them, or night shifts. But they were all showing up, kids in tow, at 7:30 on a Saturday night.

"Once folks know there's a good way to protect their kids, they're gonna do it," Leroy had said at the leadership meeting.

"Give the people a chance to stand up for themselves, and they will," Jimmy had replied.

That was truth. Spend enough time unable to protect yourself or your family, and enough time struggling for the basics, all while being ground down, day to day, and something broke inside.

Leroy looked over at me then, a question in his eyes. He was looking fine tonight, paisley shirt tucked into his bell-bottom jeans. I nodded, and he walked to the center of concentric rows of chairs.

"Power to the people!" Leroy said.

"Power to the people!" the group responded. The kids who attended breakfast every morning were the loudest voices.

There was magic in words. My mother had taught me that. So much folk magic relied on cantrips—those little magical poems—and Bible verses, because the words both tuned the mind and carried the power of breath and intention, both things magic needed. Especially witch magic, or spells, or the high ceremonial stuff some mages used.

Sorcery wasn't as tied to words, but we had to learn how to use that magic anyway.

Leroy was speaking again. "I know some of you were out at Little Bobby Hutton Park—or DeFremary—the night of the standoff. You saw what magic could do, when we all worked together. And many of you worked with Doreen and Jasmine here, getting together protection for your homes. Well, they want to teach you how to do more for yourselves and your kids."

A few people shifted in their seats. A couple of people coughed.

One man, who hadn't bothered to take off his coat yet and had taken a seat closest to the door, raised his hand.

"Yes, brother."

"How do we know this is safe?"

Leroy nodded. "That's a question I'm going to let Doreen and Jasmine answer."

Okay then, that's good, I thought. He was setting them up as authorities in the room. Transfer of power.

"But first, I want to tell you something. Huey Newton, our brother who is still doing time in jail for a crime he did *not* commit, sent a message to us all. Huey said, 'Black Power is giving power to people who have not had power to determine their destiny.' Now, leadership here agrees, that if magic is going to give power to more people than have it now? We're gonna take advantage of that. Right?"

Leroy paused, scanning the faces gathered there. Several of the parents nodded. The man in the back crossed his arms over his chest. Good enough for now.

"Doreen?"

Okay. It was time.

Doreen nodded at Drake and Patrice, who stepped forward with her. She looked at me and I met them in the front of the arcs of chairs.

Doreen raised her hands. Patrice, Drake, and I followed her lead.

Doreen was launching us straight in with no explanation.

Patrice and Drake began to hum. I took a breath and deepened my focus, feeling for their magic.

Doreen and I used their humming as a base for our sorcery, letting Fire and Water flow up our bodies and out our hands.

"Open your hands, let yourselves feel," Doreen said to the room.

The children were the first to respond. They opened up their palms and, as the magic built inside the room, lifted their arms into the air. Several of the parents followed suit, some with eyes closed, others with eyes opened wide with fear.

A few people look surprised, like this was something familiar, but they had figured it was just something they knew. We'd need to check in with those folks later. They must have some magic in their ancestral lines.

Panther leadership ringed the room, along with other key members of the Party. I could tell the shifters were trying not to change. They were sniffing at the sorcery in the air.

The other members stood, hands holding wrists in front of their waistlines. They had been instructed to feel the power and let it surround them, but not open to it yet.

A few of them were clearly itching to get at their guns, freaked out by the power in the room.

Damn. I made a note of that, too. They would need to be trained to open up their feet. To let the magic move.

I hoped they would listen to me.

I was impressed with whatever magic it was Drake and Patrice were laying down.

Doreen wasn't going all out, which was likely good. Just enough to give the room a taste. And oh, some of the people were digging it. Some were scared.

Scanning the room, I could sense the folks who'd been at the park for the standoff. They were less freaked out and had already opened up their hands, following Patrice and Drake's lead.

The other people ran the gamut from wide-eyed and amazed to freaked, to shutting down fast.

Doreen had talked to us about that beforehand. "Let folks be however they need to be. We don't need to win them over by force. We'll persuade them honestly, or we won't."

She nodded at me then, cinnamon wreathing her head, Fire reaching out to my Water.

I stepped forward to stand next to her, between the pillars of Drake on the left and Patrice on the right. By the Powers, this felt good. It reminded me of the time Helen and Doreen had braided our elements together. It gave me a taste of what magic could be if the sorcerers or witches were interested in lateral power, instead of propping up a damn hierarchy.

This was magic the Black Panther Party could be down with. I felt it now, fully. The park had been a bit of a fluke—it was mostly Doreen and I and a bunch of charged-up spell bags and trusting people.

This, though? This was magic worked from each according to their ability, going out to each according to their need.

About half the room had joined Patrice and Drake in the humming, and two thirds were holding their hands, palms out, arms raised. It looked like some Baptist meeting.

I tapped a stream of Elemental power from the bay and fed it to Doreen. Fire and Water twined together, buoyed and bolstered by what I could only think of as human magic. The basic stuff that we were proving anyone could access.

The magic of breath and spit and sheer life.

The shifters were really struggling to keep it together. I could feel them on the edges of the room, and the scent of musk was increasing.

A few of the less disciplined cats couldn't hold out anymore. I heard joints popping as fingers and hands turned into paws and arms shifted to legs.

How long was Doreen going to go on?

I looked at her. She was smiling, a blissed-out look on her face. Drake and Patrice were smiling, too.

Then she raised her arms higher, like a conductor with a baton. I mirrored her. The magic grew thick, steady, tasty.

Beautiful.

Then she opened out her fingers and drew them closed, tracing her hands sideways, outward in the air.

Drake and Patrice elongated the hum. The sound stretched itself toward silence.

The sense of humming remained in the air, along with the scent of salt water tinged with cinnamon and musk.

The three Panthers who had shifted circled the room, whuffing at the air.

I felt reverence. And elation. Tears ran down several of the faces, men, women, and children.

The ones who had been freaked out or shutting down felt softer now, except for one man who had curled up on the floor, arms wrapped around his chest. He was keening softly, and still wore his coat, despite the fact that the temperature in the room had increased by several degrees.

It was the man who had asked how we knew this was safe. I went to move toward him, but Leroy gestured for me to stay.

One of the panther shifters laid its black body down next to the man. The man reached out one hand and laid it across a big, furred paw. The man started weeping then.

I guessed that was good.

CHAPTER FORTY
JASMINE

"We just made magic together," Doreen was saying. "All of us." She gestured toward the table with the herbs and shells and small bags laid out.

"We also charged up all the ingredients we're going to use to help keep our families safe. Some of you have already worked with us before. You helped Drake and I get together the spell bags to hang in your homes, and the objects that tied our web together to defend DeFremary Park. We're going to call on you for assistance."

Folks stirred in their seats, coming back now from the sorcery and the magic that still ran through the Father Neil's church hall.

The scent of salty water and cinnamon fire settled themselves over the powerful smell of the big cats.

Tanya raised her hand.

"Yes, Tanya?" Doreen said.

Tanya smoothed her pressed hair behind her ears, and cleared her throat.

"I just want the people here to know that, like Leroy said, Panther leadership is behind this, but so are the rest of us in the Party. Brother Malcolm declared our right to bring about respect by any means necessary. And if that means we learn magic? I'm down with that, dig?"

"Yes, sister," an older woman called out.

"Right on," said a teenaged boy, who looked like he was about to leap up from his seat.

I stepped forward then, heart filled with a sense of love and pride. This. This was what I was meant to be doing with all my training. This was the work I could offer the Party, and the damn Association, too.

"You feel this magic? *You* made this magic. You did. Drake and Patrice? They never thought they could do magic before a few weeks ago." I looked at the two of them. "Right?"

They both nodded in agreement.

"Now, Doreen and I are trained sorcerers. That's a different kind of magic than what we'll be teaching you. Our magic is tied to the Elements—I'm Water and she's Fire. We can do some spooky shit"—I smiled—"but you all? You have the power of *life*. And that's enough to make the magic we need right now."

"But how?" It was a young girl, hair in two plump braids that couldn't quite contain the frizzy curls escaping around her sweet, round face. She wore a white sweater over a navy skirt and white blouse. Her brown eyes were filled with questions.

I recognized her. She was one of the kids who came every morning to breakfast.

"What's your name, sister?"

"Imani."

"You feel what we just did, Imani?"

The girl nodded and held up her hands. I could see the palms were still slightly reddish. The magic must have been pouring through her.

"How did you do it?"

She paused. I could see the thoughts turning over in her head. Good. We were going to need people who could think about this.

"I did what Mrs. Doreen told us to. I felt the magic and I opened up my hands and feet to it."

Doreen spoke. "And then what did you do?"

Imani took a little breath, and her eyes widened. "I...I think I felt something. Like a—like a click inside me."

"Like a key in a lock?" I asked.

"Yeah. Like that. Once I let that click happen, everything in the room got filled with swirling light. And I could feel it when they changed." She pointed at the big black cats who were still walking around, letting people touch them.

To see they didn't need to be afraid. Huh. If our little demonstration didn't do another thing, that was good. These people needed to know the Panthers, no matter what form they took, were firmly on their side.

"Thank you, Imani. That's just right."

I nodded at Doreen. She had this next part.

"Everything Imani just talked about? We can teach you. It's what Drake and Patrice have learned, just in a few weeks. If you are willing to be trained, and to let us train your children, we can make our communities stronger."

Leroy spoke up then, from the back of the room. "You all see how things are for us right now. The more powerful we grow, the more of a threat we are."

He ran a hand over his ruddy sideburns and continued, "We're under fire. I'm not gonna lie to you about that. But the more you all can protect yourselves, the more it frees the Party up to do what we do best. Running the clinics and the food and education programs. All that other stuff we do when the pigs are breathing down our necks."

"And what if it puts us in more danger?" a woman's voice called out.

"How can any of us be in any more danger than we already are?" I asked then, pitching my voice low. Quiet.

The room grew still.

I pressed a ball of blue ocean fire out of my right hand and held it up.

"I have this," I said. "But you each have your own magic. And if teaching you how to use your magic doesn't do anything but make you feel more comfortable walking home at night, or getting your children safely home from school, why wouldn't you use it?"

I sent the blue sphere free. It floated toward the ceiling. Half the eyes remained on it, and half were riveted on me. Come on, Jasmine. Bring it home.

"The Black Panther Party only exists because our neighborhoods and families were already in danger. We aren't in danger now because the government is mad at the Panthers. The Panthers exist because the government, and this society, wants to eradicate our people. You all *know* this. It's our job to not forget it."

I held out my hands and felt Doreen grab one and Drake grab the other. Patrice was holding Doreen's other hand.

"They will try to crush us, like they always have, since the day they brought our ancestors here on that first stinking ship, half dead and in chains. Are you gonna let them have their way without a fight?"

"Easy for you to say, when you got magic coming out of you like that."

A man's deep voice. I didn't see who said it. It didn't matter.

"The point is, brother, that we all have our own magic and that we're willing to train you so when they come to bust down your door or take away your job, or shoot you down in the street, you have another way to defend yourself."

Leroy and Jimmy came and flanked us. So did all the Panthers who weren't on guard duty, including the three who'd shifted into cats.

"We aren't forcing you to take what's being offered, any more than we force you to come to the clinic when you're sick," Jimmy said. Huh. He and Leroy hadn't shifted, I just realized. "But what they're offering is as good as it gets, protection-wise. We'll keep training folks in physical self-defense, but this magic? Seems to me anyone can do it, even the littlest ones. So we're in."

Leroy spoke up then. "Meet here once a week if you want to. Talk about it with each other in between. Ask these four comrades questions. Make your own decisions. All we ask is that you do what you need to to hold your heads high. Proud and black."

Then he raised his right fist in the air.

"All Power to the people!"

CHAPTER FORTY-ONE
CAROL

The man was fading fast. Carol had to do something.

Flames flickered in and out of her scratched glasses. The snakes were getting fatter, twining and writhing around the ghostly figure of the man.

Her bell-bottoms were wet through to her skin now, and wrapping around her boots. Hands on the wet grass, Carol tried to clear her mind.

The man was trying to contact her, mind to mind, but nothing other than his name and that repeated "Help me" was getting through. Could she…?

She reached toward the man—Lizard?—with her mind, opening her field out to the grass, the earth, the waning moon, tapping on the roots of the manzanita and the soil beneath the grass.

Carol drew on her power, the Element of Earth, filling with all the layers of grass and loam, the insects that burrowed. She drew it upward, as if her body itself had roots, until the power of Earth solidified under her knees, supported muscle and bone, filling her with strength.

Filling her with sorcery, the magic that moved between all of the planes of existence, stitching them together, or blowing them apart.

On a mighty breath, she *reached* for the man with her mind.

Nothing. She felt nothing from the man. Couldn't even feel his body, though she could feel the writhing snakes, muscular, dry, papery smooth in places, slightly rough where the scales rose and dropped from the flexing.

Why could she feel the snakes, and hear the flames, but not be able to touch the man?

Carol needed help, but didn't want to leave the garden. The man might disappear.

If she couldn't reach him, maybe she could reach Ernesto. They were keyed into each other's energy signatures as mentor and student and now with whatever it was she hoped they were becoming.

She cast his image clearly in her mind. Ernesto Alvarez. Handsome. Black hair swooping back from a broad forehead, shot with a few strands of silvery gray. Tortoiseshell glasses barely hiding laughing eyes. Strong arms, with golden skin peeking out from beneath shirt sleeves rolled just so. Pressed slacks. Shined shoes. And a heavy wolf's head done in silver on the pointer finger of his left hand.

"Ernesto," she whispered against the sound of rising wind and crackling flames. "Ernesto." She breathed in the scent of grass and fire. The scent of skunk and whatever had died in the bushes nearby.

She drew on all the Earth stored in her bones, green, and brown, and black.

Then Carol breathed out, and threw a link through the pain that split her head, straight through toward her mentor, her teacher, her first crush, and her friend.

She just hoped he was in his suite of rooms on the second floor of the Mansion tonight, and not out somewhere.

He caught her thread, just as she'd hoped he would. And he was nearby. Carol flashed him an image of the garden, the flames, the snakes, and the manzanita trees.

Carol felt, more than heard, his "On my way!"

Drawing her energy back home, she built the Earth power in her belly, constructing a cube around herself. The more she could resonate with all the powers and symbols of Earth, the more help she could be.

She also had the feeling they were going to need a protective cube, one way or another.

Looking back at the man, who flickered in and out of view, she stilled herself inside and tried to feel inside her cells, her bones, her teeth... What was needed?

There was a muffled bang behind her. The patio door slamming shut. Good.

She felt Ernesto coming toward her, the mingled power of his Elements churning around him. The particular warmth of him.

Hands on her shoulders. Ernesto crouched behind her, his voice in her ear. "Are you all right, maga?"

Carol nodded, then winced. Nodding was a mistake.

"Can you see him?"

"I can. Who is he?"

"I don't know yet. I think his name is Lizard, but I can't really reach him. Didn't you hear the boom?"

She felt Ernesto shake his head. "No. I was...in the middle of something. I thought I felt something, but figured someone in the Mansion was working on a casting."

In the middle of something.

Carol turned to look at him. His hair was disheveled, and under the wool sweater, his shirt was untucked over black corduroy trousers.

She could smell it then. The slight hint of sex. Her heart squeezed like the snake around the man in the ring of fire, and her molars clamped together.

Damn her aching head. And damn Ernesto, anyway.

He must have felt the change, because his hands moved off her shoulders.

"I'll see if I can get through. But you'll need to give me your hand, since it seems he wants to connect with you."

She really didn't want touch Ernesto now, but the man in front of her still mouthed his pitiful litany in the middle of a nest of snakes and fire.

Grabbing Ernesto's right hand with her left, she felt how warm he was, and how cold her hands had gotten from gripping the wet grass.

Ernesto hissed in through his teeth.

"Maga. It isn't what you think..."

"Just reach," she said, through gritted teeth. The man was wavering, flickering, starting to fade.

Carol took a deep breath and forced herself back down into her center, tapping once again on the power of Earth. As the structure and solidity of the soil and grass beneath her rose up, she fed it through her hand into Ernesto's waiting palm.

She felt him flow outward, toward the man.

The snakes grew agitated as Ernesto approached.

"Hold tight, maga."

Carol rooted more deeply in the soil beneath the grass. Why in the world wasn't anyone in the Mansion noticing what was going on out here? She hadn't even shielded.

Then she felt him. Mr. Sterling. He knew, all right. He knew something was going on, and he was just sitting there, cowering in his darkened office, cradling a tumbler of Glenlivet. The fumes of the scotch burned her nostrils.

"Damn you, Terrance," she said.

"Maga! Pay attention."

Carol snapped back to the garden. The fire ring around the manzanita burned and sputtered still, but the flames were smaller, as though they were losing heat. The snakes, though. The snakes were writhing as though an electric coil had been dropped in the center of them.

The naked man pushed outward with his hands and Carol felt Ernesto tugging and pulling.

"Should I help?" she asked.

"Just keep feeding me energy," he said.

His hand was sweating under hers, and Carol adjusted her grip, trying to hold on.

She had come out here to scry. She should practice scrying. She needed to See.

The energy flow needed to run without her input for her to pull this off. Dropping a deeper anchor, she felt it sink all the way to the center of the earth. Iron red mingled with the green fire she'd been feeding Ernesto. She felt him grunt in surprise.

Opening the channel, she let the energy pour through the space around her skin and directly into Ernesto. Once that was set, she stepped back inside herself and breathed into her inner eyes.

Then she Looked. The thing Rosalia had been teaching her. Adding Air to Earth. Allowing herself to fly.

"Fuck," she whispered.

Flashing in and out behind the struggling man was a white man in a black suit and dark glasses. He held one hand up, pointing toward the bound man.

Around his finger coiled a silver snake. It raised its head and its tongue shot out, hissing at Carol.

But the thing that disturbed her more?

From Terrance Sterling's office, where she had felt him sitting, just moments before? There was now a void.

Like Mr. Sterling's soul was gone.

Carol felt herself start to panic, breath coming in shallow pants.

"Maga!"

Her head snapped back as though Ernesto had slapped her, and she took in a heaving, shuddering breath.

Then she looked into the ring of fire.

Ernesto hadn't been able to free the ghostly man, but it seemed he'd bought him some space from the binding serpents. A little breathing room, so to speak.

The black suited man wavered in and out of her Sight.

Carol reached for as much Earth as her body would hold, and set it free through her body.

An arc of green Earth fire shot from her hands, passing over the bound man.

The green fire hit the white man in the chest. His body jerked back with the force of it. Carol's mouth pulled back from her teeth in a wild grin.

Carol felt the link he had to the bound-up man flare and spark.

Then she and Ernesto collapsed onto the wet grass, and the flaming circle extinguished itself.

Carol looked up. The serpents and the two men were gone.

CHAPTER FORTY-TWO
JASMINE

It was a Sunday morning in West Oakland. The sun was out, but the moisture from the bay made it feel cooler than it probably was.

I'd been happy for my leather jacket on my walk here, and had bought a new pair of purple corduroy bell-bottoms, so I was feeling pretty groovy. Nina Simone sang "I'm Feelin' Good" inside my head, keeping me company on my walk through the sleepy morning streets, and the folks heading off to church.

Even the disturbance clawing at the back of my head couldn't keep my mood down on such a gorgeous December day.

The guards waved me up the front porch of the ramshackle white Victorian with a smile. That was a change from some of the scowls I'd gotten recently.

I walked into HQ and was hit with a face full of warm air and energy, and the electric hum of excitement and activity. A group was in the kitchen area, drinking coffee and joking with each other. They'd just come in from self-defense class, from the sounds of it.

HQ felt like a different place. Almost overnight. It had gone from a tense, armed camp to a place of wild possibility.

The Emory Douglas propaganda posters, with their bold lines and bright colors were the same. The ratty old kitchen chairs were the same. The overflowing coat rack by the door was the same.

But yeah, the day after our meeting in Father Neil's church—where people stayed for two *hours* after Doreen's demonstration, talking, planning, and figuring out training schedules—I could sense anticipation in the air like I never had before.

It was as though all the coordinated attacks on the Panthers around the country were having the opposite effect from what the Feds must have expected.

Fred Hampton was alive. Deborah was alive. Roland Freeman and everyone involved in the Los Angeles shoot-out were still alive.

I spared a thought for Bunchy Carter and John Huggins, two Party members whose deaths by Ron Karenga's US group were pretty suspect. They weren't shifters, just dedicated soldiers of the revolution

I kept wondering whether the snake was involved in all that. If the Feds had planned the hit of those two brothers, blaming it on US.

But the faces here in Oakland were jubilant. Alive.

People were on *fire*. Everyone was training extra in self-defense. We had more volunteers for the food programs than we ever had. Community members were showing up with casseroles for the Panthers, wanting to make sure "you young people were keeping up your strength."

It turned out that having actual, shape-shifting panthers in the organization was a good thing. And that people were willing to accept that, and the sorcery and magic, too. Anything that gave power to the people was right on, dig?

As long as the shifters and sorcerers believed in power for the people, the people were cool.

I just had to tip the Association that direction. Or tear it down.

There'd been another disturbing phone call from down south that morning, so the energy in HQ was a welcome balm to my soul.

"What do you mean, Terrance Sterling's soul is gone?" I'd heard Doreen talking to Helen on the phone.

Those words made my spine grow cold. That was something I never wanted to hear about anyone, let alone the head of the Association for Magical Arts and Sorcery.

Besides, how was that even possible? How could someone be alive and not have their soul intact?

I had stopped in the kitchen to pour myself a cup of coffee from the percolator. Doreen's face had not looked good, despite having spent the night with Patrice.

Yeah, that all was still freaking me out.

"Hey, Jasmine!" Leroy poked his head around the corner. "I'm glad you showed. Leadership has some questions about a training schedule."

That knocked me back into the present again, which was where I belonged. Doreen and I had both agreed on that. She would get more information from Helen and check in with my mother, Cecelia. I shook my head. This all meant Carol and I were going to have to get over the little fissure my trip down south had opened.

As Chairman Fred said, "If you dare not struggle, then damn it, you don't deserve to win." I just never thought the struggle would be with my best friend.

"Jasmine?" Leroy was still staring at me. I smiled at him. The man needed to trim his ruddy sideburns, but the ladies would still be swooning over those broad shoulders of his.

"Sorry. I'm preoccupied this morning. Let me just hang my coat up and I'll be right there."

I nodded to the folks in the kitchen, noticing for the first time that some of them had stopped talking and were staring at me. Huh. I guess battling snakes with Fred Hampton in the room and then getting called into planning meetings with leadership had made an impression.

Suddenly, I was the badass Rosalia had said I was.

I wasn't exactly sure how I felt about that.

Slipping my arms out of my leather coat, I found room on the overly laden tree by the front door, and adjusted the leather belt around my new cords. My hips were still too skinny, but nothing to be done for that right now.

I licked my teeth behind my lips. Why was I nervous all of a sudden?

The stakes had been raised. For all of us. But I was feeling the particular way the stakes had been raised for me.

"Come on, Jasmine. Be cool," I whispered. I let the breath whistle out from between my open lips, then drew on some Water to soothe myself.

Time to face leadership and take my place.

Right?

I walked down the dim hallway, wood floors creaking under my feet. Posters lined the walls, even here. The rumble of voices reached me the same time as the mixed musk of cats, acrid cigarettes, and coffee. And the slight pressure on my skin that I now recognized so easily as shifter magic.

Three quick knocks on the door and it was opened. Jimmy's warm grin was waiting for me. That eased some of the gripping feeling in my belly, though the tension in my shoulders was rising.

What if Rosalia was right? If she was, I was standing on the precipice of my own destiny right now. Stepping through this doorway was going to change…everything. For me. And just as likely for every cat in the room.

I drew on more Water and stepped on through.

They were all in the room, seven of them crowded into the space. My leaders, my lover, and my comrades. Picked-out naturals, turtlenecks, jeans, slacks. Cigarettes smoking in full ashtrays, bodies crowded on chairs and a half collapsing sofa jammed against metal filing cabinets.

"We need you to pass a security check, Jasmine." Leroy was speaking, but I could tell the words came from Tarika or some of the other heavy hitters in the room. For some reason, Leroy had become the one-who-dealt-with-Jasmine-Jones.

I stood in front of the closed wood door, arms crossed over my chest. I should have expected this.

He continued. "To be honest, we don't know exactly how to make sure a sorcerer doesn't betray the Party, so here's how it's going to go: we will choose to trust you and Doreen, and trust you to vet any other sorcerers you decide to bring in to help."

"Okay…?" I wasn't sure exactly what he wanted from me.

"And we need you to tell us right now that we can trust you to act as a member of the Black Panther Party. Right now."

The air in the room was suddenly tense. I lowered my hands to my sides. Took a breath deep in my belly, to stabilize myself. I looked at Jimmy's face. His gold-tinged eyes were trained on the floor at his feet.

Right. He'd been told not to give anything away.

I swallowed, trying to get some moisture flowing back into my mouth. A Water sorcerer shouldn't have that problem, but there it was. I cleared my throat.

"I'm a proud member of the Black Panther Party and will do everything within my power to protect the Party and serve the people."

The words hung in the air like an incantation. I supposed they were. There was magic in every promise, every oath. Especially when spoken by someone with power.

It felt like everything in the room paused for a moment. Then someone coughed.

Leroy held up his fist in salute. My own fist rose in an automatic answer.

"Good. Now let's bring you on board the new plan."

CHAPTER FORTY-THREE
JASMINE

I told leadership they had to let me talk to Doreen. There was no way I could help plan this large of an operation without her.

At least explaining magical tactics to folks already trained in self-defense was easier than explaining it to people who never had to defend themselves in their lives.

So Jimmy, Leroy, Doreen, and I were all gathered around the red Formica table in Doreen's bright kitchen that Sunday afternoon.

It was a gray day outside, and the overhead globe was on to warm up the light coming in from the window above the sink.

Cups of coffee steamed in front of everybody. Leroy's spoon clinked against the white coffee cup as he stirred a pile of sugar in.

No sugar for me. The slightly bitter taste of the coffee kept me grounded. I needed that. To be rooted in the here and now, and in what came next, rather than floating in the æthers, trying to figure out all the shit my little journey with Rosalia had stirred up in me.

Jimmy and I were deliberately not touching one another, though I could feel his hand wanting to reach across the table, to grasp my fingers. I smiled, and curled my own fingers more firmly around the warm white cup.

"So, what are the next steps?" Jimmy asked. "What do we need to know?"

"That's a very large question, Jimmy." Doreen set her coffee cup down and looked at him. "This is a huge operation you all are talking about. And Jasmine and I don't even know if we're *actually* capable of helping you."

Jimmy looked at me. I shrugged. Doreen was right about that. We had no way to know whether our magic, coupled with the shifter's strength, could actually pull off what they wanted.

The thing they finally realized might be possible, *because* of our magic.

Busting Huey Newton out of prison.

Turns out he was a shifter, too, which I should have known. But on his own? He could still end up like my Uncle Hector. Dead.

With a coordinated group of us? It was possible he would survive.

"We're going to need to tell more people," I said. "And I know that's a security risk, but there are at least three people in Los Angeles I would trust with this. And we're gonna need their help. A base in LA will help us anyway. It's that much closer to San Luis Obispo, and the California Men's Colony where he's being held."

Leroy nodded. "I can dig that. The security issue is heavy, though. We don't even know who to trust in L.A. headquarters right now. Clearly there are plants everywhere. The shootout proved that. And with Bunchy and John dead, too…" His voice trailed off, but the message was clear.

I didn't say anything. I didn't need to. I'd uncovered a possible plant in Oakland, and everyone knew it. It was one of the things that had people angry with me for awhile. And now they needed me. There were plants in Chicago and Los Angeles, and probably everywhere else, too.

The Panthers needed tighter security, now that it was too late. It was almost good that word was getting out about the shifters. We could use that to our advantage. Shifters were going to be harder to control. And we'd already proven they were harder to kill.

"What we'll need for a job this big is a sorcerer from every Element," I said. "That's me and Doreen. Water and Fire. Ernesto Alvarez and Carol Johannson. Air and Earth."

I paused to think a minute. The red-and-white–striped curtains framed the window over the white kitchen sink. I looked out on the green trees moving outside.

"So then…" Leroy started.

"Give me a minute, brother," I said.

I looked at Doreen then. She was solid as a rock. Like she'd been built for this day. Her face was determined. She'd dressed carefully, in navy slacks and a cream-colored jersey shirt that skimmed over the curve of her chest.

Doreen was wearing Momma Beatrice's amulet, a silver disc that just looked like a piece of metal to anyone who didn't know. But it represented the full moon, and I knew the back was inscribed with a prayer to the ancestors.

She must have decided we needed extra help, because I'd never seen her wear it before, had only seen it on the dresser in her room.

"Doreen?"

Her right hand came up and held that metal moon for a moment. She just waited for me to continue.

"I think we're going to need a magical wild card. We can't just go in all structured and expect the penitentiary to fold. Fighting structure with structure feels like we'll just end up bashing equal forces together."

"You think we need a wild card," Doreen repeated.

"Don't you think Huey being a shifter is enough?" Jimmy asked. "And other shifters will be there with you, babe."

I sipped some coffee, then scraped my padded red kitchen chair backwards. The orange light still glowed on the percolator on the white counter. I needed a warm-up. And to buy a little more time to think.

After filling my white cup with more coffee, I turned and leaned back against the counter.

Jimmy, Leroy, and Doreen all looked so serious, sitting around the red Formica table. We were living in serious times.

"Here's the thing, I'm gonna talk my way through some thoughts, and I'll start with something maybe only Doreen will understand. But I need to be able to get clear on this, okay?"

Leroy shifted in his chair. Jimmy nodded. Doreen waved a hand at me to continue.

"First off, we're counting on a group of Panthers to scope out the facility, figure out whether Huey's in solitary or general, and what schedules and all that are like."

Leroy huffed impatiently at that. "Yeah. You know we're on that."

"I'm just covering all the bases. It's gonna help me think better." Revolutionary men. Still struggling with their sexism.

"So, the thing to understand about sorcery is that it mirrors natural structures. But when we have all four Elements working together, yeah, they're way more powerful and can do more, but in a way, they're weaker, because they risk forming a static structure."

I moved back to the table and shifted the salt and pepper shakers apart, added the jelly jar, and set down my coffee cup. A rough, four-cornered square was defined in the middle of the Formica table.

"Pretend all four objects are roughly the same size. They form a stable shape. Now what's the problem?"

I looked at Doreen with a *you keep quiet for now* look. Jimmy and Leroy both stared at the table, looking puzzled.

Then Jimmy let out a breath and sat back. His gold-rimmed eyes caught mine. "It's too stable. Too much static structure becomes brittle. It can break."

Doreen nodded at that.

"Yes," she said. "But Jasmine is also getting at something else. *That* structure mirrors the structure we're trying to break *into* too closely. We can use that to our advantage, to mask ourselves, but it can also trap us."

"That's why we need a wild card. We need a different, but equally powerful magic," I said.

"Who's that?" Leroy asked.

"Rosalia. She's a wicked-tough Chicana sorcerer. Works with the Brown Berets. And that's just the kind of sorcery we need."

Leroy grinned, a feral look crossing his face.

"Sounds far out. Let us know what you need."

CHAPTER FORTY-FOUR
DOREEN

Drake and Patrice had just left, and Doreen had her feet up on the coffee table in the sitting room. She gazed up at the framed portrait of Dr. King on the wall.

"Wish we had been able to save you, Dr. King. Hell, Malcolm, too. But we're doing the work to save some others."

And that felt good. Damn the Association, and whatever the hell was going on with Terrance.

Patrice and Drake both had their orders, and all the supplies they needed. They were going to head up the trainings for a while.

She felt bad about it, but Doreen couldn't tell them about the new plan. They just knew they needed to take over some responsibilities for now. That she'd be busy.

The fewer people who knew about the operation, the more likely it was the plan would succeed. Just like certain magical operations. The more the sorcery or spellwork was held to the chest, the more power could gather.

Not all magic worked like that, but a project this potent and this delicate? It needed the cauldron of silence in order to build.

Besides, they didn't all want to end up dead before they began. The shifters may have had an easier time healing from bullets, but Jasmine and Doreen would die from them just like any ordinary human.

Even with that on the table, Doreen had never felt more alive in her life.

She would normally say she hadn't felt so alive since Hector had been murdered by the Los Angeles County Sheriff's Department.

But she actually thought this feeling she was having was brand new.

She got up off the couch and walked down the wood floor through the hallway, until it met the black and white square kitchen tiles. Her stomach was telling her it was dinner time.

The feeling she was having wasn't love. It wasn't lust and sex. It wasn't the vibrancy of youth, or the newness of coming into her magic.

It felt like all of that. And more than that.

She had her magic back, full force. She had a sex life again. And a good one, at that.

But mostly? Doreen had a purpose now like never before. It felt... exhilarating.

She grabbed a pot from one of the low white wood cabinets that ringed the room. Spaghetti would have to do. She was too distracted to cook anything more complicated. And she didn't want to take the time.

There was still canned sauce in the pantry from summer's tomatoes, and some sausages in the refrigerator, left over from breakfast with Patrice a few days before. Needed to be used.

The front door opened and clicked shut. Doreen heard Jasmine's boots in the hallway.

Doreen finished filling the pot and put it on the old white stove with the cast iron burners. Jasmine said it reminded her of the big old stove at the church, and didn't Doreen want a newer stove?

Doreen liked the old stove. She shook some salt into the water and turned burner knob. The blue fire came on with a soft *whoomf.*

"What's for dinner?" Jasmine asked. Unlike Doreen, Jasmine looked tired. Like the big old fringed leather bag she always carried was dragging at her shoulder. Her pretty face looked drawn, and her usually carefully picked-out natural was looking a little raggedy near the back.

The black leather coat looked heavy today, too. Though Doreen couldn't have said why. Everything about the girl telegraphed a need for rest.

But none of them were going to get much of that right now.

"Spaghetti. I've got too much going on to fuss with much else tonight."

"Sounds good. Just let me drop my stuff."

Jasmine continued through the kitchen to her bedroom in the back. Doreen heard the thump of her bag, some rustling, and the the thump, thump of her boots on the floor.

Funny, just a year ago, Doreen would have been worried about the girl. But Jasmine was a different person than the sheltered girl from Crenshaw, fresh to magic and the world.

Jasmine was a woman now. That was clear. And her sorcery grew more powerful every day.

So why so tired?

Doreen thought about it as the top of the glass jar popped open under her hands. Pouring the rich, herbed tomato sauce into Momma's copper-bottomed Revere Ware pan, she sniffed in appreciation. Momma had saved and saved for that pan, and cooking in it and the cast iron skillet reminded Doreen of where she'd come from as surely as the Chokwe mask up in the attic.

The warming sauce smelled like late summer. Tomatoes. Basil. Rosemary. Garlic. Ground red pepper.

Okay. Mushroom and sausages came next.

She was chopping happily away when Jasmine came in.

"You okay?" she asked her niece.

Jasmine slumped into one of the padded kitchen chairs, all bones and sinew. The girl had definitely gotten too skinny for her own good.

"I've been feeling so good, you know? But today? I just feel exhausted." Doreen's niece traced the grey patterns on the red Formica table top with one finger.

"There's too much going on all of a sudden. Fred and Deborah getting shot up and surviving. The shoot-out in LA. Roland surviving. The snakes. The spiders. Whoever that Fed is who's after us. And now, the new plan."

Doreen scraped the mushrooms and cooked sausages into the sauce, stirred the mixture with a wooden spoon, and turned the heat down.

She sat her own comfortable backside across from Jasmine at the table, and trained her eyes on the young woman's aura.

This wasn't just exhaustion. Something else was going on. And it was connected with how much weight Jasmine was losing, too.

"How are you coping with it all, Doreen?"

"Ssh. Be still a moment. I'm trying to see what's wrong."

"Besides the cops, the Feds, Vietnam, and everything else?"

"Ssh." Doreen was a little irritated. And scared. The thing that was wrong was hard to pinpoint, but it was palpable all the same.

Why hadn't Doreen seen it before?

They'd been too busy, prepping everyone in the neighborhood. And wasting time arguing with Powers-be-damned Terrance Sterling instead of just doing whatever the hell needed to be done.

There it was. A gray strand threading its way through Jasmine's aura. Her usual teal blue and warm silver auric egg was riddled with dim patches. Like something was draining her.

Or eating her.

Doreen closed her eyes, tuning out the scent of tomato sauce bubbling, the sound of water hitting boil, and the feel of the kitchen.

All she wanted to see or hear or sense was Jasmine.

"Jasmine Jones," she whispered, using her niece's name to anchor her own Sight more cleanly to the person she knew and loved.

"Say your name for me," Doreen said.

"Jasmine Jones."

The name still resonated in her niece's aura. That was good. Her core was still strong, too. Doreen could feel it pulsing, just behind her belly button. But what was that…

"The snake," Doreen said. "It's that damn snake."

"What?" Jasmine said.

Doreen's eyes snapped open. The glass lid was rattling against the pot. Ready for the noodles.

"Sorry, give me a minute and I'll explain."

She got up from the table and dumped half a box of spaghetti into the salted water, adding a dollop of oil to the mix. She turned the heat down a little and sat back down.

"Okay. Here's what's going on. That damn snake of a man has infected your energy field. He somehow wove a tracker into you and it's been spreading. It looks like it keeps itself powered by slowly eating your energy."

"*That's* why I feel so tired. Can you get it off me?"

Doreen got up again to stir the noodles, separating them out with a fork, making sure they weren't sticking together. She hated globs of spaghetti. They never cooked right that way.

"When do you think he got to you?"

Jasmine thought a moment.

"It must have been that last time he attacked me. When he was trying to get to Fred."

"Or that whole thing was a distraction, and what he really wanted was a clear opening into you, when you were looking the other way."

Jasmine heaved herself up from the table and got two yellow daisy-rimmed plates down from the cupboard.

"I was so busy trying to protect Fred and the rest of the room, I didn't even notice. I figured the headache I got that night was just from overwork."

"Well, we're going to fortify ourselves with this spaghetti, and then I'm calling Patrice over. We're going to try to do an extraction."

CHAPTER FORTY-FIVE
CAROL

It was just after noon and the December sun slanted through the multipaned windows of the round Mansion foyer. The light sliced across the Spanish tiled floor leading to the blue carpeted hallway and living room beyond.

Carol, in a purple granny skirt and lace-up boots, shook nervous energy from her hands as she walked behind Ernesto toward the big wooden front door.

Maybe calling Rosalia had been a bad idea, but Carol was angry and didn't know what else to do.

A small group of ten-year-olds came thundering down the Mansion stairs just then, scrambling and laughing, on their way to class.

"S'cuse us!" they called out as they darted past Carol.

Carol glanced at their retreating backs. She so was not cut out to be a teacher. But what the hell else was she going to do?

Rosalia cleared her throat.

Right.

Her tiny frame filled the foyer of the Mansion. Ernesto was still closing the heavy wood paneled door when Rosalia's voice rang out.

"Where is the pendejo? He is not allowed to disappear."

The hechicera clapped her hands, palms sounding like a shot, bracelets smacking into one another.

Carol never knew someone so small could feel so large. She kind of wished she could disappear herself. Or crawl into her room and sneak a few puffs of MJ. She couldn't smoke under the manzanita anymore, that was for sure.

The gardener was out there fussing with the burnt out-ring of grass right now. He was probably going to have to replace the sod.

Terrance Sterling hadn't even said a word about that. About any of it.

After the men disappeared, she and Ernesto had run back into the Mansion, leaving trails of wet grass on the carpeting, and burst into Terrance's office. The only thing there was the glass of scotch on an end table.

Terrance wasn't there.

But Carol could feel him.

Terrance had come down to breakfast the next morning, all trim and neat in one of his sharp suits.

As though not a thing had happened.

"Oh, I just went up to bed," he said.

It was all Carol could do to not shout "bullshit, man!" in his face. Ernesto laid a hand on her shoulder and poured them all some orange juice from the sweating pitcher on the sideboard.

Carol drank her juice, which tasted bitter on her tongue. And then rose to call Rosalia.

Who was here now. And pissed off. Thank the Powers the children had made it into class before this little explosion.

"Abuela, calm down just a moment."

Rosalia whirled on Ernesto, who held up his hands in defense. His deep brown eyes were wary behind his glasses, and he looked hot as hell in his gold shirt and brown striped trousers.

Carol was still mad at him for smelling like sex the other night, but he still looked good to her. She bit that thought off, and shoved it to the back of her mind.

"I mean no disrespect to you," Ernesto said. "I only intend to suggest that Terrance is in his office right now, and that shouting down the Mansion isn't usually the best way to approach him."

"As though I care what Mr. Mighty thinks about how Las Manos shall approach the *Association*."

Rosalia whipped her head toward Carol, who froze, right hand still on the stem of her glasses.

"You, girl, stop cowering. If you are going to do this work, you must be strong. You've had long enough now. *Respect* yourself."

Carol's hand lowered slowly to her side, and she nodded. Then she found her center again. Rosalia was right. She'd been knocked off since the night before, and Terrance had been making sure she stayed that way.

Screw that.

The hechicera looked around Carol's body, gazing at the edges of her energy field with those uncanny citrine eyes, and gave a sharp nod.

"Bueno." Not taking her eyes off Carol, who took a big breath and held the older woman's gaze, she spoke over her shoulder. "Ernesto. Please show me to Señor Sterling."

Ernesto led the way down the blue carpet, Carol following Rosalia, whose tiny frame was straight as an arrow, velvet skirts swirling around her legs. Her hair was still black as a scrying bowl at midnight, twisted back with a hammered silver clasp.

She smelled like copal and frankincense. And something else. Warm and wild. The way Carol imagined a fox would smell, running in the hills.

Ernesto's hand was on the door, ready to knock, when Rosalia shoved her small frame past him, grabbed the knob, and thrust open the door.

Terrance and Helen were sitting at the matching love seats and chairs grouped near the big fireplace. They both held delicate cups of tea in their hands, and had clearly been deep in conversation.

Terrance's face flushed red for an instance before he got it back under control. He sat, one leg crossed over the other, blue-gray trousers sharply creased, silver cufflinks winking at his French cuffs. The blue faience ring was on his right hand as usual, but today he wasn't wearing the tree of life that usually tacked down his sumptuous tie. Burgundy silk today.

Helen's heavy brown hair was in its usual Jackie O bob. She wore an orange skirt suit today.

Carol took all of this in, along with the walls of books and statuary, the occult art, and the sideboard that held the tea service.

She noticed Helen had been about to stand, but was gestured back to stillness by Terrance's hand.

"Rosalia!" Terrance's voice was a bit too sharp and bright. "Has Las Manos decided to join the Association after all?"

Rosalia was so still it hardly seemed as if she were breathing. The air in the room grew thick with sorcery. The hechicera and the sorcerer just stared at one another, green eyes to blue.

Terrance's fingers on the china saucer were pink with effort. The tips grew white from the strain of gripping the porcelain. The cup itself lifted from the saucer, floating through the air to Rosalia's upturned left palm.

It descended, and the hechicera calmly gripped the slender handle with two fingers and her thumb. Raising the cup to her mouth, she took a sip of tea.

"Hm. I prefer Oolong. But this is very good. Thank you."

There was a cracking sound, and Carol saw a piece of the china saucer in Terrance's hand break off. He dropped the pieces to the carpeted floor.

Helen set her own cup and saucer down on the coffee table between the couches.

"Please sit down, Rosalia. Ernesto." Helen spoke to the room, but never took her eyes off Terrance's face.

There weren't enough chairs and no way was Carol sitting on the couch next to Terrance, so she wandered over to lean against his desk.

"What brings you here without an appointment, Rosalia?" Terrance said.

"I think you know."

He gave a bark of laughter at that. "No. No I don't think I do. No offense, but we have more pressing things to do than keep track of Las Manos and your wishes."

"Carol, maga, would you pour me some more tea?" Rosalia asked. "And get another cup for Mr. Sterling."

Oh shit. This was so not good. But Carol did as the hechicera asked.

After handing out the tea, she raised on eyebrow to Ernesto, who gave a small shake of his head. He was looking a little sick. Or maybe angry.

Huh. She couldn't read him right now. Of course, given that he was having sex with someone in the Mansion and she never knew it, maybe Carol had never been able to read him at all.

She returned to the desk. The long mahogany slab of held several artifacts, as though Terrance had been seeking something. Or making a catalog. A black obelisk. An irregular hunk of rose quartz as big as Carol's hand. A green malachite pyramid. A blue scarab beetle the size of a large man's thumb.

"I'm here because there has been fighting on the æthers as well as in the streets. And Las Manos wants to know what the Association is going to do about it," Rosalia said, then took another sip of tea.

Terrance started to speak, but she held up a hand.

"I'm not through yet," she said. "We also felt you disappear last night."

One manzanita-colored finger traced the edge of the porcelain cup, then the hechicera raised her eyes.

"We want to know where you went," she continued.

Barely moving, Terrance set his cup down on the coffee table. Then he stood.

"I have never answered to you, or to your organization, señora. And I will not start today."

He began to step around the table, but Rosalia shot out an arm to stop him.

"You must answer soon. We are not going away. The troubles are only increasing."

Terrance removed her hand from his white shirt, and took his suit coat from the arm of the couch.

"Helen?"

She rose and followed, leaving Carol, Ernesto, and Rosalia alone in the big office, sun streaming through the windows.

The tension left the room.

"I believe you won that round, abuela."

Rosalia smiled, and drank more tea.

"I believe you are correct, mijo. But I am not sure that it helped."

Then Carol saw something on the desk she hadn't noticed before.

A small, silver tree of life, missing the tiger eye stone that usually rested in the bottom sphere.

Terrance's tie tack. It was missing the sphere of Earth.

She had no idea what that meant. But she knew it wasn't good.

CHAPTER FORTY-SIX
JASMINE

I so did not want to be doing this thing. We had to get down south. We had to make sure Carol, Ernesto, and Rosalia were ready.

We had shit to set up. We didn't have time to be worrying about me.

Doreen finally convinced me that *I* was the Powers-be-damned security breach and that I ran the possibility of compromising the entire operation.

"What if they're tracking you, girl? What if they're tracking Fred and who knows who else because of you?"

Doreen was angry. And she was right.

That shut me up and sat me down to listen.

The Fed must have tagged me that day under the trees at school. No wonder he hadn't come after me when I ran.

So here I was, sitting in a chair under the sloped roof of the attic, facing down that spooky-as-shit Chokwe ancestor mask and Momma Beatrice's crystal ball.

Patrice was lighting candles as Doreen bustled and hummed.

I was nervous. I tried to sit still in that hard wood chair and slow my breathing down, but frankly, I wasn't doing such a good job of it.

Sweat beaded on my upper lip and I swiped it away. The blank eyes of the big red-and-black mask kept holding my attention. Like they were asking me to walk through them to face whatever was on the other side.

All I wanted to face were the damn guards holding Huey prisoner.

I licked my lips. Dry where they should have been moist.

This was so not cool. Damn it. I needed to be strong, and here I was, freaking out inside.

"You ready, Jasmine?" Doreen placed her hands on my shoulders. I jumped at the gentle pressure.

"Ssh, girl. It's gonna be okay. I'm going to use this crystal tip to try to get that thing out of you." She showed me the long piece of quartz in her right hand. Not her usual tool, but I wasn't going to argue.

"Patrice?" Doreen said.

I felt Patrice come up beside me. She offered me a cup of water.

"Drink this," she said.

Water. Cool. Clear. Clean.

Then *fuckohfuckohfuck* the cup slipped from my hands, spilling water down my shirt.

It felt like Doreen's crystal was digging a hole into the hollow of my shoulder, right beneath my collarbone.

Biting my lips, I could feel my feet scrabbling on the floor, my body heaving itself up from the chair. Patrice holding me down.

The eyes. The blank eyes of the Chokwe mask pinned me in place. I dropped into the chair, eyes rolling back in my skull.

And there was a woman staring at me. Red mud covered her thick hair and when she smiled at me, I saw her left incisor was missing.

"Hello," I said.

Then I passed out from the pain.

CHAPTER FORTY-SEVEN
LIZARD

Lizard was amazed he'd gotten in on this operation. How could they still trust him, when he must stink with the sweat of guilt and fear?

But meeting after meeting, they hadn't said anything. Still treated him like a comrade. Like they had his back as usual.

Like Lizard meant something to them. Like he was something more than cannon fodder, or a stupid black boy who shouldn't have had any dreams, let alone dreams of liberation.

The Panthers took in his eighteen-year-old self and convinced him he could be part of something real. Something important.

They had made Lizard believe. And they still believed in him.

When he finally found out where Roland and the other cats were holed up, Lizard just told them he'd gone into hiding a few days, figured he'd ride out the confusion.

They seemed to take him at his word. Which meant that damn Feeb now had another plant inside the Party.

Lizard hated that it was him.

It was twilight, out in a place that would have been beautiful if it weren't for the sprawling prison complex floodlit behind cyclone fences and razor wire marring the landscape.

Lizard lay down flat, feeling the dried-out grass under his fingers, smelling the scents of coming night, and the oil from his gun. It was about all that was holding him together right now, that feel of solid ground. An owl hooted nearby. Damn. He'd never heard a real owl before.

At least Cotton, the other traitor, wasn't in on this operation. Leadership needed him to help shore up things in South Central.

Lizard didn't know if that was better or worse for the Panthers. Having the two informants split up, keeping watch on two different places, or having them both in on some shit as big as busting Huey Newton out of prison.

He didn't trust Cotton at all now. Lizard combed back over every conversation, every action, trying to see where Cotton was sowing discord in the ranks, and where he was asking questions that no one ever should have asked. Not in a million years.

Lizard had tried to figure out a way to warn Roland about Cotton, but couldn't think on how to do it without blowing his own position.

Damn, man. How the hell had Lizard gotten trapped like this?

And what the fuck was he gonna do now? Trapped like a mother-fucker by a white man in a black suit.

Last thing he wanted to do was take out Huey P. Newton. Head of the Oakland Panthers. One of the *founders* of the Party. That cat was righteous, man.

That cat meant *everything* to the people. Just like Fred Hampton.

The snake squeezed him, just a little. Letting Lizard know it was still there. Lizard panted from the pressure, then willed his breathing slower. Tried to clear his mind.

Lizard was terrified. The Panthers were all around him now, hiding in the shadows of the setting sun. They'd parked the cars in a copse of live oaks, about two miles outside the Men's Colony.

Now they were all crouched or lying flat, spread here and there, just outside the deadly gates. The razor wire was outlined against the sky, orange of the setting sun reflecting off the knife-like slashes of wire.

The snake kept squeezing. Sweat popped out all over Lizard's body, adding another layer to the stink of his body in the cool California evening. His breath shuddered in his lungs.

Lizard tried to distract himself. To think about the operation. What he was gonna do.

The gates outside the Colony were supposed to blow. Lizard had no idea how. He wasn't part of those conversations. That was leadership shit.

All he knew was his job: provide cover and distraction with gunfire while the shifters took care of any guards on Huey.

And then there was his other job. From the Feeb. The magic man.

The one that made a sick bile taste fill his mouth.

Lizard turned his head and spat on the grass. It was starting to poke through his shirt, irritating his skin. He rolled a little, before settling into the breathing patterns Geronimo Pratt taught him, trying to calm every little thing back down.

Lizard was supposed to make sure Huey Newton ended up dead tonight.

In the confusion, he could do it. Didn't matter who else he took out, guards or Panthers. Didn't matter if he died.

Huey wasn't going to make it out.

The squeezing eased up. Yeah. The goddamned snake knew what he was thinking.

Gonna take out Huey Newton. Gonna get myself out the gates alive.

Lizard repeated those thoughts. Put them on a loop inside his head, then calmed himself back down. Just like he was taught: Breathe deep. Breathe slow. Keep it calm. Keep it clear.

Gonna take out Huey Newton. Gonna get myself out the gates alive.

"We're going in. Get ready" Geronimo's voice crackled over the two-way radio.

Heat ran down Lizard's skin. Fear? Excitement? Didn't matter. He had no idea how the hell they were supposed to get in the fortress.

He tensed up his muscles anyway. Ready to run.

CHAPTER FORTY-EIGHT
JASMINE

Everyone was in place.

It was a cool evening in Southern California, and my leather coat provided me with comfort, and a reminder of who I was, and what mattered. Doreen had been able to do the extraction, though, damn, that had hurt.

Rolling my shoulder, I tested the muscles. Everything seemed okay, though the extraction point still ached.

I just hoped I was strong enough now to do what needed to be done. We were planning sorcery I'd barely even heard of, let alone done.

And we hadn't had enough time to prepare. But I knew we'd never have that kind of time.

In the middle of revolution, there was never enough time.

The hills behind us were gorgeous. The sun was setting rapidly off over the ocean, staining the sky with salmon, purple, and gold. A falcon screamed overhead, then dove toward her prey.

I could sense the Panthers down near the Men's Colony. Some of them were getting ready to shift. There was no way I should smell Jimmy this far away, but I swore I could. His scent mixed with the combined smells of gun oil, steel, wire, manzanita, and dried grass waiting for rain.

I could sense Leroy, too. And Carlos. The two men I'd worked with most—at Father Neil's kitchen, or in leadership meetings—and knew best.

And I could sense the fear and lust and bodies of a thousand caged men. I shouldn't have been able to smell anything but the grass and manzanita, but whether it was a trick of the breeze, or just my imagination, the scents were all there, solidifying our purpose.

We couldn't free every man in the penal colony, but we sure as hell could free one. Our brother. Our leader.

And maybe, all together, we could shut down the whole stinking system someday.

All my psychic senses had heightened after the extraction, making me wonder what other gunk Doreen had cleared out of my aura.

The extraction had also sent my energy roaring back into me. It was as if all the oceans in the world were running through me. I could see and touch and taste everything more clearly than before.

I felt as powerful as a tsunami. Now I just needed to trust it. Trust the sorcery. Trust my connection to Water.

The last week was a blur of motion. I'd barely slept, barely ate. It was as if I didn't need to. All the meetings. All the training. All the coded conversations. They fed me like nothing ever had.

Doreen and I had flown down to Los Angeles and Helen made sure the Association paid for it, which was good, because no way could we afford plane tickets. What she told Terrance it was for, I didn't care. This was the second time she'd pulled strings like this.

I kind of wondered why. What Helen even thought we were doing. Who knew that, either.

The Oakland Panthers rode down in a convoy, trading off driving. They'd met in secret with leadership in LA.

We sorcerers met in East Los Angeles, behind the door with the golden triangle and the blue hand.

Rosalia was the baddest sorcerer I'd ever met. Once all this was over, I hoped to be able to work with her again.

And Carol had figured out how to get her backbone shored up before Doreen and I ever set foot in the Burbank airport.

I was glad.

No way could I do what was necessary if she and I were in some weird power battle. I had to lead this charge and she had to damn well not get her feelings hurt about it.

Besides, I liked knowing my best friend had my back.

"You ready?" Roland Freeman's deep voice crackled through the two-way radio. We'd met for the first time just a few days ago, but I was already impressed. He and Geronimo Pratt were two bad cats.

"Just about."

I looked at Doreen, Ernesto, and Carol. They all nodded. Ready. Rosalia was already in trance, flying out in the æthers, making sure everything was copacetic. She lay on the dried-out golden grass in the middle of we four, head pillowed by a jacket, well wrapped up in a brightly striped wool blanket

I felt her spirit hovering above our circle.

We were working with no candles, no fire, nothing but the sorcery inside us and the Elements all around.

Just the way we'd been trained. This was what made sorcery a force to reckon with. The tools we needed pumped through our breath, our bones, and our spit. No spells. No altars. No blades or wands. Nothing but raw power.

"Yes. Looks like we're ready to go here," I said. "When should we start?"

There was static on the radio, then Roland's voice was back. "Three minutes. They're just about to transfer. Get ready to blow."

Blow the gates, is what he meant. The guards were getting ready to transfer Huey from from one building to the other. Huey P. Newton, our fearless leader. One of the two founders of the Black Panther Party.

The man I'd never met, but who had greeted me my first day in Oakland anyway, through the bodies of his supporters crowding the courthouse steps, shouting for his freedom.

Chanting his name.

I grinned, feeling half-feral, as the evening air swirled around my face and rustled the hem of my black leather coat.

The entire Pacific Ocean was at my disposal. Carol had a whole mountain range to draw from. Doreen was already well rooted, having dropped a cord all the way to the center of the earth, tapping the molten fire there. And Ernesto had a breeze that I knew could become a mighty windstorm in an instant if he needed it.

Rosalia? We weren't sure what she was using, or what she was going to do. A wild card needed to remain wild in order to be effective.

We trusted her. That was enough.

The four Elemental sorcerers would provide the structure. Rosalia would provide the ability to shift and move at will.

There was no way to tell if this would work. We probably should have taken another month to plan.

But we were going to try it anyway. All the energies said now was the time. So…

"Ready?" I said, voice pitched low.

"Ready." Carol grasped my hand for a moment. I held on to her hand before she could let go, and grabbed Doreen. Ernesto completed the circle, with the trancing hechicera in the middle of it all.

Mountains, ocean, golden grasses, wind.

And blocks of bars, razor wire, steel, and humanity down the hill below.

"Let's do this."

We unlinked our hands then, replacing flesh with cool evening air, but the energy connecting us remained.

The wind grew stronger. Ernesto was pulling strands of Air out of the sky, shaping it with his breath. He threw it to Doreen who added a blast of Fire straight from the heart of the earth. Air and Fire slammed toward me, shocking laughter from my throat. I drew from the Pacific and sent out a rush of ocean, meeting Air and Fire.

Air, Fire, and Water all met Earth. Carol was solid, rooted, beaming. Her face was serene as a carved statue. Blond hair whipped around her face.

The energy built and built, one Element feeding power into the other. I felt Rosalia flying up above, cackling, crooning. Singing some strange song.

"Ready!" I screamed into the mighty elemental storm.

"Aim!" Ernesto called out.

"Fire!" Doreen bellowed.

The combined energies shot straight down the hillside, blowing all four gates at once. Klaxons sounded; lights began to flash and strobe. A siren wailed.

Above it all, I swear I heard the coughing roar of panthers, heading toward their prey.

Rosalia snapped upright, eyes wide, and shouted, "Hold steady. Give me what you have!"

We dropped the energy for a moment, forming a solid base, making sure the Panthers down the hill were still fed the energy they needed.

Then Ernesto and Carol, working together, began to weave the lighter energies into a complicated braiding I'd never seen before. It formed a giant kite shape weaving over and around the four of us, with Rosalia at the eye.

That's what it was. I had seen this, in the doorways of East LA.

Ojos. The Eyes of God.

Once I figured that out, I started helping, bringing Doreen in, too. We wove faster and faster. It felt like shaping lightning.

Rosalia's body began to rise in the middle of it all, supported by the eye. Held aloft by magic.

I never knew that was possible. Fear spiked inside me, causing me to wobble.

Carol cursed and grabbed the thread of fire and ocean I'd dropped. Doreen and Ernesto helped her.

"Come on!" I spat out between clenched teeth. I had to get my shit in order or I was going to take them all down.

My spirit wanted to travel upwards, following Rosalia. I wanted to see what she saw. I wanted to help her.

And I knew that would mess everything up. I was lifting in my feet anyway.

"*Jasmine!*" Carol's voice cracked through the sorcery.

Heaving a breath, I slammed back into my body and pulled more ocean in. We were going to do this, if it killed me.

Huey needed to be free. Until Huey was free, every one of us was good as locked inside a cage.

Besides, Jimmy was down there, and my other comrades.

If this was the revolution, I was going to do this thing.

CHAPTER FORTY-NINE
LIZARD

*B*OOM!

Lizard ducked his head, ears throbbing from the concussion of sound.

Electricity. Purple. Orange. Blue. Yellow. Green.

Smell of ozone.

Razor wire and cyclone fence flying through the air.

Then he was up, running toward the blown-out gate, gun gripped in his hand. Fucking actual panthers streaked past him, bodies black and huge against the multicolored electric static still swirling through the air.

Beneath the colored wisps of fire, there were patches of darkness and light. Some of the flood lights must have blown.

Heart smashing like a hammer against his breastbone, he ran as fast as he could, gun in hand. He fired a few shots into the air.

Get in. Kill Huey. Get out. The words became like one of those mantras the hippies were always chanting. Over and over and over.

Every part of Lizard wanted to run the opposite direction. His body screamed with it. He just needed to keep that out of his mind.

Get in. Kill Huey. Get out.

Then he was through the twisted gates, running toward a maelstrom of fire and light, snarling panthers, and bullets.

Damn it all to hell.

The closer he got, the harder he wanted to run away. Tears poured down his face.

A white guard, red-faced and bellowing, swung a heavy Sig Sauer Lizard's way. Lizard sobbed, and shot the guard between the eyes.

He inhaled the scent of cordite and smoke and watched the man fall, crashing into a second guard. The guards were all facing inward, toward a white armored prison van.

Panthers snarled and swiped, opening red slashes on the tan and khaki uniforms. One guard fell, body convulsing, head tumbling from his body.

In the center of it all, someone in pale blue prison clothes was shifting, clothing absorbing into black fur. Lizard saw his face through the crazed movement all around him. Half panther. Half man.

It had to be Huey P. Newton.

The sight of the man shifting into beast rocked Lizard to his knees.

He was caught by a mighty squeezing at his chest, and in the confusion, his mind cleared enough to start the mantra up again.

Get in. Kill Huey. Get out.

Get in. Kill Huey. Get out.

Get in. Kill Huey. Get out.

The squeezing eased again. Lizard staggered to his feet.

The klaxons were still screaming. Then the sound of boots running toward them en masse. More guards heading their way.

Lizard shot the three remaining guards surrounding Huey.

Get in. Kill Huey. Get out.

Huey glanced at Lizard, then shifted all the way, becoming a magnificent black panther, coat gleaming in the floodlights.

Lizard raised his gun. Huey looked at him with black eyes. One split second.

Are you a man, Lizard? The thought spiked through his mind. *What kind of man?*

Lizard dropped gun and ran.

Panting desperately, arms pumping, he headed for the blasted open gate, heedless of the guards shouting and the shots cracking behind him.

Get in. Kill Huey. Get out.

The panthers roared.

Lizard didn't stay ahead of them for long. Two magnificent cats sprinted past him. So much more powerful than his human legs. His eighteen-year-old body that just wanted...

Get in. Kill Huey. Get out.

He just hoped he could get out of there alive. Either way, he knew what kind of man he was now.

Lizard smiled.

A line of heat seared his left ear. Bullet.

Get in. Kill Huey. Get out.

He chanted the words in his mind.

Get in. Kill Huey. Get out.

A flash. A sudden pain. A burst.

Gone.

Chapter Fifty
Carol

The green fire whooshed and left her fingers. Carol fell to the hard ground, then felt Ernesto's arms around her.

Her whole body shook with the aftermath of sorcery.

She wanted to burrow into the earth, dragging Ernesto with her. She wanted to open to his lips. To taste his magic in her mouth.

To make love in the dried grass that poked under the hem of her jeans.

The sounds of mayhem and confusion down the hill seemed so loud, even from a distance.

Klaxons were still sounding and horns blared. She caught the flash of searchlights every time they made their big, arcing sweep across the ground.

They had to get up. Get out of there. Get to safety.

"Carol," Ernesto said, then paused and kissed her hair.

They needed to run.

"What?" she whispered.

"The other night…I wasn't with anyone else. I was…you know… pleasuring myself. I was thinking about you."

Carol gave a small gasp, then sat up and lightly smacked his shoulder.

"Why didn't you tell me?"

He cleared his throat. "It was a little embarrassing, and we haven't exactly had time alone to talk."

The light flashed again, lighting his face for an instant. His glasses were crooked on his face. His beautiful brown eyes half shadowed.

Carol kissed him then. His lips were warm in the cold night air. He tasted like sunrise.

"We have to move!" Doreen's call was just loud enough to carry beneath the noise from the Men's Colony yard.

Carol scrambled off Ernesto, face flushed. Caught. As if Doreen would care.

"Hey." Ernesto grabbed her hand before she could pull away completely. "Thanks for the kiss."

"I need *help!*" Doreen called again, voice pitched low to carry across the hill, without giving their position away.

They both scrambled to their feet.

A few yards away, Carol saw Doreen crouched over the hechicera. She poured water from a canteen over Rosalia's lips. Rosalia coughed, then waved Doreen away, struggling to sit up.

"I've got to go help," Ernesto said.

Carol nodded. Felt his lips on her forehead. Then the warmth of his body was gone. She ached. All that Earth pouring through her filled every part of her with a sense of power and desire.

The energy of her Element had lubricated every muscle, sinew, and joint. And the kiss had done the same. Her body had never felt like this.

Rolling her shoulders and slapping dried grass from her jeans, she realized that she should have been terrified, but she actually felt really good.

Carol saw Jasmine was picking herself up, too. The magic must have knocked them all on their asses. She ran over and hugged her friend.

"Okay?"

"Okay," Jasmine replied. "Let's get down this hill."

Now that the sorcery had left her, Carol was cold. She shivered in the night wind despite her sweater and coat.

It was hard to tell what was going on down the hill, but with the klaxons and sirens, and the searchlights, she was sure they were running out of time.

Who knew when guards and dogs would start to search up here.

Carol just hoped the Panthers were able to get away.

They hurried over to Doreen and Ernesto.

One sweep of light showed low, dark shapes speeding away from the prison complex. Five of them. The panthers. And two men's shapes, arms pumping as they ran.

That was strange, she thought. Jasmine had said there were *three* non-shifter Panthers helping with backup. Carol hadn't met them— there just wasn't time, and security concerns meant they'd coordinated their actions separately—but they'd gone over the plan enough with Jimmy and Jasmine that Carol was almost certain that was right.

So who was missing?

Then she remembered, the flash from Rosalia's mind as the hechicera hovered over the land, sharing a vision of what was happening down the hill below, flooding information into their minds as they poured their combined power into her, weaving protection, helping her stay aloft inside the maelstrom.

It was the man from the garden. Lizard. Carol had seen him in the confusion down the hill.

Carol replayed it in her mind as the dried grass crunched softly under her boots. The roaring. The running. The bodies on the ground.

Then the bright spray of red. The back of a man's head exploding as he ran for the gates.

The man they'd tried to help was dead. But what did it mean that he had been there at all?

Carol shook her head. That worried her. A lot.

Ernesto and Doreen were trying to get Rosalia up. Carol hurried, and bent down, offering an arm and shoulder. Between the three of them, they got the small hechicera to her feet.

"Okay, abuela. We've got you. We don't have far to go," Ernesto said.

Carol hoped that was correct. She hoped the car was still there.

Jasmine and Doreen led the way down into the sloping darkness, risking only one tiny flashlight beam, shining it toward their feet to guide the way.

Rosalia didn't weigh much, but she dragged on Carol's shoulder all the same, barely able to support herself, though her feet and legs were moving just fine. Nothing broken then, just exhaustion or some magical backlash.

The dry grass rustled around their legs, and the scent of grass, guns, and Elemental magic mingled on a slight breeze coming in from the ocean.

Carol remembered more, then. About the vision. The man who'd been held captive, squeezed alive by all the snakes?

This time, he hadn't been asking for her help.

This time, right before the bullet took him, he'd looked at her and smiled. Like he was free.

She hoped that was true.

Carol cast her attention down the hill, toward the direction the shapes had run, seeking the man's energy, trying to catch the sense of him among the others.

He wasn't there. She couldn't sense him anymore.

But around Rosalia's back, Carol could feel Ernesto's hand, seeking her own.

And she could feel the hill underneath her feet. Earth.

There were questions that still needed answering, but for now? Carol knew that she was one step closer to becoming whatever, whomever, it was her destiny to be.

"You okay, Rosalia?" she asked.

"I'm fine, maga. Just please get me down this hill."

CHAPTER FIFTY-ONE
JASMINE

All of a sudden, I felt tired and scared.

We were back in Rosalia's shop, surrounded by the soft glow of a dozen candles, and the scent of the tea Ernesto and Carol were ferrying out from behind the burgundy curtain.

The high of sorcery I'd felt up on the hilltop was gone. I just felt bruised and small, and a little weepy, though I was keeping that under control.

Jimmy was preparing to leave. I knew it was necessary, but I hated it.

Huey was in the back room, changing into borrowed clothes. We would burn the prison garb once they were gone. Leroy and Carlos were off somewhere, getting supplies, I guessed.

The clock was ticking.

They had to get Huey to a safe house. Every second he was on the streets was one second closer to capture. I knew that. Understood it with my mind. But my heart said something different.

Jimmy came over with a cup of tea, and encircled my waist with one warm arm. The peppermint and sage twined together with his musk and amber. I just wanted to fall into him. To curl up in a bed somewhere and not leave for days.

But we were a long way from home.

"I don't want you to go," I whispered in his ear.

That hurt me to say, as if gravel scraped at my throat. And like some-one had stuck pins into my heart.

Revolutionary Jasmine Jones, badass sorcerer, clinging to her man like she was helpless.

Jimmy leaned back a few inches so he could see my face. I didn't want to meet his gaze. It all felt like too much.

"I've gotta go, babe. It was always part of the plan. And the other part of the plan is coming back to you once we get our man safe, dig? It's Huey, babe. Huey."

There was excitement in his voice. But though I was amazed to finally be in the presence of Huey myself, the roiling emotions were still taking over.

And the emotions in the middle of it all were sadness and fear.

And the knowledge that this war was far from over.

"Yeah. It's cool. I get it. But I just…" I gestured toward the steaming mug. He handed it over. The clay warmed my hand, the way Jimmy's body warmed my side, and the tea was just the right combination of soothing and fortifying. I hoped it would help.

"The sorcery just overwhelms me. Makes me all emotional." I let out a snort of disgust. "I help bust a prison open to liberate Huey P. Newton, and it makes me want to cry."

"Hey," Jimmy said. "Look at me."

I did. His gold-ringed eyes beamed love my way. I nodded, and pressed my lips against his. He kissed me back, and I knew he meant it.

Then I pulled my mouth away.

Because he had work to do. And the other thing I saw in his eyes? Was a sense of power that hadn't been there before.

The night's sorcery had affected me, that was certain, and it was looking like the operation had affected us all.

The bell clattered as the shop door opened and Carlos and Leroy came in with bags smelling of hamburgers and fries.

"We gotta get on the road," Carlos said, handing one of the bags of food to Ernesto. "Car's outside, running."

Leroy handed Huey a coat. "Here, man, we brought your leather down from Oakland."

Huey's eyes lit up. It was a funny thing, seeing a powerful shifter so happy about a coat. A man so many people all over the country had lobbied to get free, just busted out from behind bars, slipped on that leather coat like it was a favorite friend.

Then I remembered why I'd gotten a leather coat myself. It was a symbol. A piece of magic to remind me I was a member of something larger than myself. That I was a Panther.

Of course a founder of the movement wanted his coat back.

Carlos shoved a burger in his mouth. He had first shift driving. The others would eat in the car, I guessed.

Huey looked good with the black leather swirling around his legs. He turned to shake Carol and Doreen's hands. Ernesto's too.

When he got to me, I almost burst into tears again. Groovy, Jasmine. Way to impress a man. With a breath, I clamped it down, but he'd already moved on to Doreen.

Then the other Panthers were all in motion, picking up duffles, getting ready to go. Jimmy hugged me tight. I breathed him in, memorizing the scent, then let him go.

"Come back safe," I said.

"I will. Always."

That was it, then. All that planning. All that sorcery. And the operation was just...done.

Huey stood by the door, waiting for Jimmy, who squeezed my shoulder one last time, then grabbed bags of food. Leroy held the duffles and Carlos balled up the burger wrapper and tossed it in a small can by the door. Then he stood, keys in hand, waiting for the word.

"You did good work for the revolution today," Huey said.

"The first lesson a revolutionary must learn is that he is a doomed man," Huey said. "Today, I may still be doomed, but I'm also alive. Thank you. You are my strength."

Then he raised his right fist.

"All power to the people."

"All power to the people," we replied.

Then, bell on the shop door clattering, they were gone.

CHAPTER FIFTY-TWO
DOREEN

The Mansion was quiet. The dozen or so students and the three teachers who lived in house besides Ernesto were long in bed.

Doreen was just off one of the long, sapphire-blue–carpeted Mansion hallways, tucked into a little wood-paneled closet just large enough for a padded chair with a built-in phone stand.

"Hey baby. We did it," she said.

Doreen couldn't say too much over the phone, but she needed to hear Patrice's voice. Needed to let her know she was all right.

Needed to reach out and touch that woman in whatever way she could.

"I'm not sure how long until I'm home. No more than a few days, I hope. But there's still things to work out here."

Including the confrontation with Terrance that they all decided couldn't wait until morning.

But by all the Powers, it was good to hear her lover's voice. Doreen could almost taste her skin down the coiled wire. Could smell the barest hint of cocoa butter and Aqua Net.

She heard the muffled sound of the large front door opening, and a low clamor of voices. She hoped it was her sister, Cecelia, arriving.

"I'll call you as soon as I know. But the others are all here now and we really need to meet. I have to go."

Then, for the first time since Hector died, three simple words set fire to the wires strung the length of California, entering the whorl of her right ear and lighting up Doreen's whole body.

"I love you too, baby," Doreen replied, then placed the black receiver down into the cradle with a click.

She closed her eyes for just a moment, staying with the magic Patrice had just sent her, allowing it to kiss the larger Fire that was her own.

Letting that Elemental Fire run down her hands and legs, she stood, straightened her spine, and set her feet to walk down the long hallway.

Terrance Sterling wasn't going to like what was about to hit him.

Doreen smiled.

She realized, deep in her soul, she just didn't care anymore.

For the first time in years, Doreen felt free.

CHAPTER FIFTY-THREE
JASMINE

It was close to midnight and we were still gathered in Terrance's fancy damn office.

Doreen, my mother, and I squeezed ourselves onto one love seat, with Carol and Helen in the matching tufted chairs set around a long, low, polished mahogany coffee table.

Terrance sat on the other love seat.

Ernesto stood, leaning against the wooden side board that served as a bar. An old, framed, Euro-centric map was on the wall above his head.

It had already been such a long day, but we all agreed this needed to be dealt with now, before something worse happened.

Looking at my former mentor, I could definitely tell that Terrance was missing something. It was more than just his usual well-groomed sheen being gone, but I couldn't quite name what it was.

Carol insisted it was his soul. That his soul had gotten trapped in the æthers somewhere, and didn't know how to come back.

That would make a sorcerer pretty damn easy to manipulate.

But how had he let it happen?

Rosalia showed up around an hour into the confrontation, and gave Terrance hell.

"You have no right!" Terrance was yelling. He stood up, straining forward onto his toes, leaning in toward Rosalia's placid face. "No authority here! You and your damned group of *witches!*"

The word burst from his lips on a spray of spit.

Rosalia put up a wall of sorcery between them and then shoved. He fell back onto the love seat, head snapping so hard I heard his teeth crack together.

"I have all the authority I need," Rosalia said. "And Las Manos will do what is necessary to stop the destructive magic you have brought into our city."

Terrance looked as though a demon had taken up residence in his chest. He coughed, red-faced, hair rumpled, shoes slightly scuffed at the toes. Breath heaved through his half-opened mouth with a whine.

I just stared at him. Thought about the evidence, piece by piece. The police raids and attacks. The sigils. Carol's visions. The snake. The spiders. The Feds. The Association...

We might not have had all the puzzle pieces together yet, but we knew they were all connected. And the head of the Association was a key player.

Terrance sat on his sofa, alone, rubbing his face. It was clear from the beginning of this meeting: none of us wanted to be near him.

"I don't know what you're talking about, you crazy bitch!" he said into his hands. He wouldn't dare look Rosalia in the eyes and say that.

Carol and Ernesto both gasped. I was ready to punch Terrance in the mouth. What was *wrong* with the man?

Rosalia raised her hands, fingers ready to send out another burst, then stopped herself. She bit off words I could almost taste, as if they hovered in the air.

My mother and Doreen sat, tight-lipped and stern, bookending me on the tufted love seat.

Yeah. It was late. Really damn late. Whiskey had replaced tea on the long wood coffee table, the talking had gone to shouting, and now here we were, back to angry silence.

I was done. Time to act, Jasmine Jones.

"Terrance Sterling." I stood and stepped out from behind the coffee table, giving myself space. I towered over him in my picked-out natural, low-heeled boots sinking into the plush blue carpeting, arms loose at my sides.

He looked up at me with red-rimmed eyes from under his disheveled, silver hair.

"You aren't thinking to challenge me, are you, girl?" he rasped out.

Okay, that pissed me off. No one was allowed to call me *girl* but family. I don't care how long Terrance Sterling had known me. He was a wealthy white man who still thought he was in charge.

"I think the Elements have already challenged you."

Confusion crossed his face. I felt Rosalia stop her pacing.

"How dare you..." he said.

"Let her speak," Rosalia said, coming closer, not standing next to me, but near enough to signal clear support.

I sent my attention outward then, reaching for the Pacific Ocean, from Malibu to Laguna Beach. It flowed rapidly toward me, whispering into my veins. Increasing my power.

"Terrance Sterling, you have abdicated your responsibility to the people. You have consolidated the efforts, energy, and resources of the Association of Magical Arts and Sorcery, only serving the few, instead of the many."

He set his cut glass whiskey tumbler on the coffee table with a loud crack.

"You have done untold damage to the Association itself, putting its members at risk, while risking the lives and well-being of communities you should have been protecting. You have lied..."

"You ungrateful..." He began to rise.

"Sit down, Terrance," Helen snapped.

"You, too?"

"You need to hear her out," Helen replied.

"Actually, Cecelia?" I kept my gaze trained firmly on Terrance, sensing my mother, sitting at attention to my left. Her sorcery was building.

"Would you care to outline the rest?" I said.

I felt the power of Earth push into the room as she readied herself to speak.

Then my mother stood, cleared her throat, and began a recitation that electrified the edges of my skin.

"Terrance Sterling, the Association is concerned with your increasingly aberrant behavior. You have grown lax in your duties. You have gone into fits during trance, putting yourself and other sorcerers in danger. Formal concerns have been lodged with the Officers of the Association."

My mother's voice softened as she spoke the next words.

"Terrance, the Officers were concerned enough to call upon me in my role as Healer."

"Helen? Is this true?" His voice cracked, and a tongue shot out to lick dry lips.

Helen pursed her lips and nodded.

"You need to say the words, Helen," I said.

Helen Price took a shuddering sigh, then stood.

"Terrance Sterling, if you do not consent to a series of healing sessions, possibly leading to a soul retrieval, you run the risk of losing your place as head of the Association."

It wasn't enough, in my mind, but until we confirmed all of our suspicions about his activities, it would have to do.

Carol and Ernesto stood up, too. All of us were standing except the man who should have been our leader.

"You all agree with this?" he screeched, the red of his face shading to purple. "You are all betraying me? Betraying your oaths?"

"You betrayed the oaths, Terrance. And who knows what else." Ernesto spoke quietly, then turned and walked across the plush blue carpet, toward the office door.

Carol grabbed her rust leather jacket from the chair and followed, clutching onto Ernesto's hand as they both left.

I heard the door open, but it didn't shut.

Helen looked like she was going to cry. She just stood there as Doreen nodded at Cecelia, and they both headed for the open door.

Tears started running down Helen's face.

"Fuck all of you. You think you have power? Just…" Terrance flicked his fingers, as though sending out a curse. Then he picked up his whiskey glass and started drinking.

"Helen?" I asked.

Helen just shook her head and stood there, not even wiping at the tears.

I felt Rosalia's hand upon my shoulder.

"Come now, hechicera," she said. "It is time."

"Goodbye, Terrance," I said.

He didn't reply.

But at least it was clear now, his days as head of the Association would be over soon. It might take us some time to wind our way out of his reign, but change?

It was gonna come.

CHAPTER FIFTY-FOUR
SNAKES AND SPIDERS

*T*he Master paced the circle on the stone floor, a sick, crooning chant emerging from his throat. The leather soles of his slippers made a soft slapping sound that bounced inside of Samuels' skull.

Samuels' craned his neck, trying to see what was happening. All his discipline told him not to look. To remain still, counting each breath, reciting the sacred formulae.

But he couldn't. The animal part of his nature had won this battle, and he was bathed in primal fear.

Must be an effect of that damned tattoo under his right arm. It made the shields he'd diligently erected over the past twenty years more susceptible to being breached.

Damn the Master.

Dimly, Samuels knew he shouldn't be thinking that.

The candles flickered, piercing his exposed and naked eyes. Too much light.

His back ached from his bonds. The chains were short, dragging his arms and legs toward the eyebolts sunken in between the dark gray slabs.

The methamphetamine stink of the Master's sweat mingled with the candle smoke, melting beeswax, and frankincense and cedar. Samuels fought to swallow down the bile rising up his gullet.

He knew enough to not vomit while on his back.

The slapping of the slipper soles stopped. So did the whining croon.

Samuels' stomach cramped. Clawing for one scrap of his magician-trained mind, he fought again to control his breath.

All his body wanted was to pant like a chained dog.

Noooo. In breath. Hold. Out breath. Hold. In.

"You failed," the Master said. "And you have thoughts above your station. Do you think we should let a failure like you advance? Do you think you are ready for the next initiation into the Greater Mysteries?"

Samuels tensed his muscles against the hard floor and clenched his eyes shut, willing himself to be still.

The animal inside his brain howled with fear.

The Master's stink came closer.

He said nothing. The Master said nothing. Why did the Master say nothing?

Samuels opened his eyes. The Master stared down at him, face slick, emitting the sour stink of sweat and drugs.

One drop of sweat clung to the end of the smashed, white, potato nose, threatening to drop on Samuels' face.

It did. A burning sensation arose under Samuels' left eye, as though a drop of acid had touched down.

"I should strip you of your office. Sand the memories from your brain. I should let you loose on the streets, mad and itching, and raving at the sky."

The Master walked away again. Samuels heard the heavy doors open and the sound of the feet of many men, heavy on the gray slabs.

The men, other operatives, placed themselves around the circle, and began a low chanting. "Come, come, come, come, come..."

They would always do his bidding.

The Master drew a sigil that hovered in the smoky air above Samuels' chained body.

The tattoo beneath Samuels' right arm felt like it caught fire. His back arched off the floor as he screamed.

This wasn't supposed to be happening.

He'd done everything the Master asked.

It was that Panther bitch.

She took it all away.

Someday...

Samuels screamed again, bellowing as the sigil under his right armpit writhed and burned, as the chanting voices grew louder in his ears.

Someday she would pay.

CHAPTER FIFTY-FIVE
JASMINE

Jimmy had finally made it home to Oakland, after getting Huey safely who knows where.

We were curled up in my too-small bed off Aunt Doreen's kitchen. Doreen had kindly given us some privacy for a reunion, and was at Patrice's for the night.

Che Guevara and the Black Power woman stared down at us from the walls. The refrigerator hummed through the walls, and Jimmy's breath slowed itself, catching, then evening out toward sleep.

Snuggling further against Jimmy's naked body, I breathed in the scent of him. The scent of *us*.

He had the right idea. Sleep.

But I was awake. Wide awake. Safe in my lover's arms for now. Huey, Deborah, Fred, and Roland, all free.

I should feel good about that. And I did, dig? The Black Panthers were only getting stronger every day.

Doreen and I had come home to find the magic lessons going strong. Patrice and Drake were both stepping up. And the Panther clinics, food pantry, and breakfast programs hadn't missed a beat.

Some young cats had even started a safe escort service for seniors, and rigged an ambulance for folks who couldn't get to the clinic or a hospital on their own.

It was power to the people, every day, all the way.

But Fred, Huey, and the others couldn't walk in public yet. That day had to be coming, but I couldn't see how yet. Jimmy said to trust the people. They'd make it all all right.

Doreen said to trust our sorcery.

But I couldn't shake the feeling that the snakes and spiders still weren't dead. And what in the Powers were we going to do with Terrance Sterling?

The challenge had been issued, but not accepted. And how can you force a person to accept healing?

Jimmy stirred at my side, and threw an arm across my waist.

"Go to sleep, Jaz," he murmured.

"I will, baby. I will."

Breathing into the night, I let the ocean cradle me. Rock me. I kept waiting for it to soothe me down toward the depths of sleep, knowing I would have to wake up soon enough.

There was always work to be done.

*

My name is Jasmine Jones. Badass sorcerer. Member in good standing of the Black Panther Party.

My name is also Jaz.

And I'm in love with a shifter named Jimmy.

I'm also figuring out that in the midst of revolution, we find home where we can, and we can let ourselves rest there.

As best we can.

Power to the people.

TO DROWN THIS FURY IN THE SEA

THE PANTHER CHRONICLES

BOOK THREE

T. THORN COYLE
author of *Like Water*

Turn the page to read a sample
of the next novel in the Panther Chronicles,
To Drown This Fury in the Sea.

CHAPTER ONE
JASMINE

My worn black lace-up boots marched through Oakland's Chinatown, supporting my feet and legs the way they must have supported whatever poor small-footed soldier had them before me.

I wasn't a middle-class, eighteen-year-old sorcerer fresh off the bus from Southern California anymore.

One year later, I was a soldier now. Fighting in an army of liberation. Looking for freedom for my people. For *all* oppressed people: black, brown, white…whatever. If they were struggling, poor, and oppressed, the Black Panther Party was there for them.

As Huey said, "Black Power is giving power to people who have not had power to determine their destiny."

I hadn't been to Father Neil's church to work the Free Breakfast for Children program in what felt like too long. The Party had taken me off duty, to free me up to train folks in community magical defense. That was cool and all. I liked it.

But days like today? I needed something simple. Something good.

A reminder of why we were doing all this revolutionary action in the first place.

My boots took me up to busy San Pablo Avenue, where the delivery trucks rolled by. To Saint Augustine's. The old, red-brick church that was home to so many of us.

It took us all in, believers or not. Embracing us in warm, forgiving arms.

Even though I knew my work was righteous, I felt a little bruised all the same.

Some forgiveness, a warm kitchen, and the faces of some little kids?

That would suit my day just fine.

"Hey Tanya!"

I walked into the steamy kitchen through the back door. The rust-colored tiles and long steel countertops embraced me, as did the humming fluorescent lights, the crashing of the scrambled egg pans coming out of the oven, and the cinnamon oats in the big pot on the battered gas stove.

"Jasmine! I thought you weren't coming here for a while." Tanya was a marvel.

Pressed hair with perfect edges, always dressed for her bank job, Tanya was the most dedicated Panther I knew. Not part of leadership, and a person too many others overlooked, Tanya pretty much kept the Free Breakfast for Children program running, often starting and ending her day in the kitchen, between getting her own two kids to school and putting in her time as a bank teller downtown.

Today she wore burgundy slacks and a cream-colored blouse under a flowered apron. She set the shallow baking pan of eggs on the stove top and kicked the heavy oven door closed.

"I wasn't, but I missed it too much," I replied.

Tanya took off the battered gray oven mitts and ran the back of her hand across her forehead, smoothing down the edges of her hair.

"Come here, girl," she said, arms opened wide. I dropped my big fringed leather purse on the counter and walked into her arms.

I smelled cocoa butter, a whiff of pressing iron, and eggs. Her arms were bony despite all the kitchen work, but her chest was soft against mine. The hug was quick, but surprising all the same. I'd never had a hug from a party member besides my boyfriend Jimmy. And Tanya and I? We liked each other, and respected one another, but weren't particularly close. She was a woman I always wished could become a friend, but there was never enough spare time.

"Thanks for the welcome, Tanya. What can I do to help?"

"Start serving up the food. The kids'll be here any minute, and then you know how things get."

I grabbed paper plates for the eggs and melamine bowls for the oatmeal and stacked them on the counter next to the long metal serving trays.

Tanya's hug was strange, but a lot of things were strange these days. Ever since the standoff at DeFremary Park, people had started treating me different. And then word got out that I'd taken part in busting Oakland Party founder Huey Newton out of prison. People were either terrified of me, or wanted to take care of me somehow.

I was grateful that some folks just treated me like a friend. Maybe Tanya and I would get there. Seemed like it.

"Who else is here?" I asked.

"Leroy and George are setting up the dining room, but that's it today. We're a little short, so…" She scooped eggs onto the paper plates with a metal serving spoon and handed them to me to set onto the trays. "It's a good thing you stopped by."

"Tanya." I stopped myself. Wasn't sure exactly how to ask what I needed to.

One tray was full, so I scooted the full one aside and started on a second.

"What?" she asked, still scooping egg onto plates.

I kept up with her pace, trying to think. How in the Powers could I put this?

"Have you ever noticed anything strange here at the kitchen?"

She snorted at that. "You mean, besides finding out that honest-to-Goddamn shape-shifting panthers are bringing in the powdered milk and oats and spouting off about Frantz Fanon?"

I grinned at that. She had a point. She also seemed to have the eggs under control. I set out a couple more empty trays, then moved over to the ten-gallon pot of oatmeal on the stove, grabbing a ladle from the hood overhead.

"No. I mean like that snake thing I was battling at HQ. Or white spiders."

Tanya's brow wrinkled at that. "White spiders? That's strange. The only spiders I see in the kitchen are daddy longlegs or the little brown ones. We shoo those outside. Should I be watching for white spiders now?"

I stopped ladling out the oatmeal, because even with my back to her, I could feel Tanya had stopped scooping eggs and was staring at me. So I turned. Sure enough, hands on her aproned hips, small scowl on her face, Tanya was waiting for an answer.

Hoping I hadn't just blown it, I took in a big breath and dropped into my center to steady myself. As much experience as I had with this sorcerous shit, talking to mundanes about it still made me feel uneasy. But we were all part of this army now.

Children's voices filtered through the swinging wood door that led into the church hall where breakfast was served. Damn. I could hear Leroy and George greeting the kids. Hear the voices, excited for a warm meal, happy to see their friends, excited even for the little lecture that accompanied breakfast. Black history. Black power. Black pride.

What we all needed right about now. I dug it. And I had other work to do here. And I still had to figure out the right way to talk to people about it, and to make sure danger wasn't creeping around behind my back, undermining everything the Panthers worked for.

"Let's get this breakfast ready. I'll keep talking as we work."

Tanya nodded and turned to scrape the last of the eggs onto plates. Then I felt her at my side, sliding the bowls I'd filled onto more serving trays.

"So. There's a weird cosmic battle going on. And we've seen white spiders appearing in strange places where spiders had no right to be. We think they're magic. Maybe even spies."

I could smell Tanya's nervousness rising. Couldn't blame her.

"This is so not what I signed up for, you dig?" She shoved a full tray down the counter next to the stove and slammed another down, grabbing more bowls.

Great, Jasmine. You've terrified your comrade. I shook my head. Should be used to it by now. But I likely never would.

"None of us did. But it's what's happening. The cops are killing people and the Feds have us under magical attack."

"The Feds?" She backed away from me. "The Feds have magic?"

I nodded. "Straight up Solomonic Temple magic. Old. As strong as my sorcery. Maybe stronger."

"I don't know what any of that means…but… How do you know? And is leadership hip to all this?"

"Doreen and I told them just last night. We had to. It's part of what went down when we broke Huey out. And part of how me and Fred got attacked at HQ."

"The snake thing," she whispered.

"The snake thing. And these white spiders are part of it, somehow. I've got a pretty good handle on the snakes, but the spiders need watching. And we need more help with that."

We loaded up the last of the bowls onto the trays. The children's voices had quieted down; there was just George's voice, rising and falling through the kitchen door. They were going to be ready for breakfast any minute.

"So I got permission from leadership to talk to you about it."

Tanya clutched her arms in front of her chest. "Why me?"

"Because I trust you, Tanya. You work hard for the Party. But more than that. You watch. You listen. And you keep your mouth shut."

She nodded at that, face tight, mouth small. "Yeah."

"You now have security clearance, Tanya. Leadership told me I could give it to you."

"But you're not…"

"I'm not leadership exactly. But I am in charge of sorcery. And I say we need your help."

Leroy came loping through the swinging door, his shoulders practically filling the whole doorway, crammed into a tight red turtleneck shirt tucked into bell-bottom jeans cinched at his waist with a tooled leather belt and hammered brass buckle. The man was just big, from his raggedy red-tinged natural and impressive sideburns on down to his boots.

He nodded at Tanya and then grinned wide when he saw me. It was good to be back at Father Neil's church for breakfast. I really had missed it.

"Breakfast ready?" he rumbled.

"It is," Tanya replied. "But"—she looked at me—"can I ask him, Jasmine?"

"He knows."

Tanya just looked up at Leroy, who dwarfed her. He put a hand on her slender shoulder and looked her in the eyes.

"I know, sister. And it's about damn time."

Tanya took in a jagged breath, then shook out her hands.

"Okay. I'm gonna ponder this, Jasmine."

Then she nodded at the trays lining the counter.

"Let's get this food out to the children," she said.

We all grabbed a tray. Leroy led the way through the swinging door.

In the church hall turned into dining room, three dozen bright faces looked up from the long tables and turned our way, smiles and all.

Take that, Federal Agents.

The revolution begins with breakfast, your spiders and snakes be damned.

AUTHOR'S NOTE & BIBLIOGRAPHY

This series came about because for many years I've wondered what racial justice in the United States would look like if Fred Hampton had not been brutally assassinated by the FBI and Chicago PD, and if J. Edgar Hoover's COINTELPRO had not purposefully decimated so many groups and coalitions working toward equity, autonomy, and justice.

With encouragement from others, what started off as a 10,000 word short story turned into a four book series.

Am I the right person to tell this tale of sorcery, shape-shifters, and the Black Panther Party? There are likely far better candidates for the task, but the story pushed its way through me nonetheless, for better or worse.

There's a lot of history in this alt-history fantasy. 1968–69 was a time in which so much happened, it is almost impossible to keep track of events. The infiltration, assassinations, psychological warfare, disruption, and attacks on anti-war and civil rights groups by the FBI was far worse and more comprehensive than I could even being to include in these novels. Many of these tactics continue into contemporary times.

I chose only a few key events to highlight in the story, and concentrated on Oakland and Los Angeles, though events were going down in cities across the U.S.

When possible, I used the words of Panther organizers like Fred Hampton and Huey Newton. I also tried to remain respectful of the

Panthers still living and doing good work in the world. That is why so many key historical players are barely mentioned, or appear as very minor characters. I didn't want to put words in their mouths. That is not my place. Many of them have told their stories, and you can find a few in the books below. There is a wealth of information not included here.

If you are interested in more actual history, here is a resource list to get you started:

Film

- *Black Power Mix Tape*
- *1971*
- *The Black Panthers: Vanguard of the Revolution* (this film is controversial among some of the remaining Panthers)

Books

- *The Fire Next Time*, James Baldwin (not about the Panthers in particular, but a great background that frankly, everyone should read)
- *To Live and Die for the People*, Huey P. Newton
- *Revolutionary Suicide*, Huey P. Newton
- *The Nine Lives of a Black Panther*, Wayne Pharr
- *A Taste of Power*, Elaine Brown
- *Seize the Time*, Bobby Seale
- *The Ten Point Program of the Black Panther Party*, https://web.stanford.edu/group/blackpanthers/history.shtml
- *Assata: An Autobiography*, Assata Shakur (Panther history after the time period of this series)
- *J. Edgar Hoover: A Graphic Biography*, Rick Geary
- *Chicano Movement for Beginners*, Maceo Montoya
- *Youth, Identity, Power: The Chicano Movement*, Carlos Muñoz, Jr.

And of course, the repercussions from this time roll forward.

Some Additional Key Resources

- *The New Jim Crow*, Michelle Alexander
- *The 13th Movie*, Ava DuVernay
- *From #BlackLivesMatter to Black Liberation*, Keeanga-Yamahtta Taylor

Many of the Black Panther Party continue to do public work in the world.

- Fred Hampton and Deborah Johnson/Akua Njeri's son founded the Prisoners of Conscience Committee: http://chairmanfredjr.blogspot.com/
- Elaine Brown is an activist and author. http://www.elainebrown.org/
- Ericka Huggins is an activist, speaker, and spiritual teacher. http://www.erickahuggins.com/Home.html
- Bobby Seale is an educator, author, and activist. http://www.bobbyseale.com/
- Angela Davis is a professor, author, and active in the prison abolitionist movement: http://www.speakoutnow.org/speaker/davis-angela
- Tarika Lewis is a violinist, artist, activist, and art teacher: https://en.wikipedia.org/wiki/Joan_Tarika_Lewis

Acknowlegements

Every published book requires both an author working alone, and a host of friends and community.

Thank you and love to Robert and Jonathan, for helping me build a home all these years.

Thanks to first readers Leslie Claire Walker, Thealandrah Davis, and Luna Pantera. Thanks also to Al Osorio for the occasional consultation on the series! These would be lesser books without all of you.

Thank you to Dayle Dermatis, editor extraordinaire.

Thank you to Carl of Extended Imagery for the gorgeous covers.

Thanks to my first and third Saturday writing cohort. It's great working with you.

Thanks to Kris Rusch, who told me this wasn't just a short story, but a novel series.

Most of all: thanks to all of the activists and justice organizations who do the work day in and day out. May your lives and work be blessed.

ABOUT THE AUTHOR

T. Thorn Coyle writes books, drinks tea, and agitates for justice.

She is the author of the Panther Chronicles series, the novel *Like Water*, two story collections, and multiple spirituality books including *Sigil Magic for Writers, Artists & Other Creatives* and *Evolutionary Witchcraft*. Thorn's work also appears in many anthologies, magazines, and collections. She has taught people all over the world.

An interloper to the Pacific Northwest, Thorn joyfully stalks city streets, writes in cafes, and talks to crows, squirrels, and trees. Sometimes she gets arrested.

Want to learn more?

Follow Thorn on Twitter and Facebook
Sign up for her monthly newsletter at her ThornCoyle.com
Read advance copies of essays and stories via Patreon

24509624R00152

Made in the USA
Columbia, SC
25 August 2018